Staying Home

A Windsor Peak Novel

Book 2

Denise Latham

Dedication

To all of you who were so encouraging and positive when I announced I had taken this terrifying leap into publishing a book – thank you.

In loving memory of Caroline "Calle" Cronk, who fought DIPG like a warrior. She touched the world's heart with her battle and is missed every day by her family and friends.

Rachael, Kevin, Connor, and Maddie, thank you for allowing me to honor her memory in this book. I hope her spirit and joy for life shine through on every page.

Chapter 1

Dan Burrows had last felt sane on the night of his father's wedding, when he held his ex-girlfriend in his arms during the first dance. The moment had been far too brief, and the weeks since his world had completely come apart. Granted, it had started to come undone weeks before the wedding, when he had to walk away from his high-powered job in Manhattan, but things had gotten considerably worse.

He had lost the ability to have a coherent thought, he was so fixated on getting Kendra back into his arms again. The work situation needed to be resolved as well, and after spending the last few weeks talking to clients and evaluating, he was getting close to deciding his approach. Being betrayed by a person he considered a close friend stung, so the distraction of his ex-girlfriend came at a good time.

With that thought in mind, he pulled open the heavy door into Kendra's restaurant, The Windsor Peak Palace. It was midday, so there were only a handful of people inside when he entered. He saw a few of his dad's friends playing pool in the back, and a small group of women were playing mahjong at a table. Kendra Knight stood behind the bar, her back to the door, talking to a woman eating a salad. She turned to see who had entered, and her smile disappeared quickly when she saw it was him. Not one to be pushed off easily, he slid onto a barstool and waited for her to cross.

"Hi," she said as she slapped a napkin on the bar in front of him. "Want a drink?"

"Just a Pepsi is fine, thanks." He smiled at her. "How are you?"

"Great." She placed a cup in front of him. "This all?"

"No, I'm a little hungry so I think I'll look over the menu."

"Dan," she said quietly. "You must have it memorized by now. We have been doing this same thing for weeks."

"You could just agree to go to dinner with me, and then we wouldn't have to keep this up." Dan shrugged. "Otherwise, I'll just have to come sit here every afternoon and try to make you realize how much you miss me."

"I've seen you every day for weeks now. I couldn't possibly miss you, because you won't go away."

"Does that mean we're on for dinner tomorrow?"

"No, Dan." She rolled her eyes at him. "We're not going down this path again."

The door opened, and Dan turned to see his brother Jake walk into the restaurant. He crossed and slid onto the barstool to Dan's right, smiling at Kendra as he did. "What's going on? Day drinking for the unemployed?"

"Hey, Jake," Kendra greeted him.

"I'm not drinking," Dan said, pointing at his soda. "Just having a soda and trying to convince Kendra that she should give me another chance."

"She's way too smart for that." Jake grinned at her, and Kendra laughed in return as she agreed. "Stella wanted me to ask you to come to dinner at the house. She and our dad want to thank you for all you did for their wedding."

"That's really nice of them, but unnecessary. I wanted to help," Kendra replied.

"They spend a lot of time trying to figure out how to thank you, so don't be surprised if they do something crazy if you play hard to get." Jake pointed at Dan. "Just like this guy."

"Shouldn't you be in class?" Dan asked, trying to hurry his brother along. Jake had recently begun taking classes at Windsor Peak College, working towards his contractor's license.

"I'm done by one most days, so just killing some time until Shea and Charlie are done with school. We're going to Burlington to get Charlie some new skates. Kid grows too fast; his feet are bigger than mine now." Jake's son was about to turn fifteen after the holidays and was already taller than his father and two uncles. "Want to come with us? We're going to grab a bite to eat on the way back."

"No, thanks." He glanced at where Kendra was busy with customers at the end of the bar. "I'm going to stick around here for a while."

"Not a good look to beg, you know." Jake glanced at his watch. "Maybe she needs a little space?"

"I gave her all these years, didn't I?"

"Not on purpose. Or at least, I don't think it was on purpose. Did you ghost her so that you could come back all this time later and win her back?"

"Go away, Jake." Dan pointed at the door.

"Just stating facts, my brother. You're the older, wiser one, after all." Jake stood and slapped a hand on Dan's shoulder. "Try something different, that's all I'm saying. This isn't working."

Dan nodded and watched his brother leave, thinking about what he had said. So far, he had tried sending her flowers and candy, which didn't work. He tried to talk to her at social events where they were together, but she moved away as quickly as possible. Sitting at the bar every day was clearly not getting him any points. Aside from the one dance at his father's wedding, he had struck out entirely.

Watching as she made her way down to his end of the bar, he considered his options. She expected him to disappear again, so he couldn't just drop out of sight and hope she understood that it was to get her attention. "You really should come for dinner at the house. Are you free tomorrow?" He blurted it out without thinking and was surprised when it looked like she was considering it.

"Maybe," she said slowly. "I haven't seen your dad and Stella since they got back from Aruba, so it would be nice to see them. And I don't want them to think I'm avoiding them."

His day brightened up immediately. "They would love it. Come at six, okay?"

Making a move to slide off the stool before she could change her mind, he was stopped by her voice. "One thing, Dan."

"Of course, what?"

"I'd have to bring Calle." Her six-year-old daughter, who Dan had only met briefly in town and while at the restaurant.

"Not a problem. Stella will love having you both."

"Just don't start thinking this will turn into something, okay? I'm just coming to have dinner with the family, not as a date."

"Not a date, got it." Dan zipped up his jacket as he nodded.

"Dan," she waited until he looked up. "I'm serious. Especially in front of Calle, I can't have you trying to be my boyfriend. She has never seen me with anyone, and I don't want to spend the next three months answering questions. We're friends, that's it."

"Friends who also would maybe have a date in the future?"

"Dan. Don't make me regret this."

"I will be on my best behavior; you have my word." He turned to leave. "Six, tomorrow. See you then."

He drove home, tapping to the beat of the song on the radio, with a smile on his face. Finally, a tiny step in the right direction. However small, he would take it and run with it. He made the biggest mistake of his life at eighteen years old, and that included the huge error that had cost him his job. Putting his life together piece by piece would take time, and he needed to be patient, no matter how hard it was. He needed to figure out the next baby step he could take with Kendra, and he knew just who to turn to for help with it.

***

The smell of baking bread hit his nose as he entered his childhood home, where he had been living the last few months since leaving New York. His father and Stella, both of his brothers, and his nephew Charlie all lived there as well, but the house was large and had plenty of room to escape each other. In addition to the main house, there was a small guest cottage out back where Stella had lived for years, a barn and a stable.

Stella, now his stepmother, but really his mom in so many ways, was at the stove stirring a pot. He crossed the kitchen to kiss her on the head and grab a cup of coffee before sitting at the kitchen island.

"Hi, honey," she smiled at him. "What's up?"

"I just came from seeing Kendra, she's going to come to dinner tomorrow night," he told her. "She's bringing Calle as well."

"Oh, that's wonderful. I've barely seen her since we got back from the honeymoon."

"I wondered—" Hesitation to spill his emotions on the kitchen floor held his tongue.

"Wondered what?"

"If you had any advice for me. About that."

"Dinner, or Kendra?"

"I think I can manage to eat dinner okay," he smiled. "But I can't seem to get through to Kendra. She doesn't want to talk to me, won't even give me a chance to apologize to her."

"What do you need to apologize for?"

"You were here, you know."

"I do know that," she gazed at him. "But do you know what hurt her? That's something important you should be thinking about, because when the time comes if you're not sincere or don't hit what hurt her, you wasted your time."

"Do you think she'll ever give me another chance?"

"I don't know," Stella admitted. "She loved you deeply and was very hurt. But I hope she'll come to realize that you were children, and you were bound to make mistakes. The experiences and lives you have led in the time apart can help you to build a better, stronger relationship now, if you both want that."

"I hope so."

"Dan, look at me." When he complied, she continued. "She wants to be strong, but she's fragile. I love you, and I want nothing more than for you to find happiness. I also suspect that your unresolved feelings for Kendra have kept you from finding that with someone else. But I don't want you to hurt her in order to resolve your feelings. If you only want to clear the air, or be forgiven, then there are other ways to make yourself feel better about things. If you want to really consider building a life with Kendra, you also have to be committed to being here. Being a stepdad. Those are things that will not change in her life."

He nodded, taking her advice to heart. It did sting to see Kendra so friendly with his brothers while ignoring him, and it was important that he wanted her for more than his ego. If she would give him a chance, spend some time with him, maybe they could both find out if they were even still compatible. Then he could figure out the rest.

Chapter 2

Kendra parked in the driveway and took a deep breath, looking at the house she had spent so much time in as a teenager. The white farmhouse seemed to glow in the night, with light beaming out the windows and from lamps along the long front porch. The nights got dark early this time of year, and the Burrows family seemed to accommodate the darkness by turning on every light in the house.

"Mama, let me out!" Calle demanded from the backseat, plucking at the buckles on her booster seat. Kendra knew she was overprotective to still have her six-year-old strapped in, at least according to the moms in the drop-off line at school, but Calle was all she had. She wasn't risking anything happening to her so she could save thirty seconds in the school parking lot.

"I'm coming, hold on." She gathered her purse, and the gifts she had brought along, before getting out to open the rear car door. Unbuckling Calle, she then handed her a small bouquet of flowers to carry. "These are for Ms. Stella. Or Mrs. Burrows now, I suppose."

"Okay, let's go!" Calle raced up the porch steps, no regard for the snow or ice that carpeted the pathway. Fortunately, she made it safely and was ringing the doorbell as Kendra climbed the stairs slowly. They both heard dogs bark from inside the house, and Calle's wide eyes met hers. "Mama, dogs!"

"Yes, honey, you know—" She was cut off by the door opening, showing a grinning Dan in the entryway holding two Labrador retrievers by their collars.

"Hi," he said, looking from Kendra to Calle. "I'm Dan. This is Twix and this is Reese."

"I love them," Calle declared, lunging forward for the kisses the dogs were waiting to disperse. She shoved the flowers into Dan's hands as she fell to the floor, giggling and surrounded by happy dogs.

"If only your mom was so easily swayed." Dan cocked an eyebrow in Kendra's direction.

"You promised," she whispered in what she hoped was a menacing way.

"I did, and I'll stick with it. Let me take your coats."

She handed him the bottle of wine she carried first. "I brought this for Stella and your dad."

"I'll pass it along. Thanks for coming."

They stared at each other for a long moment, and she let herself get washed back in time. Years ago, standing in this same spot, ready to go to prom. Her first kiss in the barn out back. Playing games with his family at the table they would sit at shortly, watching movies cuddled on the couch with him. Forcing herself to look away, she pushed the memories aside and focused on the present.

The thud of footsteps coming down the stairs preceded Dan's nephew Charlie appearing, and Kendra gave him a quick hug. Calle had grown up idolizing Charlie, the closest thing she had to a brother or cousin. Stella had made sure they saw each other regularly, so Calle had grown up seeing him play hockey and having him as an occasional babysitter, making their bond strong. She ran to him and threw herself at his legs, squealing with delight at seeing him. He picked her up and swung her around quickly before placing her safely on the ground. "Hey squirt, how are you?"

"I love your dogs. Will you read to me?" She gazed up at him adoringly.

He grabbed the small backpack she had dropped on the floor. "Sure, let's go on the couch. But I'm not doing Princess voices."

They argued as they made their way to the family room, and Dan led her into the kitchen, where Stella was behind the stove. Ben Burrows, Dan's father, sat at the island with a glass of whiskey in front of him. Kendra greeted both with a kiss on the cheek and pointed to the wine Dan held. "I brought a bottle of red, and Calle brought you flowers, but she dropped everything for Charlie and the dogs."

"I would do the same if I were her," Stella smiled. "Have a seat, or you two can grab a drink and go sit by the fire. Jake just went to pick up Shea, they should be here any minute."

Kendra hesitated, looking at Dan. He answered for them, holding up the wine he held. "Let's open this and sit by the fire to warm up while we wait for Jake and Shea." He quickly opened the bottle and poured two glasses, handing her one before leading her to the living room off the kitchen where a fire roared.

"I've always loved this room," Kendra mused as she walked around the large space. The room spanned the entire length of the house, and the wall with the fireplace was covered in pictures of the boys as they grew up. The wood beams in the ceiling and the stone going up the wall over the fire gave the room a cozy feeling despite being so large. A piano sat in one corner, a small bar set up in another, and a large seating area was in front of the fire.

"I appreciate it more as an adult than I did as a kid," Dan admitted. "We weren't allowed in here much when we were younger. I guess we just tracked mud everywhere and Stella wasn't having it in here."

"You three were pretty wild," Kendra agreed as she walked to look at the pictures on the wall, pausing when she came to one of Charlie as an infant with his mom, Jenna. Jenna had been tragically killed in a bombing when Charlie was only three months old, and Jake had shocked everyone when he enlisted in the Army and virtually disappeared for the next fourteen years. He had come home after being shot in Afghanistan a few months ago and decided to stay. "How is Charlie doing with Jake here full time now?"

"He's adjusting. I think it helps that he didn't have to move anywhere. Since my dad and Stella got married, they have been living out in the cottage out back where Stella has lived all these years. Stella keeps saying they will come to the main house when the honeymoon phase is over, which we all prefer to block from our brains." Dan pretended to shudder, and Kendra laughed. "Jake is thinking of building a house on a clearing just past the barn, that way when he and Shea are ready to live together, Charlie could still stay here but be around all the time, if he wanted."

"That's a great idea. Are Shea and Jake ready to move in so quick?"

"Well, remember, they wrote to each other for years. So even though the relationship is new, it's moving a lot faster than two strangers getting together."

She saw the look in his eye and held her hand up. "Don't start."

"I didn't say a word," Dan insisted as Patrick came into the room.

"Hey, Kendra." Patrick hugged her quickly before sitting on the couch. Kendra quickly sat next to him, leaving Dan the other couch or the chairs as his options for sitting.

"How are you, Patrick?"

"Great, staying busy. I just got back to Vermont yesterday, I had to fly over to Japan to do a commercial shoot." He yawned and covered his mouth with his hand. "Sorry, I'm still adjusting."

"That's a long flight to shoot a commercial. You must be exhausted."

Patrick shrugged. "You get used to it. And it's not like they have me flying coach, so I can sleep on the plane. I should have stuck around a few extra days or gone to Australia or Hawaii to break it up, but I just wanted to get back here. I'm so used to being home now, it's getting harder to leave."

"When do you have to travel again?" Kendra asked, leaning back on the couch.

"Not until after the holidays. I fly out in January to do some costume fittings, then we start filming in February in Georgia. I'll get home in between the two, I hope. The script is top secret, so I might need to relocate sooner than I thought to start working on that."

"Do you have lines? I thought you just flexed and beat people up?" Dan teased him with a grin.

"Yes, Daniel, I have lines." Patrick rolled his eyes at his brother. "These movies are no joke. We work long days, it's hard physically and we have to memorize a lot of dialogue. Some of it isn't even real words, since they introduced so many aliens and other planets. It's more than just fun."

"I know, I'm just kidding. I see all the paperwork you need to sign." Dan looked at his brother suddenly with a quizzical look on his face. "Speaking of, you never told me what the paperwork was that you signed at the Palace that night. What was that?"

"It was nothing, why do you keep bringing it up?" Patrick sounded irritated to Kendra's ear.

"As your lawyer, I should read everything before you sign it."

"You don't read the autographs I sign," Patrick pointed out.

Dan shot him a look. "Big difference between an autograph and what looked like legal documents."

"I bought some land, if you must know. And I had a real estate attorney check everything over, so you don't have to worry." With a huff, Patrick stood up from the couch. "If you'll excuse me, I'm going to find a beer."

They both watched as he left the room, and Kendra turned to Dan once he was gone. "You could cut him some slack. He is an adult. And a very rich, successful adult at that."

He sighed. "I know. It's hard, he lived with me as a teenager when I was in law school, and I was responsible for him. It's hard to stop thinking of him as my kid brother who needs looking after."

"He's pretty well grown by now," Kendra pointed out. "I think you owe him an apology."

"I will, later tonight. I promise." Dan placed his glass on the table in front of them and leaned toward her with a serious look on his face. "Kendra, I know- "

The noise level suddenly rose as Jake and Shea entered the kitchen, and the sound of all the voices and dogs barking broke up whatever Dan had been about to say. Kendra stood, wanting to break the tension between them. "Let's go say hi to them."

Dan stepped forward suddenly, putting himself between the door and Kendra. "Before we go out there, I just need to say one thing. I'm sorry. I know I owe you a million apologies, and it will never be enough, but I wanted to say it sincerely. I don't know how to explain what went wrong with me back then, and I don't know why I haven't fixed it until now. I'd really like the chance to try and explain to you. I plan to keep trying to convince you to let me, so you should get used to the idea."

She stared at him for a long moment, feeling frozen. "I appreciate the apology," she finally managed to say.

He stepped aside and waved an arm, indicating for her to walk through the door in front of him. She did so, feeling a little caught off guard. Yes, he had been hitting on her for weeks now, and trying to talk to her, but this was the first time she could ever remember him issuing an apology to her. Dan was not one to ever admit he was wrong, and hearing the words from his mouth shook her more than she wanted to reveal.

Pushing the emotions that rose to the surface aside, she entered the kitchen, determined to just enjoy the night with friends. Tonight, when she was alone in her bed, she could question what it was she was feeling for Dan at this moment.

Chapter 3

Sitting around the kitchen table with his entire family, plus Kendra and Calle, was surreal for Dan. He and Kendra had eaten many meals around this table during their teenage years, and he kept drifting back into his memories while the conversation swirled around him.

"Dan?" Shea's voice broke through his reverie. "Any interest?"

"I'm sorry, interest in what?"

"We were just talking about going to cut down a Christmas tree the day after Thanksgiving. Shea, Kendra and Calle are going to come along." Stella beamed at them as she spoke. "I'm so excited to have some girls along this year, I'm so used to just me and my Burrows boys, this will be extra fun."

"Count me in," he said, trying to read Kendra's expression. He caught her quick glimpse at him and the small bite she took of her lower lip, and realized she was nervous.

"I want a big, huge tree." Calle looked at Ben Burrows as she spoke. "As big as Charlie."

"I think she just called you fat," Patrick whispered to Charlie before turning to Calle. "I think we can get one that's even bigger than Charlie, if you want."

"Really?" Her eyes widened as she looked at Patrick, and then shook her head. "No, because we live up the stairs and it's hard for mama to carry that up all by herself. I'm not strong enough yet, but soon I will be."

"What if we put the biggest tree possible here?" Stella suggested from her seat next to Ben. "We can put it in the living room by the fireplace. There is a nice tall ceiling in there, and we have plenty of strong men to carry it inside."

"But then I won't see it every day," Calle pouted.

"You can come every day," Dan said, earning a glare from Kendra.

"That might be hard, Dan. I work every day." She turned to her daughter. "We can see it as much as possible, okay? And we'll have our own tree at home."

"We should plan a day to go shopping in Burlington," Shea suggested to Stella.

"That would be fun. Maybe on a Sunday, when these men are so busy watching football, we can't get them to do anything with us." Stella looked down the table at Kendra. "Any chance you two could join us?"

"Let me check the events at the restaurant," Kendra replied. "If there is a day I can sneak out, I'll let you know."

"And speaking of Thanksgiving," Stella said. "Kendra and Shea, what are your plans?"

"Shea will be here," Jake said around a mouthful of spaghetti, earning an elbow from Patrick. "Ow. Why did you do that?"

"You're talking with your mouth full." Patrick rolled his eyes like it was obvious.

"I'd love to be here, Stella. Let me know how I can help." Shea smiled at her.

"I'm not sure what our plans are yet," Kendra hedged.

"If you don't have plans yet, you do now." Ben nodded as though the subject was closed. "We owe you a huge debt for all you did the day of our wedding. We know that wasn't easy, planning it with such short notice, and we're very grateful. A meal on Thanksgiving is the least we can do."

"Every year we do a meal at the restaurant for anyone who doesn't have a place to go or can't afford a meal. I just need to make sure I can get that done before leaving." Kendra explained, flushing slightly. "Most people prefer to pick it up quietly during the week, our neighbors aren't fond of being seen taking a handout."

Ben frowned at her. "How long have you been doing this?"

"Since I took over the restaurant."

"And we didn't know about it? That's something we could have helped with."

"I try to keep it quiet, the people who need it know about it and let me know in advance they need some help," Kendra explained. "If I made a big announcement, I think they would all be scared off. The church helps to spread the word, and the schools, since they know who needs some extra help. They get the families all the information on how to contact me, so it can be done quietly."

"You must need help financially," Ben insisted. "We can help."

Patrick nodded. "I'm happy to help, just let me know what you need."

"Nothing, honestly." Kendra glanced at Dan, and he knew she wanted help ending the conversation. She had always been shy about her good deeds, for reasons he didn't understand. Most people would be shouting from the rooftops, but Kendra preferred to help without recognition.

"Charlie, any games this weekend?" Dan turned to his nephew, knowing he would engage everyone in conversation. He saw the frown on his father's lips and shook his head quickly at him, seeing his dad nod grudgingly in return.

Charlie lit up when he talked about his hockey team, and the whole family got engaged quickly. Even Calle wanted to know if she could get a cheerleader's uniform, an idea that Kendra quickly shut down by agreeing to let her wear one of Charlie's old jerseys to games, since it was too cold in the rink for a skirt.

Dan could see Kendra relaxing as the conversation turned the focus off her, and he wished he could reach for her hand. The urge was strong, but he knew it would only cause her to tense up again. He needed to figure out what he could do to get her to agree to spend time with him, and he needed to figure it out fast, before he needed to head back to New York to figure out his professional life.

Chapter 4

Kendra relaxed with Shea and Stella as the men cleaned the kitchen, laughing at the bickering happening between them all. She knew too many cooks in the kitchen was trouble, and apparently too many dishwashers were just as big a problem. Calle had gone back to the family room with the dogs and her books, content and quiet for a change.

"She really is adorable," Shea commented, seeing Kendra's look towards the room where her daughter was.

"She is," Kendra agreed. "A handful, but adorable."

"Is she loving being at school full time?"

"It's been a transition for sure, going from half day kindergarten to full day this year. But she has adjusted well, and her teacher is wonderful."

"That's great. I have a few years before I'll see her in school, but I give those first and second grade teachers credit. It's hard enough getting my students to sit still, never mind if they were six or seven."

"They did a Halloween event at the school," Kendra shared. "The kids were so wild; I couldn't believe it. And the teachers would give them one look and they would all quiet right down. I wish I had that skill."

"Me too," Stella laughed, pointing at the chaos at the kitchen sink.

"It's nice to see them all together." Kendra saw Dan glance her way as he laughed at something Patrick had said.

"Yes, having them all at home for these last few months has been amazing. Not to mention seeing Jake heal and open up with Shea as he has." Stella patted Shea's arm.

"It's been pretty amazing for me as well," Shea admitted. "My family lives so far away, I feel like I hit the lottery that in addition to getting Jake in my life, I get the whole Burrows clan. I couldn't be luckier."

Kendra smiled at them, thinking back to when she had been a regular member of the Burrows family. They had been some of the happiest days of her life, when she was cocooned in her relationship with Dan and enveloped in this family. Then it had all fallen apart, and she had tried to pull away from Stella and Ben, despite knowing it had hurt them. She couldn't handle any reminder of Dan, and every time she saw them, she was desperate to beg for information, which wasn't a good look.

Stella had refused to accept Kendra's withdrawal from her life, showing up at the restaurant where she was working and dropping by her small apartment. They had finally come to an agreement that they would remain close, but no mention of Dan would be made. With that assurance in place, Kendra had leaned on Stella heavily over the years, especially when she was pregnant and as the truth about the man she married came to light.

"Any thought of you two moving in together?" Kendra asked Shea, trying to redirect her thoughts.

"Yes, we plan to. We don't want to live at my house, though, because Charlie is here. It makes more sense to wait until Jake is able to build the house next door, and we can move in there. The plan is to get one level up quickly that we can live in, and then he can add on to the original structure with a second floor and more space downstairs." Shea laughed. "It might be a puzzle put together, but we don't need much when it's just the two of us."

"Any plans to make it more than the two of you?" Stella asked with a smile, surprising Kendra with the question.

"Yes, one day. He is doing great in therapy, which helps us both feel safe with the idea of having an infant. And I'd like to be married first, I know that's old fashioned, but it's important to me." Shea smiled while looking at Jake across the room. "Don't tell him that, I don't want him to feel rushed. I'm only just thirty, so we have some time."

Stella patted her arm. "Your secret is safe with us."

Kendra nodded, agreeing. There was a lump in her throat at the thought of Jake having a baby with someone other than Jenna, but she didn't want Shea to think she was upset at the thought. Clearly Jake needed to move on, and he couldn't ask for a better partner than Shea.

"Well, if you two want to live together sooner than later, Ben and I can always move into the main house, and you two can take the cabin," Stella offered.

Shea looked towards Jake thoughtfully. "I'll talk to him, see what he thinks. I don't want him to rush to start building and permits take forever anyway. He was grumbling last night about needing to wait until spring if they didn't come in soon, so we may take you up on that."

"Just say the word. I don't mind at all, and I know Ben doesn't. Last night we discussed adding a first-floor suite for when we hit our old age and won't want to do the stairs." Stella smiled at Ben as he came to sit next to her. "The girls and I were just talking about you and I moving back here, so Jake and Shea could have the cabin."

"Fine by me, I don't mind where I sleep as long as its next to you." He kissed her on the cheek, and she beamed at him.

"All this romance is getting to me," Shea said before she stood up and crossed to where Jake was drying the last dish. "Charlie, do you mind if I steal your dad for the night? I don't want him to drive back up after bringing me home, and I don't have my car here to leave him behind. It looks like it's starting to snow and I'm sure it will get icy fast."

Kendra glanced out the window, shocked to see snow coming down heavily. It wasn't unusual to see snow in Vermont, but she hadn't paid close attention to the weather forecast that morning, so this was a surprise. "I should get going myself, before the roads get bad. Shea, I can drive you home if you want."

Dan stopped fooling around with his brothers and turned to her. "Why don't I drive you home? I can bring your car down first thing in the morning."

"That's silly," Stella said. "The girls should just stay here. We have plenty of space."

"Oh, we couldn't possibly—" She was cut off by the scrape of a chair as Ben stood up.

"Stella is right, no point in anyone going out in this. Everyone is staying here tonight." He held up a hand to the objections coming from Kendra and Shea. "I know we're all well equipped with our four-wheel drive, and no one is scared to drive in the snow. But I also know there is no point in doing so when you're already inside, safe and sound, and don't have to go anywhere."

"Calle has school in the morning," Kendra tried to explain.

"If they have school, we can drive her and Charlie down bright and early. Plenty of time to stop at your place so she can change and grab her things." Ben dismissed her concerns as he stood from the table. "Come on, Stella. Let's make sure the guest rooms are made up and find the girls something to sleep in. Shea, I assume you'll be with Jake, but we can all pretend you're sleeping down the hall."

Shea blushed as Jake laughed, and they all watched the older couple walk down the hall.

"No offense to you all, but I'm going to turn in. I'm still jetlagged and exhausted, so I can barely keep my eyes open." Patrick smiled at all of them as he hung the kitchen towel up and started out of the room.

"I'm going to go up and play online with my friends." Charlie and Patrick walked out of the kitchen together, heading upstairs behind Ben and Stella.

"What time does Calle go to bed?" Dan asked, glancing at Kendra.

"Eight, usually." She glanced at her watch and saw it was already half past seven. "I should probably get her settled."

"I'll help you," Dan offered, which she quickly tried to object to before he continued. "I know where the toothbrushes and everything you'll need is stashed, so let me help."

Kendra stuck her head in the family room, seeing her daughter lying on the couch with the dogs. "Hey, honey, what do you think about sleeping over here tonight?"

"Really? That would be so fun." Calle bounced off the couch, making the dogs bark in excitement. "Can Twix and Reese sleep with me?"

"As long as you don't tell Stella." Dan winked at her and held a finger to his lips.

"That's not lying, is it?" Her face scrunched up as she considered.

"I'm only teasing, she knows the dogs sleep upstairs. She just likes to give us a hard time for spoiling them."

"Okay, then yes, I want them to sleep with me. Will I have my own room?"

"You will, you'll probably just be on the other side of a bathroom from your mom, if I had to guess."

"Can I see?"

"Yes, let's go up." He started toward the stairs, and Kendra's heart skipped three beats when her tiny daughter ran to catch up and slipped her hand into Dan's.

Her heart was one thing, but there was no way she could risk Calle's.

Chapter 5

Dan found himself reading a book to a sleepy Calle as he sat perched on the edge of the bed in the guest room. He hadn't remembered the theatrics that were required when it came to reading to a child, but although he knew Patrick would be better at this, he was enjoying his time with Calle. Her eyes slid closed as he neared the end of the book, so he closed it and quietly stood, turning off the bedside lamp before he snuck from the room.

Kendra had been leaning in the doorway as he read, and she stepped into the hall with him. "You did a good job."

"Thanks," he said softly. "First time reading to a kid since Charlie was little."

"Seems like a lifetime ago, when he was this age. And Calle is a lot more to handle, Charlie was always so easygoing."

He studied her, shocked to realize she had spent time with Charlie as a young child. "I didn't know you spent time with him when he was little."

Her cheeks turned pink, and she studied her fingernails suddenly. "Yes."

"Can we go downstairs and talk for a bit? Maybe open another bottle of wine? It's barely eight o'clock."

She hesitated, then looked up and met his gaze. "Sure."

His heart thumped as he followed her back down the stairs, wondering if this was when the tide would turn for him. He reminded himself to slow down, not push too hard, and let her come to him if possible. Lifting a bottle of red from the wine rack, he waited for her nod before pulling the cork and grabbing two glasses from the shelf. "Let's take this by the fire."

They settled back in front of the fire, this time on the same couch. Kendra accepted the glass he passed her, and he took a long sip of his before he spoke again. "Tell me how you knew Charlie at Calle's age."

"Stella and I were always close, back when we were kids. When you disappeared, I tried to drop out of your family life. She refused, and Jenna was right there with her, telling me that I was a part of their lives like it or not." She looked over to the picture on the wall of Jenna and Jake with a newborn Charlie, a sad look in her eye. "When Jenna got pregnant, she came over to talk to me, she was scared. But she knew Jake would be there for her, and I envied her a little. I was jealous. That's hard to admit."

"Jealous of the pregnancy?"

"No, of her and Jake. He was so devoted to her, and you had dropped me like I was nothing."

"I'm sorry," he started to say before she waved her hand.

"Let's not do that right now, let me finish." She took a sip of her wine and continued. "Jenna and I got closer during her pregnancy, and I was so happy for them when Charlie was born. I was here a lot those first few weeks, helping her when Jake was at work. When she died, I was devastated. I lost my friend, my little sister in my heart, but Charlie lost his mom. Then Jake left, which rocked everyone's world all over again. I vowed to help and be there for Charlie for Jenna, and I have followed through."

"I didn't know any of this."

"I swore Stella to secrecy. Your dad knew that I would babysit for them, but he thought it was more of a financial arrangement, I think. But I was around more than that, spending time with Charlie during the day when Stella was busy and watching him grow up."

"I'm surprised Charlie didn't mention it when I was home." Dan had visited frequently, or he thought he had.

"You weren't here often, and I kept myself busy when you were." She gave him a rueful smile. "Not hard to do when you would only pop up for a day at a time."

"Wow," he said as he put a hand over his heart. "You wound me."

"Truth hurts," she said with a small smile.

"It does. I was busy with work, but I wish I had been able to come more."

"When Calle was born, Charlie was like a big brother to her. Even now, he should be bothered by her as a teenager, but he loves spending time with her. He stops by a lot after school when he doesn't have practice and will sit and color with her or play outside for hours. He's such a good kid."

"I can't believe I didn't know any of this. I've been here for months now and still had no idea."

"Your family knows how difficult things are with us, so I'm not surprised."

"Can we maybe talk about things with us? Just let me say my piece, at least?"

She looked down, and he was sure she would say no. But then she met his gaze and nodded, and his heart skipped a beat. This was the chance he had been waiting for.

"I know I was wrong. One hundred percent. You thinking you were pregnant freaked me out more than I'd even like to admit now. I was going to NYU, and you were staying here in Windsor Peak. If you were pregnant, all my plans were going to go out the window. I knew I'd have to stay, and I thought my life was over. Instead of reassuring you, or thinking about how you must be feeling, I took the opportunity to drive a wedge between us, and I will never understand why I did that." He ran a hand through his hair, thinking back to the day he left for college. "We fought more those last few days than we ever had. Even when you told me you weren't pregnant, I could only think about myself, and worry that it could happen again, and I wouldn't get so lucky. But then I got to school and started worrying that you had lied to me."

"About not being pregnant?"

"Yeah. I know it's crazy. But I started thinking maybe you were trying to let me be free, and I was so upset that you had told me that you wanted a break when I left."

"I was just so raw, so upset about it all. For a minute I had the fairy tale thought of a family with you, and then I saw that being tied to me forever was a nightmare for you."

"No! That's the opposite, it had nothing to do with you. It was just that I knew I would have to give up my dreams."

"And I wasn't one of them." She gave him a sad smile as she looked down at the couch, and he saw a tear sneak out before she wiped it away.

"I wish I could go back and shake that kid," Dan said, feeling the frustration he had felt all those years ago. "But I took the easy way out. You told me to go, that we needed the time apart, and I jumped at it."

"I was pretty shocked," she admitted. "I was sure you would come over before you left, tell me it wasn't what you wanted. When I found out you had left, I was crushed."

"I knew within days what a mistake I had made. Everything I saw, every new experience I had, I only wanted to tell you about. I tried to call a few times and you never answered, so I decided to wait until I could make the trip back. Then next thing I knew, it was October, I had just been so busy with school the time flew without me knowing." He shook his head, wanting to go back and kick that kid for all the mistakes he had made. "When I got back here, you wouldn't talk to me. Told me it was over."

"Dan, it had been six weeks. Nothing from you for six weeks."

"I know. God, I was stupid."

"You have no idea how it hurt. I was still here, still seeing the same people, living the same life. Only now I had to keep telling everyone you were doing great at school and pretending I knew anything about your life. Meanwhile I cried myself to sleep every single night." She shook her head, as if shaking off the memory.

"I have no excuse, other than being a dumb teenage boy. I let your anger justify my actions, and threw myself into school, trying to forget you. It worked until Jenna died, and then suddenly I couldn't figure out what I had done wrong with my life. Jake was alone and not by choice, and here I was, having thrown you away."

"Yes, you did."

"I tried then too, hoping I could fix things."

"You tried to talk to me at Jenna's funeral. Not exactly the time or place." She leveled him with a look as she said the words.

"True. I was just so shaken up. I had spent days looking for her in New York with Jake. You can't imagine what that did to me." He sighed, flashing back to those frantic days spent running from hospital to hospital, searching fruitlessly. "Obviously not at Jake's level, but it rocked my whole world. And instead of running back to you, clinging to you, and devoting my life to making things better between us, I doubled down on my future. You know me, you know I need order and for things to make sense. Jenna dying didn't make sense. Jake enlisting didn't make sense. So, I buried myself in books, where things had clear rules."

"That's actually really sad," Kendra said. "You used to be so connected to everyone around you, so in touch with what your family needed."

"I know. And I couldn't explain why I needed to shut down, I don't think it was even a choice I made."

"Did you push me away because we were too close? Less risk if you don't care about the people around you, I guess."

"Was I scared to get hurt? Probably. But I feel like that's an easy excuse. Not that what I'm saying isn't, but it's just factual. Jenna died, I panicked, and I completely immersed myself into my education. Then I moved to California so Patrick could live with me, and I threw myself into helping him and getting my law degree."

She sighed, thinking back to how far away he felt all those years. "The space between us just kept growing. And I must admit, I got angrier every time you came home, and I was just nothing to you."

He leaned forward, closer to her. "You were never nothing to me. Never."

"But that's how it felt, Dan." She wiped a tear from her eye. "I was so in love with you. We talked about our future together, having a family. And for one shiny moment, I thought we would have it, even if the timing wasn't ideal. Then suddenly, you were gone and didn't look back, and I was so alone."

"Imagine how I felt when I heard you were getting married," he grimaced. "I came home then. I was determined to stop you; sure that I could make you realize what a mistake it was and that we should be together. Even then, years after we had broken up and hadn't spoken, I knew it should've been me. I came home, and you looked happy. Walking away was the hardest thing I've ever done, but I thought I was doing what was right. And I admit, I stayed away after that, because I felt betrayed that you had moved on and loved someone else."

"I don't think I ever loved him," she said sadly. "I tried to. But I was just so sad and felt lonely, and I didn't think you would ever come back. Then I found out I was pregnant, and he was adamant we get married. It was easier to go along than to fight it, and I guess I was happy at the time, or at least would have looked like it from the outside. I didn't know you came back then; no one told me. Before I got married, when you came home, you didn't really try. Yes, you said things sometimes, but never really tried."

"I'm trying now." He started to lean toward her and stopped himself suddenly. Kissing her would feel amazing, but she was vulnerable right now and they were a bottle of wine deep. Better to wait than to push things, he decided. As much as he regretted the decision, he forced himself to sit back again.

Chapter 6

The restaurant was quiet when Kendra let herself in from the back door after putting Calle on the school bus. They had woken up early, the streets freshly plowed and school on as scheduled, so they had rushed out of the Burrows house. Turning down breakfast from Stella had been difficult, but Kendra knew if she saw Dan this morning, she might have caved to his charm.

Half the night she had stared at the ceiling and thought about what he said. Was she being unreasonable, still being so angry? They had been teenagers, and heaven knows they both had made mistakes in their relationship. Both stubborn and opinionated, they were prone to passionate arguments and heated debates. Holding a grudge this many years later was probably over the top, even for her.

Her feelings for Dan had run deep and strong, even though they were so young. Her parents had worked constantly when she was a child, and since she didn't have siblings, most of her life she felt alone. She had been unplanned, as her mother had recounted once, and neither parent wanted to step back from their career to raise a child. Not to mention, they were efficient as parents, but not necessarily warm and fuzzy. The bond she had formed with Dan had filled a void in her, and she had relied heavily on him. Not only with him, she realized, but with the Burrows, who had given her the first sense of what a family truly was. Being a part of their family unit again for one night had felt like slipping on a favorite cozy sweater.

The conversation with Dan last night had impacted her more than she let on in the moment, but she could feel her resolve weakening. If he were to walk in right now and ask her to dinner, or even just kiss her, she wouldn't be able to say no. The thought scared her because he still held so much power over her. There was no way Dan would stay in Windsor Peak forever, and her whole life was here. Getting involved with him again was a recipe for disaster, but she had no idea how to resist.

"Hi." Kendra was startled out of her thoughts by her new chef, Zoe. She had started the previous week and had a habit of showing up hours before the restaurant opened.

"Morning," Kendra replied. "What are you doing here so early?"

"I'm still on France time, so I'm up way too early. Figured I might as well get the walk-in freezer organized." Zoe was a petite blonde with a pixie haircut and a half French, half Canadian accent. She had grown up in Canada, relocated to France for culinary school, and had turned up in Windsor Peak for reasons unknown.

"I'm sure the freezer will appreciate your early wake up," Kendra replied.

"Are you alright? You looked upset."

"Yes, I'm fine. Just a matter of the heart."

"I'm French, I know all about love. Tell me." Zoe perched on a barstool and looked ready to listen.

Kendra had two close friends who had been by her side since she was a young girl, but found she clicked with less people as she got older. Maybe she was fussier about who she spent time with, or simply didn't have time for new friends with Calle. Most likely, the reason had to do with her unwillingness to trust new people, which she could credit her ex-husband with.

Deciding it was worth hearing an outsider's perspective, especially one she was quickly growing to like, she opted to share with Zoe.

"My high school boyfriend came back to town a few months ago. It's causing me some heartache."

"He's the one who sits here at the bar looking sad and handsome when we're supposed to be getting things done between lunch and dinner?"

"Yes."
"But he is not Calle's father?"

"No, we broke up when he went to college. Calle's dad came later."

"And where is he?"

Kendra shrugged. "I have no idea. I don't want to know."

"But this one, you care about him still?"

"I think so." She sighed, weighing her thoughts. "I was so angry for so many years, that's all I knew. But when I spend time with him, it's like he never left."

"Maybe this is a good thing."

"Or maybe he'll break my heart again."

Zoe shrugged, pushing off the barstool. "What is life if it doesn't hurt sometimes? How would we know what is good if we don't also see the bad? We were all fools as children, he must have changed the same way you have. If he makes you smile, you should try. You could be surprised."

"Thanks, Zoe."

"What is the point of having a French chef if you can't talk about love?" She headed for the kitchen, humming a tune as she went.

Kendra watched her leave, then did a quick inventory of the bar and decided to go for a quick run before opening for lunch. Some exercise and fresh air, then a shower, would invigorate her for the day. Not to mention take her mind off Dan.

***

Dan was stopped by a table full of skiers as he entered the restaurant late that afternoon, so Kendra had a chance to study him from afar. Despite the years that had passed, he was still as handsome as ever, if not more so. The five o'clock shadow he could never seem to avoid added to his tall and dark good looks, and his body had clearly enjoyed time in the gym. As a teenager he had been on the thinner side, but he had filled out nicely as an adult.

She watched as he said goodbye to the table full of people and crossed to sit at the midway point of the bar. "Friends of yours?" she asked, indicating the table.

"People I knew in New York; they came up for some early skiing when they heard we were due for fresh snow."

"You must miss the city."

"Not as much as I thought I would," he replied. "Some things here are more appealing than Manhattan."

She decided to leave the subject alone and poured him a soda, placing it on a coaster in front of him.

"Thanks. I'm sorry I missed seeing you this morning."

"Dan," she whispered, looking around. "You make it sound like we spent the night together."

"Well, we did, technically. Under the same roof at least."

"Still, you know how fast rumors fly in this town."

"You can't be worried about that. I'm a safe bet to be linked with, especially now. If you weren't worried about being associated with me when I was a wild teenager, this shouldn't be a problem."

"I have Calle to think about."

He shook his head. "They aren't talking about us at the elementary school. And I think you're using her as an excuse."

"I'm sorry?"

"You're using her as an excuse to not date. I don't know what happened with your ex, but I would like to know. And I'd like to make up for what he did, and what I did, to your heart. I wish you would stop hiding behind Calle."

She felt her cheeks turning red and couldn't decide if she was mad or embarrassed. Yes, she was probably using her daughter as a reason to not get close to anyone. Calle was the most important thing in her life, and she was going to protect her at all costs. "You really don't know what you're talking about."

"Prove me wrong," he dared. "Go to dinner with me tomorrow."

Of all her weaknesses, being unable to resist a dare was her least favorite. Dan knew the button to push, and since she had already been halfway to convincing herself to give him another chance, she found herself nodding. "Fine. As long as you agree that if it doesn't go well, we go our separate ways as friends. Deal?"

"Deal." He was beaming as he stood up, grabbing his jacket from the back of the chair. "I'm going to go make a reservation now. Pick you up at seven? Or would you rather bring Calle to the house and have her stay there with Stella? She could sleep over again; they would love it."

Always the problem solver, he was three steps ahead of her in anticipating any excuse she could make. "I'll let you know, let me check with her regular sitter first."

"Okay. I'll touch base with you later. I'm leaving before you change your mind." He grinned at her and headed out, feeling happier than he had in weeks.

She shook her head as she watched him leave, equal parts frustrated and looking forward to the date. It was probably inevitable that he would get his way and convince her to give him another chance, so maybe it was a good thing that she had agreed to this one night to get it out of his system. One night, and then they could maybe be friends. That was all this could be. Firmly resolved, she turned back to finish her tasks before thoughts of the past or future could completely throw her off schedule.

Chapter 7

"What are you doing?" Patrick asked as he entered the kitchen and leaned over Dan's shoulder to look at his cell phone.

"Trying to decide where to go to dinner tomorrow night."

"With who?" Patrick opened the refrigerator and grabbed a bottle of water.

"Kendra."

"She finally said yes? What came over her?"

"My wit and charm."

Patrick laughed. "No, really. What changed her mind?"

"Not really sure," Dan said as he leaned back in his chair. "But I'm running with it. I need to find the perfect spot to take her, somewhere romantic and amazing."

"I tried a new place in Stowe a few weeks ago, it was great. It's very small, exclusive, just a few tables but well spread out. Nice fire going, might fit the bill."

"What's the name of it?" Dan opened a browser on his phone to search for the phone number.

"I think it was called Fireside."

Dan found the number and called, only to be quickly rebuffed by the person who answered the phone and assured him they were booked solid for months.

"Go ahead, you can ask me." Patrick was leaning on the counter, listening as Dan hung up the phone.

"Could you get me a table?" Dan couldn't believe he was asking his youngest brother for such a favor, but desperate times called for desperate measures.

"I didn't hear a please in there."

"Please, Patrick, can you get me a reservation?"

"And maybe that you think I'm the greatest-"

"Patrick."

"Fine. I'll have my agent call, what time do you want it for?"

"Seven thirty. Thank you."

Patrick nodded, already texting on his phone. "Want to hit the gym with me? Can't have you slacking now that you finally got Kendra to agree to go out with you again."

Dan stood up, checking his watch. "Think we have time to go before it gets busy? I can't deal with all the girls standing around watching you."

"If we go now, we should be alright." Patrick groaned. "We really need to put a gym in here. It probably will be a little crazy, I should have gone hours ago."

"Alright, get your hat on, maybe we can stay out of sight. At some point people have to realize you're sticking around." Dan bumped his brother with his shoulder as they walked down the hall. "Not that I know what all the fuss is about. If they got to know you, they would probably fade away."

"Very funny. Maybe I should just text my agent back again and tell her we're all set."

"No, I'm sorry. You know I think you're the greatest actor of all time." Dan laughed as Patrick put the phone back into his pocket. "Besides, you want Kendra to have a nice night as much as I do."

"In that case, maybe I should take her."

"Not in this lifetime, buddy. I'm winning her back and never letting go."

***

Dan was surprised at how nervous he was when he knocked on Kendra's door the following night. She had texted him earlier, stating that her babysitter was available, and he could pick her up for their date. He had stopped at the florist earlier in the day and clutched two bouquets in his hand as he waited for the door to open.

"Hi," Kendra said breathlessly as she answered, stepping out to where he stood on the porch. She took his breath away in a classic little black dress that she had paired with a pair of cowgirl boots and a jean jacket. "I'm sorry, I should have met you downstairs."

"It's okay," Dan replied, cut off from saying anything else when the door opened again to reveal Calle.

"Hi! What are you doing here?"

"I brought you some flowers," he answered, handing her one of the bouquets he held.

"Who are those for?" She pointed at the flowers still in his hand.

"Your mom." He offered them to Kendra with a smile.

"Thank you, that was very sweet. Calle, let's put this inside." Kendra hesitated, then indicated he could come in as well. "Come in while I find some vases."

Calle bounced around the kitchen, dancing to music playing in the adjacent living room. The space was cozy, he noted. The kitchen was updated with stainless appliances and granite countertops, and what looked like new hardwood floors that ran into the next room. He waved to who he assumed was the babysitter on the comfortable looking sectional sofa facing the television. A shelf full of toys and books against the wall, pictures of Kendra and Calle mixed in with everything. An open door off the kitchen looked to be a bathroom, and a hallway in the living room likely led to the bedrooms. It was clean and well decorated, and obvious that a six-year-old girl lived there, with dolls and glitter everywhere the eye could see.

"Dan, will you take me skiing this weekend? Mama is busy at the restaurant, but I want to ski."

Kendra stooped down, whispering in Calle's ear frantically. Calle shook her head and gave her mom such a look of determination that he had to laugh, knowing that stubborn streak had come from Kendra.

"Mama, he's our friend and I want to ski with him." Calle crossed her arms across her chest and scowled at her mother, clearly determined to get her way.

He looked to Kendra, seeing the uncertainty on her face. "If your mom says it's okay, I'd love to take you."

"Really?" Both Kendra and Calle looked at him with the same wide eyes.

"Sure, my skis are ready to go. If you're alright with it, that is."

Kendra nodded slowly. "You'll have to take it easy. No black diamonds."

"I can do the bunny slope with the best of them."

"No bunny slope," Calle declared. "That's for babies."

"She's pretty good, but she has no fear. I don't want to have her go flying into trees or off the side of the mountain."

"Mama, you can't fall off a mountain."

"Still, Dan will pick the runs and you'll go along, understood?"

"Yes." She nodded solemnly before turning back to Dan. "Can Charlie come too?"

"I'll ask him. If he doesn't have a hockey game, I'm sure he'll want to come. Patrick too, I bet."

Calle clapped her hands in delight, running over to hug him around his legs. "I'm so excited."

"Me too," he said as he patted her head.

"Okay, time to go settle down and watch a movie with Nora." Kendra leaned down and kissed her daughter good night, whispering in her ear.

Calle turned to face him again. "Thank you for the flowers."

He smiled. "You're very welcome. I'll see you on Saturday for skiing."

"Bright and early?"

"You got it." He watched her run off to the couch, where her teenage babysitter was waiting, before turning to Kendra. "Ready?"

He followed her down the stairs, rushing to the car to open the passenger door for her. She settled into the passenger seat and sighed. "I might have to move into your car, this is so nice."

"Wait until I turn on the seat warmer," he promised, closing the door. When he got in and turned the car on, he hit a few buttons on the dashboard before turning to her. "As much as I'd love to be the one warming your buns, this will help."

"*Dan*," she laughed. "How do you manage to make the simplest things sound dirty?"

As he drove, they talked about her day at the restaurant and the changes her new chef was hoping to make to the menu. "I'm not sure people will go for a lot of it," she admitted. "But she's so good, I can't risk losing her. I think we will have a very wide array of food, from burgers to finer French cuisine."

"Something for everyone, probably a good business model."

"True, I got lucky when she turned up looking for a job. Like a magical fairy who just arrives when you need them the most, so I try not to question it too much."

"She didn't live here before she started working for you? What happened to your last chef?"

"No, she had been living in France, finishing her culinary training. Honestly, I get the sense she had been planning to stay there, or at least go to a big city in Canada or the US, but somehow, she found Windsor Peak. She had stellar references and she made me a meal as we talked about the job, and I would have hired her based on the food alone. My chef had just taken a job at a new restaurant in Burlington, some trendy spot that's already struggling from what I've heard." She turned toward him in her car seat. "Some people can't help chasing the bright light, even when the risk of it going out are high."

"Touché."

"Since we're on the subject, what happened with your job?"

"Oh, we're jumping right into it, huh?" He glanced at her and saw the curiosity in her eyes. "I was distracted when Jake came home. We were all worried about him, and as much as I tried to keep up with work, I wasn't fully focused. I slipped on a contract, let something in that should never have gotten past me. I could have fixed it, but a colleague spotted it first and ran to the client, saying I would have gotten them in trouble but that he had caught it. Then he started approaching all my clients, saying the same, that I was slipping and not all in. He also made some claims that get me too fired up to repeat right now, but suffice it to say, they were lies. One by one the big corporate clients were asking to be moved to him, and my bosses noticed."

"That's not fair. You would have caught it eventually. And if he lied, you should have pointed that out."

"I probably would have caught it, but I had sent it for signatures. It could have ended badly for my client, and I was distracted. The lies bothered me more than anything else, honestly." He was trying hard to keep himself emotionally uninvolved in the retelling, so he wouldn't express the anger and frustration he had felt over the whole situation. He had given his life to this firm, and they turned on him in an instant, but that wasn't going to ruin this night for him.

"He stole all your clients?"

"No, obviously Patrick is still with me, and all his Hollywood friends. Who would have thought I would be an entertainment lawyer?" He laughed, thinking back to his younger days, when he was sure he would pick the greater good over greed. "I left the firm when it was clear what was happening, and that no one would have my back. At the end of the day, I should have been able to take some time off for a family emergency. What kind of job doesn't let you even take a vacation?"

"Owning a restaurant," she quipped. "And apparently, being a big shot lawyer."

"Well, I realized that there were more important things in life. Honestly, I could just work for Patrick and no one else, but I have my pride to worry about."

"He can't be hard to work for."

"No, but he's my baby brother. I can't rely just on him for my income."

"Do you want to go back to the law you were practicing in New York?"

"I have to admit, I'm enjoying what I'm doing now. It's not nearly as busy, and I enjoy the people that I work with. Obviously, Patrick is easy, and most of the other actors are the same. They don't want to deal with the nitty gritty of their contracts, they just want to know that what they were promised is included." He shrugged. "It's a lot more interesting some days than corporate mergers."

"I can imagine. I always thought you would be trying to save the world. Or at least, save the little guy from the big, bad guys."

"I thought so too. I guess I got distracted by all the flash and the competitiveness of it. Somehow, I ended up where I was, and I can't even remember how I got there."

"That's not good." She looked out as he pulled into the parking lot. "Oh, I've heard about this place. You must have had to pull some strings to get a reservation."

"You could say that," he laughed as he jumped out to open her door for her.

They settled into the table they were led to by the hostess, a private two-seater nestled by the fireplace behind a wall of plants that shielded them from the view of others. It was as if they were all alone, other than the attentive waitstaff filling water glasses and offering a wine list.

Dan half listened as the waiter expounded on the menu, touting the virtues of the prix fixe option that included five courses. He knew Kendra well enough to know that she would enjoy all the courses, and that she would never order it for herself because she would worry about the cost. Handing his menu back to the waiter, he asked him to put them both down for the fixed option.

"Dan, that's too much." Kendra objected, but he nodded at the waiter, who disappeared.

"It's not too much. I'm trying to woo you, remember?"

"Oh, is this a wooing? I don't think I know how that works."

"Ouch. I thought I did that years ago."

She laughed. "I don't think teenagers ever know how to be romantic. I'm sure we thought we did, but we had no idea what we were doing. You must have gotten lots of practice in New York."

"Less than you think," he said as he swirled his glass of wine. "I worked eighty-hour weeks most of the time. When I did socialize, it was usually client events. Yes, I dated, but honestly didn't have the energy or interest in a relationship."

"That's sad," she said softly.

"Not really," he shrugged. "I was happy until I knew better."

"That I understand."

He gazed into her eyes, wanting to break down all the walls between them. The biggest hurdle might be the hardest to jump, since he knew that whatever had happened with her ex-husband had scarred her heart. But he had to know if they had any chance of being together. "Will you tell me about Calle's dad?"

Chapter 8

"Oh, that's a lot." She sipped her wine and used the time to compose her thoughts. She didn't talk about Brad to anyone, ever, other than her therapist. But Dan was the person she had trusted more than anyone, and if she were to find herself in a crisis, she knew that she could still lean on him. He would be able to handle the truth, and if she was even entertaining the idea of a future for them, he had to know. "We met at the restaurant. He was a salesman with one of the big ski brands, moved to Vermont from Colorado. Swooped me off my feet, and right into bed. Next thing I knew, I was pregnant with Calle and thought the sun rose and set on him."

"When did that change?"

"I wish I could say it was the first time he hit me." She knew the detachment was evident in her voice and was glad she was able to say it out loud without emotion. Her therapist had worked with her for a long time to separate who she was from what happened to her, and she could look at the incident now almost as an outsider.

"Oh, Kendra." She saw the pain in his eyes, and how he shifted back in his chair slightly, as if ready to get up and go find Brad. "I had no idea."

"No one does. I can't believe I even just told you that." She sighed, playing with her silverware. "That's actually not true, people know now, they just didn't know when it was happening. The Holmes' knew. They were the ones who saved me."

"What happened?"

"He had isolated me, broken me away from my friends and family. I was completely reliant on him; he controlled the money, and I had no idea where we were financially. I think he was both happy and mad that I was pregnant, because it took my attention off him. He used to come home from traveling and tell me these disgusting stories about women coming on to him, trying to sneak into his hotel room." She shuddered. "I should have kicked him out a hundred times over. But I didn't, I was foolish and thought he was choosing me over all these women who wanted him so badly. Plus, I had no one to turn to."

"I wish you could have called me."

"Me too," she said softly. "But he checked my phone records anyway. And I never was able to have privacy if I did talk to someone. He read my text messages, sent vile things to my family that looked like they came from me. Then when I had Calle, she was about six months old when he decided I had looked at another man. He hit me so hard I saw stars. I couldn't leave the house for days until the bruises faded."

He groaned, running his hand down his face as if he was in pain himself.

"I could never make him happy; I was never good enough. One day I went into the restaurant with Calle, and Janet Holmes took one look at me and went to get Ron. He left for a few hours, and when he came back, he said Brad was gone. I didn't have to worry about him again." She allowed herself a small smile. "You know how protective Ron was, he was my pseudo-dad once my parents moved to South Carolina. I think he would have happily driven Ron to a cliff and thrown him over, but he knew it would come back on me if he did."

"You haven't heard from Brad since?"

"Other than signing divorce papers, nothing."

"What did Ron say to him?"

"I have no idea. He would never tell me. Just said he had taken care of it, and that Calle and I were safe with them until we felt like we could go home. But then they asked if I would move in upstairs and manage the restaurant full time, and obviously I needed the roof over our heads and the pay." She met his eyes as the first course was delivered to the table. "And the rest is history."

"I hope you had someone to talk to about all this," Dan said.

"Yes, I went to therapy for a few years, and Janet was a shoulder to cry on. I think Stella figured it out as well, I spent a lot of time with her. I used to have panic attacks, just out of nowhere. Suddenly the air would be gone from the room, and I had almost tunnel vision. It was terrifying, I wouldn't be able to move." She took a bite of her food and almost moaned in pleasure as the flavors hit her tongue. "I had to go to therapy to get better for Calle."

"You're a good mom."

"You don't know that. You've seen us together a handful of times. But I try really hard."

"I don't have to see you with her all the time, I know how caring you are and from what I've seen, she's lucky to have you."

"I'm lucky to have her," she said softly. "It really made me see the damage I did to my parents in a new light."

"What damage?"

"When Brad decided he wanted them out of my life, he stopped at nothing to remove them. He caused so many fights, and so much drama, and then would just step away and let me fight them for him. He played victim so well, I fell for it every time, never even stopping to think that it wasn't in my parent's nature to act the way he was accusing them of." She took a deep breath, trying not to wallow in the memories. "He managed to completely break me away from them, and it broke their hearts. I had turned on them, treated them horribly, and kicked them out of my life. Seeing that from their perspective and thinking about how I would feel if Calle had done that to me was enlightening."

"You weren't of right mind," he said, giving her an excuse.

"I should have been. I should be stronger than that. Yes, he controlled me, he even controlled my thoughts and actions. But I was weak enough to let him."

"Kendra," he said softly. "I'm sorry. I don't think you're weak at all."

"I was then," she insisted. "I was so down on myself after you left, so lacking any confidence in myself, that I was easily pushed into the mold he wanted. Before I even knew what was happening, I had no control over my own life. Money, phone, friends, social media, nothing. By the time he got physical with me, I had nowhere to turn."

"Did it happen often?"

"The hitting?" She thought back, allowing her mind to revisit it briefly. "Not really. Just enough to keep me scared, I guess. He was a big drinker, and it usually happened when he was drunk. I think he took drugs too, but I can't say for sure. But he was usually on something that he could blame the next day, saying he was blacked out and it wasn't him that did it."

"No amount of alcohol should cause a man to put his hands on a woman."

"Agreed." She picked up her wine glass, ready for a change in topic. "Enough about all these sad stories. Let's talk about something happy. Your dad and Stella seem to be enjoying the honeymoon phase, and Jake looks to be over the moon for Shea."

"Over it and then some. I think he'll propose soon, if I had to guess." He pushed his empty plate away from him, prompting the busboy to come and clear the table. "My dad, I don't think I've ever seen him so happy. They still haven't told us how long this has been going on, but I tend to think it was from when we were little."

"You think they kept it a secret this whole time?"

"Think about it. Neither one of them ever dated anyone else. My dad was widowed in his early thirties, and Stella never married." He held up a hand. "I don't think anything happened when my mom was alive, what little memory I have of her, they were always laughing and dancing together. But I think when he was ready to move on, the best friend in the guest cottage was the perfect fit."

"That's nice that you remember that about your mom. And yes, I actually think I agree with you, now that I think about it. They came into dinner together once or twice a week all these years and looked better suited for each other than half the married couples I would see." She laughed, amused at how she had completely missed it. "I can't believe she kept it a secret from me all these years."

"You and me both," he said. "But then again, I was the son, and I sure didn't want to be thinking about my dad's sex life. Or Stella's, for that matter."

"No, I can't imagine you did." They laughed together, and her breath caught as their gaze locked. The waiter interrupted to deliver the next course before she could lose herself completely in his eyes, and for that, she was grateful.

This was her first date with a man since Brad, and it shocked her how comfortable she was. Granted, she had such a history with Dan, it was like slipping on a worn pair of jeans. But all the years she had spent thinking it was better to be alone, that she should never risk her heart again, and here she sat. Her heart halfway to falling, her mind still trying to fight it. She wanted to say this was a good test to get her back into the dating pool and ready for a new relationship, but she knew that unless it was the man across the table, she would never be ready. Her heart wanted Dan, and no one else.

Chapter 9

Dan's stomach was rolling, and he couldn't imagine putting another bite of food in his mouth, but he didn't want Kendra to see how much her story had upset him. He knew she hated pity, and although it wasn't what he was feeling, that's how she would interpret it.

"Dan," she touched his hand where it sat on the table, playing with his knife. "I can see you're upset about what I told you. I don't want that to be the case. I've moved on, and there is nothing you can do to change the past."

"No, but if I wasn't an idiot when I was eighteen, it wouldn't have happened at all."

"You can't know that," she responded. "We could have broken up at any point when you were away in college, or when you were in California. You never had a future here in Windsor Peak, you were too big for this little town."

"That's not true." He shook his head, but she knew he understood what she was saying. "I would have come back here to be with you, or you could have come to California or New York to be with me."

She tilted her head to the side and gave him a small smile. "Can you really picture me in either of those places?"

He laughed, thinking of what a tomboy Kendra had been as a teen. She had spent most of her time without makeup, hair pulled back, in jeans and a sweatshirt. The most expensive clothing item she owned was a pair of boots she wore when riding a horse, and they were not the fashionable cowgirl boots he saw in Los Angeles so often. Hers had usually been covered in mud, were worn down on the inside where they rubbed against the horse and were molded to her feet perfectly.

That girl wouldn't have fit in where he lived in California, or in the high-power circles he was a part of in Manhattan. However, the woman across from him, who had her black hair hanging down her back, in a dress that showed all her curves, would turn heads in either location.

"Maybe not then, but now, yes."

"Now I have Calle. And I want her to have the same small-town life I had, where it's safe for her to run down the street alone to meet a friend, and I don't have to worry about school shootings or drugs."

"There is bad everywhere, Kendra. Look at Brad."

"Yes, that's true." She looked thoughtful as she pushed her plate away from her. "I feel like he was a fluke, he only ended up here because he ran out of money. He was a gambler, and not a good one, even tried to be a day trader for a while. Blew through the little he earned and had to come live with an aunt to get his feet under him. He told me that he moved here because she was getting older and needed help, so he convinced his company to transfer him here. Turns out that was a lie too, he had just run out of money and people to scam in Colorado, and his aunt was willing to fall for his sob story. She ran the old antique store, and he helped her manage it."

"Is that still in business?"

"No, he bled her dry too."

"Too?"

She nodded, not meeting his eyes. "I didn't have any control over our finances, so when he left, I found out there was nothing. He had gambled it all, or spent it on drugs, anything other than what he said he was doing. My credit was destroyed, I'm still recovering from that."

"Shit, Kendra." He ran a hand over his forehead, trying to will away a stress headache.

"No." She met his gaze with a look of steely determination. "I will not let him have any more control over my life. Yes, it was horrible. Yes, I regret ever getting caught up in his lies. But I don't regret Calle, and I refuse to let him continue to have a negative impact on my life."

"Okay," he said slowly, unsure of where to go next.

"Let's finish this meal, talking about anything that doesn't give one of us heartburn." Her eyes softened as they met his. "I actually want to enjoy this night, Danny."

"Me too," he said softly, reaching for her hand and thrilled when she accepted it.

They spent the rest of the meal talking about lighter topics, from Calle's attempts at playing soccer to tales from the Burrow's household. Letting go of her hand to enjoy the delicious meal had been a sacrifice, but he savored every second he spent gazing into her eyes and getting to know her again. When they finished their last course, he helped her with her coat and escorted her to the parking lot.

"This was nice," she admitted as he started the car.

"It was," he smiled at her. "I'm glad I finally wore you down."

She sighed. "You do have a history of always getting your way."

He chuckled, and she shot him a questioning look. "Just thinking ahead to whether I'll get a kiss goodnight. Should I start my arguments now in favor?"

She squeezed his hand. "Save your breath, I think you're in good shape."

"Does this mean I could take you out again?"

"Yes, I suppose it does. I've told myself for years that I would never go down this road again, and now I've fallen under your spell in record time. I should be ashamed of myself."

"No." He signaled to exit the highway, slowing the SUV down to prolong the time he had with her. "Don't think like that. This is a second chance for us, we were stupid kids back then. I can tell you that adult me is very interested in a future with adult you, and we would be bigger fools to not explore this."

"Just promise me one thing."

"Anything."

"Don't let Calle get hurt in this. I can handle my own broken heart if this all falls apart, but I can't handle hers."

"I'm not going to break any hearts."

"You can't promise that. So just be aware of how much time and attention you give her, don't let her start depending on you if you're not sure you'll be here next week. Deal?"

"I will be here—"

"Dan."

"Okay, deal." He pulled into the driveway that ran to next to the restaurant to a small parking lot, where the stairs to her apartment were hidden. After parking, he jumped out and went to the passenger side to open her door.

"We should probably say goodnight out here," she said, glancing up at the small balcony outside her door.

"I'm a gentleman, and I'll have to walk you to your door. Otherwise, Stella will find out somehow and I'll never hear the end of it." He offered her a hand, and she hesitated, then slid her hand into his. As she stepped out of the car, her heel caught on the running board of his SUV and she stumbled into him, landing against his chest. "Are you okay?"

"Yes, sorry." She looked up, her eyes looking dazed.

His restraint thrown off by the sudden full body contact, he skimmed his hand along her jawline and into her hair and lowered his lips to hers. Tasting the wine and hint of chocolate from dessert on her lips, he released her hand to wrap an arm around her lower back, so she was sealed to him. Suddenly he was seventeen again, wanting to explore every inch of her.

Sudden noise from the kitchen reached his ear, and he became aware that someone was dumping a bucket of water out of the side door, feet away from where they were making out like teenagers. He waited until the door closed again before stepping back from her. "I should get you inside before we get carried away out here."

"That would be a little embarrassing, since these people all work for me now." She cast a glance over at the door before crossing the dark lot towards the stairs, leading him by the hand.

When they reached the landing, she held a finger to her lips. "We have to be quiet, or Calle will hear us."

"I can be quiet," he whispered, taking her in his arms again.

What felt like seconds later the door behind them suddenly opened, and Kendra jumped away. Her lips were swollen and her hair wild where his hands had been, an image that he would happily have in his head as he drifted off to sleep later.

"Mama, what are you doing out here?" Calle stood in the doorway, in her pajamas, clinging a teddy bear to her chest.

"The bigger question is why are you still awake, young lady." Kendra tried to usher her daughter inside, casting a look over her shoulder at Dan. "I'll see you later. Thank you, Dan. This was a good night."

"I'll walk your babysitter to her car," he offered, pulling out his wallet. "I wanted to pay her for the night."

"That's not necessary."

"I know, but I invited you out, and I'd like to do this. And I want to make sure she gets home safely before I leave."

Kendra smiled at him before looking to where the teenager was pulling on her jacket, ready to go. "Dan will walk you to your car, Nora."

"Thanks." She accepted a hug from Calle and then slid a backpack on her shoulder before joining Dan on the porch. He offered her cash, which she took with a sharp intake of breath that told him it was too much, but she quickly tucked it away.

He drove home after seeing Nora's taillights disappear, satisfied with how the night had gone and feeling hopeful about his future for the first time in months.

Chapter 10

Kendra was up early the next morning, helping a hyper Calle get ready for school and count the hours until her ski date with Dan. Getting her into her leggings and sweater was a struggle, as she was jumping all over the room in excitement.

"Mama, I can't wait to ski tomorrow!"

"I know, sweetheart. But try to stay still so I can braid your hair, okay?"

"He won't believe how fast I'm."

"No, I think he'll be surprised."

"Do you think he wears a helmet too?"

Kendra made a mental note to text Dan, making sure he would bring his helmet. She assumed he would, as he tended to lean towards safety in most areas of his life, and yet he might consider an easy day of skiing with a six-year-old safe.

Finally sending her daughter off to the bus with a hug and a kiss, she collapsed at her kitchen table with a cup of coffee and allowed herself to relive the night before. Being with Dan had filled her with the comfort of an old friend, and the excitement of a new man. She didn't know the Dan who was a high-powered attorney in Manhattan or have any idea what his dating life had been like for the last sixteen years. They had avoided any talk about their love lives, other than discussing Brad, and she wondered if that was intentional on his part.

It would appear he was single, as he hadn't brought a date to Ben and Stella's wedding weeks ago. He also hadn't mentioned anyone visiting, and she had seen him daily since the wedding. He was also the kind of guy you would never suspect of being unfaithful, she had always felt secure in their relationship when they were younger. His deep routed sense of right and wrong could be infuriating, but it also gave her some reassurance that he wouldn't be on a date last night if he was involved with someone in New York.

Thinking about the end of their night filled her with heat again, a feeling she hadn't had in a long time. Going from refusing to think about their time together years ago to being consumed with thoughts about him was giving her whiplash, but she needed to spend some time thinking about what this meant going forward. Trusting Dan was a huge jump she wasn't entirely sure she could make.

***

A knock on the door startled her just before she was about to leave for work. Checking the doorbell camera that she had installed, she saw a delivery person holding a vase of flowers. She pulled open the door and smiled at the man, who frequented the bar.

"Morning," he said, offering the flowers. "Delivery for you."

"Thank you! Beautiful."

"They sure are, biggest bouquet I have on my route." He turned to jog down the stairs before she could react.

"Wait, I need to give you a tip!" She shouted down the stairs, to which he waved her away.

"Buy me a drink next time I'm in, and we're even." He jumped into the driver's seat of the running van and drove off with a wave.

Carrying the flowers inside, she noted the card poking out of the top. She placed the vase down and allowed herself a moment to stick her face in and breathe in the deep smell of the fresh cut sunflower, snapdragons, and dahlia's. The bright, cheery autumn colors and the smell brought a smile to her face before she even opened the card.

K – Here's to the second part of our story – D

Tucking the card into the back pocket of her jeans, she headed down to the bar, deciding to wait and text Dan once her butterflies settled.

***

Finding her accountant parked in her office, with his laptop open on her desk, wasn't a huge surprise. He came by often for a quarterly review, to have her sign paperwork, or to add new employees to the payroll system, knowing he would get a free meal for making it more convenient for her. She sank into the seat across from her desk and waited for him to finish typing away when he then pushed his glasses up on his head and smiled at her.

"How's it going?"

"Great, Pete. How are you?" She sat back and crossed her legs, happy to catch up with her old friend.

"I'm good. I have some business things to discuss, thought it might be better to do it in here than at the bar."

"Anything wrong?" The look he was giving her made her concerned, although she had thought the bar was doing well.

"I don't know." He turned the laptop so she could see the screen. "Do you know what these transactions are?"

She looked, seeing several transfers for a few thousand dollars apiece, to an account she didn't know about. Her stomach sank, guessing what he was about to tell her. "No. I didn't make those. You know I almost never log in to the banking account, I prefer to go in and do deposits the old-fashioned way."

"That's what I thought." He sighed, crossing his arms. "I asked the bank to investigate, and to freeze any further transfers. They can also put a stop payment on any outstanding checks if you want, but I don't see anything unusual there."

"I don't even have a checkbook. I have everyone invoice me and I send them to your office."

"Just because you don't have one doesn't mean someone else does. I use the bank system to send payments out for you, so I asked them to keep an eye out for anything that is handwritten rather than processed electronically. That should help, but they can't inspect everything." Pete leaned forward, his elbows on the desk. "You have any other trouble?"

"No," she sighed, feeling weary suddenly. Her good mood from earlier was gone, lost in the swirling of her stomach. "I haven't heard anything from him for a long time. How could he even get into the account?"

Pete shrugged, looking back at the screen. "Your account number hasn't changed, and you haven't switched banks. We might need to do that now, I'll warn you. These wires are difficult to trace, and I don't know if we will be able to recover the money. Fortunately, he didn't want to wipe you out, it seems like he just wanted to skim a little each month and hope no one noticed."

She managed a small smile. "He doesn't know you, I guess."

"No, he doesn't." He closed the laptop and slipped it into a messenger bag. "I'll head over to the bank and see what they think we should do. I know changing accounts will be a nightmare for your automatic payments and payroll, but I'll take care of all that if you want. I know this is a lot to digest."

"Thanks, Pete. I'm lucky to have you."

"Remember that when you start your holiday shopping." He stopped before leaving the small office, placing a hand on her shoulder. "Call me if you need anything at all, okay?"

"I will, thanks." She heard the door click close behind her and her shoulders hunched as she placed her face in her hands. She would *not* cry. It had been years and she refused to let him have any control over her, even to draw tears from her eyes. Taking a shaky breath, she pushed to her feet and made her way through the kitchen, seeing her staff hard at work.

She lost her brief battle with tears when she saw her two best friends sitting at the bar waiting for her. They weren't open yet, but that had never stopped Julie and Tina from coming in through the kitchen door to catch up on some gossip over their lunch breaks. They came a couple days a week at least, trying to get in right when they opened so it would be a little quieter for her.

"What's wrong?" Tina jumped off her stool and wrapped her in a hug that managed to crumble the rest of her resolve.

"Brad."

"What?" Julie erupted, looking around the empty room. "Where? What did he do?"

"Pete was just here. He got into my bank account somehow, took money."

"Oh, no." Tina rubbed her back. "Can we help?"

"No but thank you." Kendra rubbed her cheeks, letting a long sigh escape. "He didn't take everything, just giving himself a little income for a few months."

"He has no right to do that." Julie sounded irate. "He's a loser, maybe he should get a job and support himself for once. Or pay some child support."

"I know. I was hoping if I didn't push for any support for Calle, he would just go away. All I care about is keeping her safe. And this place."

"Pete will fix it."

Tina sounded more confident than Kendra felt. It took all her willpower to avoid racing to the school to get Calle, then spend the next several weeks behind a locked door waiting for the threat to pass. Instead, she plastered a fake smile on her face and chatted with her friends, trying to keep them from seeing how rattled she really was. The pit in her stomach told her this was just the beginning, and she was afraid of what was to come.

Chapter 11

"Ready?" Dan asked Patrick and Jake as they came into the kitchen dressed for their workout.

"Yeah, did you grab our waters?" Patrick asked.

Dan held up the refillable bottles that Stella had given them one morning, telling them that bottled water was out of style. He tossed his brothers their bottles and they all headed out the door, climbing into Dan's SUV.

"How's the shoulder?" Dan asked Jake, who was still recovering from being shot overseas.

"Better. The stretching helps, but I'll never have full range of motion again." He rolled his shoulder a few times. "But at least I can move without pain, and the strength is coming back to my left arm."

"You finished your physical therapy, right?" Patrick asked from the back seat.

"They said I was as good as it would get with them, so I guess so."

"But still going for regular therapy?" Dan asked, glancing over at his brother. Jake's struggles with PTSD were well known within the family, and the more they talked about it, the less likely Jake was to hide an incident from them. Dan was a big believer in having all the facts to confront all issues, and his brother's mental health was no different.

"I still go a couple times a week. Probably will go regularly for the rest of my life, or so Dr. Katz tells me."

"Better to stay on top of it." Dan nodded to Patrick's words.

"What about you, Dan? You ever going to tell us what happened with work?" Jake tossed the question out easily, but it still caused Dan to tense up.

"I will. Still figuring it out, honestly."

"We could help," Patrick offered.

Dan let out a rough laugh. "I wish you could, but I'm afraid not."

"My friends want to pull their business from the firm. They ask me all the time when you'll be set up somewhere else so they can move." Patrick unclipped his seat belt as they pulled into the gym parking lot. "I heard from a few of them that some asshat had called and been a real jerk to them. Jeb something?"

Dan's stomach churned; a long-forgotten ulcer ready to rear its ugly head. "I'm sure. Tell them to give me a couple of weeks, alright? I will figure out my next steps as soon as I can."

"Any chance you can look at a contract for Liam this week? He's not willing to sign it unless you do, and the studio is getting antsy."

"Have him send it to my personal email, I'll call him later." Dan climbed from the car, ready to burn off some aggression in the gym. The thought of the person who had betrayed him going after his clients made him want to hit something. "I'm going to head to the punching bags first, if you guys want to go somewhere else, I'll meet you."

"No, I'm game to hit something." Jake agreed as he scanned his membership pass, and Patrick nodded.

As usual, getting through the lobby with Patrick was a challenge. Even though they went to the gym nearly every day, and rotated their workout times during the slower periods, they inevitably ran into a small group of fans hoping to spot him. Today he had worn a ski cap pulled down low, and a hoodie that further obscured his face, but they spotted him anyway.

"I'll just do this and then meet you down there," Patrick said, indicating the small crowd.

"I'm getting sick of this," Jake whispered to Dan. "I feel like we should do something."

"He's well known for being good to his fans. If he started blowing them off now, it would be bad for his reputation." Dan watched as Patrick was hugged by one woman who didn't seem to want to let go. "But this is a little much, they need to respect his time and space a little."

"Agreed." Jake stepped forward, gently separating the woman from Patrick's torso. "Ladies, Patrick is more than willing to take pictures with you all, but let's try to keep the groping to a minimum, okay?"

Leaving Jake to handle the small crowd, Dan followed the signs to the gym manager's office. Knocking on the open door to announce himself, he stepped in as the manager looked up from her computer. She looked young to be in charge of the gym, but her devotion to fitness was clear, and her desk looked well organized. "Hi," he said. "I'm Dan Burrows, I just joined a few weeks ago. My brother Patrick is having a little bit of an issue, and I wondered if we could figure something out to make it more comfortable for him."

She pushed back from her desk quickly, jumping to her feet. "Is there an issue right now?"

He held up a hand to stop her from charging out of her office, appreciating her dedication. "He's taking some pictures in the lobby, but our brother Jake is handling it for now."

"I can call a trainer to go out and disperse them," she offered, reaching for the phone.

"I was thinking something a little more subtle. He doesn't want his fans to think he's blowing them off, but this happens every day when we come into the lobby. Is there another entrance we could use when Patrick is with us?"

"Yes." She indicated the door, and he stepped aside to follow her. "Let me show you the staff entrance. You guys usually do the boxing or weights first, right?"

"Yes."

"If you come in this door, you can go right to the boxing area unnoticed. The weight room will have more people in it, but it usually isn't as crowded this time of day. If you come in here and skip the cardio and lobby areas, he should be able to do most of his workout without being seen."

"That would be amazing, thank you." Dan felt relief for having solved at least one of the many problems in his life, even something so small.

"Let me give you my number." She reached into her pocket and pulled out a card, then a pen to scribble a number on the back. "I'm Ashley, by the way. My cell is on the card, and I put the number for our lead trainer on the back. Call or text when you're on your way, and one of us will meet you here to open this door. I'll work on getting you a pass that will open it, but that might take a day or two."

"Thank you so much," Dan said as he pocketed the card.

"No problem. We're thrilled to have Patrick here, our membership doubled the month after he joined. But our priority is for him to be comfortable, that matters more than people joining just to catch a glimpse of him."

"We keep suggesting setting up a full gym in the barn, but he likes to be here. Unless he changes his mind, or people finally get used to him being around, this would be best. Especially when ski season really kicks off and you get more tourists on day passes, I don't know that he would make it through the lobby."

"Let me know if there is anything else I can do." She started to walk back to her office, then turned quickly. "One thing we could do, if he wants. The trainer and I both work out here for an hour before the gym opens. It's early, but it's only us here. If he wants to come, or all three of you, you're welcome."

"I'll mention that to him. Thanks again."

Dan made his way back to the lobby, meeting Patrick and Jake just as they finished with the last selfie. He told them about his meeting with the manager, seeing the relief on his brothers' face. Small victories, he told himself as he pulled on boxing gloves. He would take what he could get, personally and professionally, until things improved in his life.

Two hours later, they were all exhausted and sweaty. After grabbing their outerwear from the locker room, they exited to find the hulk of a man who had been lurking around their workout areas waiting in the hall.

"I'm Mike," he greeted them. "The head trainer here. Ashley asked me to keep an eye out to make sure you were able to work out in peace today. I also wanted to suggest you head out through the staff entrance, since a small crowd has formed in the lobby while you were exercising."

"Appreciate that." Patrick shook hands with the trainer. "Might be a good idea for me to set up an appointment with you, you make me look small."

"Anytime, man. It would be an honor."

"Jake, stand next to him. I bet he would dwarf you since you're so little."

"I'm going to put boxing gloves back on and aim for your pretty face if you keep that up." Jake cocked an eyebrow at Patrick.

"I can't help that you're a shorty." Patrick shrugged.

Mike looked between them in confusion. "You're all pretty tall."

"But Jake is the runt," Patrick said before Jake put him into a headlock.

"Excuse them," Dan said. "We can't seem to help but act like little kids when we're all together."

"Back to being about me," Patrick said as he broke away from Jake, both laughing.

"As it always is," Jake piped in.

"If you're around tomorrow and have some free time, let's plan a session." Patrick pulled his phone out, handing it to Mike. "If you want to throw your info in there, I'll text you later and we can set it up."

"Sure thing," Mike said as he entered his phone number before handing the phone back. "It might help keep the crowds at bay too, no one wants to mess with me when I'm working with a client."

The brothers said goodbye to Mike and headed for the staff door, catching a glimpse of the crowd in the lobby as they left. "Patrick, you really should consider letting us put a gym in the barn. This is getting out of hand, and it's only going to get worse."

"I'll think about it. Let's try working out with Mike and see how that goes."

"I think he's just training you." Dan stated as he unlocked his SUV.

"Oh, you two need to be whipped into shape more than me. I just didn't want you to feel bad about your dad bods."

"Dad bods? Is he kidding?" Dan stared at Jake as they got into the car.

"Hey, a paunch is a look. Don't get upset."

"I don't have a paunch." Jake growled, clipping his seatbelt on. "And I was just shot, so yeah, little out of shape but nothing I won't fix."

"Are you saying I do?" Dan looked down at his stomach as he asked.

"It's okay," Patrick patted him on the head. "We all get old someday."

"I honestly don't know why I spend any time with you two." Dan groaned as his brothers laughed. "I'm going to have to start spending time with people who appreciate me."

"Like Kendra?" Jake asked.

"Yes, like Kendra."

"How's that going?" Jake prodded further.

"Last night was great. Now I just need to convince her that we really can give this another go. I can tell she's still reluctant to think of this as long term, and I don't want to start all over again at square one and have to date for months."

"Are you already thinking of proposing?" Patrick asked from the backseat.

"No, don't be ridiculous. We need to make sure we're compatible as adults, but it would be nice to spend more time together and figure it out quickly. We're not getting any younger, as you so nicely pointed out. We need to either decide this might have a future, or get over each other once and for all. On top of all that, I don't know where I'll be in a few months, so I need to figure that out."

"Might want to do that before you jerk Kendra around," Jake said drolly.

"Oh, like you figured out your life before you fell in love with Shea? I seem to recall you not being sure if you would retire or go back to the Army." Dan shot his brother a look.

"That's different," Jake muttered.

"What about you, Jake? Rings in the future?" Patrick turned his attention to Jake, and Dan felt relief at the shift. Despite his argument, he knew Jake was right. It wasn't fair to Kendra or Calle for him to convince them to spend time with him, only to have him leave to go back to his busy life in New York. But denying himself time with either of them wasn't an option either.

Chapter 12

Kendra was restocking the bar when Dan walked in after the lunch rush. A thrill ran through her at the sight of him and the thought of the night before, and it took all her self-restraint to stay where she was. "Hey," she called to him as he pulled out a barstool.

"Hey, yourself. How are you?" His smile had a hidden intimacy only she would recognize from their past.

"Good. What have you been up to?"

"Went to the gym with the idiots."

"Jake and Patrick?"

"The very ones."

"Why are they idiots today?"

"You ask as if they aren't every other day of the week." Dan laughed and rested his elbows on the bar. "Just more annoying than usual."

She slid a soda towards him and leaned on the bar in front of him. "What else is on the agenda for today?"

"I've got some work to do. One of my clients, Patrick's friend Liam, has a contract he needs me to go through. I really need to at least set up a temporary office and LLC to officially transfer them all over from the firm."

"Can you do that here? Or is that a process?"

"Years ago, when I finished school and Dad wanted me to do his will, I applied to be admitted to the Vermont bar. Since I did that, I can practice law here without having to wait months for them to finish the process."

"That's good news. I know there is an empty space right next to the coffee shop, the first floor of that building has a few small offices. The one that is empty faces the street, so it would be a good location."

"Really? I'll have to go look at it." He rubbed his chin, looking thoughtful.

"Julie is the realtor, I can give you her number."

He smiled at her. "You sure she would want to deal with me?"

She laughed. "No, but if you went through another agent, she would really hate you."

"Okay, send it over. Maybe I can catch her while I'm down here."

"On second thought, let me just text her and ask her to stop back in. They just left a little while ago, so I know she's not far." Kendra sent a quick text and dropped her phone back into her pocket. "She works in that building. The second floor is the real estate office."

"Where is Tina working?"

"At the hospital, plus she does some home care nursing. That's what she's doing today, so she was able to come in with Julie for lunch." She pulled the phone back out. "Brace yourself, she's coming."

"Does she really despise me? We used to get along."

"Well, you broke my heart, and she holds a grudge." Kendra shrugged. "I'm sure you can understand that."

He nodded. "But if I win you back, is she going to like me again?"

"Dan, I'm not a prize to be won." She frowned as the door opened, blowing a gust of cold wind in along with Julie.

"Oh," Julie said as she spotted Dan at the bar. "I thought you said you had a customer for me?"

"Hi, Jules." Dan waved and smiled at her, getting a frown in return.

"No." She pointed at him and looked back to Kendra. "Really? You want me to help him, of all people? Why are you even talking to him?"

"Julie," Kendra's voice held a warning. "He's sitting right here. Don't be rude."

"Rude." Julie rolled her eyes so hard Kendra was surprised her whole head didn't go with them.

"I appreciate your support and that you're protective of me. But Dan and I are trying to get to a better place, and I would appreciate you allowing that to happen."

"But he—" Julie huffed out a sigh looking at Kendra, then turned to Dan. "Fine. What do you want to look at?"

"You must be top salesperson with that approach."

"Dan, don't push it." Kendra warned him, her gaze bouncing between the two of them. This could have been a mistake.

"Yeah, Dan, don't push it." Julie drew out his name in an exaggerated fashion that somehow turned the one syllable into an insult.

"I was hoping to look at the empty office space next to the coffee shop."

"In my building?" Julie looked shocked.

"Well, the same building as your office," Kendra explained. "Isn't that front office still open?"

"But we would see each other all the time." Julie looked at her friend in desperation before turning to Dan. "And how long do you plan to stay? There is a lease."

"I don't think you'll be in his office all the time, and it's not like you share a workspace." Kendra tried to keep the peace but could see the frustration on her friends face.

"I don't have long term plans. But I would prefer a month-to-month lease over a year, if we can negotiate that."

"Fine. Let's go." Julie turned and headed toward the door before looking back and pointing a finger at Kendra. "I will be back with reinforcements to discuss this in great detail."

"See you later," she yelled, watching one of her oldest friends leave with her first love.

After they left, as she restocked and prepared for the after-work rush and the flood of tourists that would hit the town for the weekend, her thoughts wandered to Dan's words. He wasn't willing to commit to a year lease. What did that mean for her?

***

At four o'clock on the dot, the door to the bar opened and her two friends trooped in, looking very serious. They chose the barstools closest to where Kendra would work most of the time, knowing it was the best place to catch her for conversation if they sat near the register and most popular drink choices.

"Hi," Kendra said as she placed napkins in front of them, then placing two frosted glasses down. Next to Julie's she placed a local IPA, and Tina got a spiked seltzer.

"Heard you had an eventful day," Tina said.

"Little bit," Julie muttered. "Were you going to tell us about Dan?"

"Of course, I was. This just happened."

"When?"

Kendra hedged, knowing her friends wouldn't be happy. "I had dinner at their house the night before last, and then Dan and I went to dinner last night."

"So, before we came in for lunch today?" Julie demanded.

"Yes. I'm sorry. I didn't know what to say, I'm still processing it myself."

"How was the dinner last night?" Tina asked.

"It was really nice, actually. We talked about a lot." Kendra poured two drinks and passed them to a server before turning back to her friends. "And at their house we had a chance to talk more about what happened between us. I've been so angry for so long, I forgot that we were kids when all that happened."

"Still old enough to know better," Julie said.

"How did it go at the office?" Kendra asked Julie.

"Fine. He signed a lease."

"For how long?"

Julie gave her a pointed look. "He was adamant it be month to month, and the owner was agreeable because it's been empty for a bit."

"Has he said anything to you about his long-term plans?" Tina asked gently.

"No," Kendra sighed. "We talked a lot about the past, not the future. But he has made it pretty clear that he would like to get involved again. I'm just nervous, because it's not just me this time. Calle could get hurt here."

"Yes, she could. And so could you." Tina's words rang out for a moment before the front door flew open and Calle came bouncing in, fresh off the school bus.

"Hi, Mama! Hi aunties." She dropped her backpack on the floor and tugged off her coat, which joined the backpack. "Guess what?"

"What?" They all chorused back to her.

"Two of my friends from school are going skiing tomorrow too, so I'll get to see them."

"You're going skiing?" Julie shot a confused look to Kendra. "How come I didn't get an invite?"

"No, not with mama. Dan is taking me." She twirled around, nearly crashing into a hostess.

"I'm sorry, what?" Julie turned back to Kendra.

"She asked if I could take her, and I can't because we will be so busy here. When Dan came to pick me up for dinner, she asked him and he agreed," Kendra explained. "I think Charlie will meet up with them too once he is done with hockey."

"We would have taken her," Tina said quietly.

"I know, I didn't really have any control over it." Kendra turned to her daughter. "Calle, will you please take your stuff upstairs? Then bring down a coloring book or something to read, Nora will be here after you eat dinner to bring you upstairs for the night."

They all watched as she gathered her things and danced towards the kitchen, where a set of stairs would bring her to their apartment. Kendra had long ago set up the apartment in a way that she felt safe with her daughter upstairs alone for short periods of time. A good lock on the exit door, an alarm system, a video monitor inside as well as the doorbell camera, helped ease her mind that nothing could harm her when she was out of sight.

"Want me to go with her?" Tina offered.

"No, she'll come right back down. Plus, the door is locked, I just always have to remind myself that no one could be in there without my knowing."

"It's normal to be nervous, after all you went through with Brad." Julie patted her hand on the bar.

"I know. I wonder sometimes if I'll ever be normal again, or if every bump in the night or minor thing will make me panic."

"You are normal," Tina objected. "And what you're feeling is normal."

"Can we go back to Dan for one minute before Calle comes back down?" Julie asked, leveling Kendra with a look. "I really don't think it's a good idea to get involved with him again."

"He may have changed," Tina said.

"I think he has. I know it's only been a couple of days, but I do think he has grown up a lot, and I think he really regrets what happened." Kendra poured a glass of water and took a sip. "I told him about spending time with Charlie when Jake was gone."

"You did?" Tina's face was shocked.

"Seems like a silly thing to keep secret now, really. He would have found out eventually, with how good Charlie is to Calle."

"Does he know how close you and Stella are?" Julie asked.

"Yes, I told him about what happened after he left."

"And about Brad?"

"I told him that too."

"Wow. I'm kind of impressed he didn't run for the hills." Tina smiled at her.

"Me too. I have to tell you guys this, and I don't want it to come back and bite me later if he leaves and I do get hurt again." Kendra glanced around and then leaned a little closer to her friends. "Being with him was the safest I have felt since before I met Brad. I honestly never once thought to be scared, or to worry about anything. That hasn't happened since Brad, even just talking one-on-one with a single guy in the bar, never mind being comfortable enough to go on a date."

"Of course, it hasn't, anyone would be terrified after what you went through." Julie huffed out a breath. "I wish I had hit him with my car when I had the chance."

"Don't be silly," Tina swatted Julie's arm. "I'm glad you feel safe, and can open up to someone, Kendra. Just be a little careful, okay? Recovering from him once was hard, the second time could be even worse."

They all watched as Calle came back into the room, carrying a doll, two books, a coloring book and a box of crayons. The little girl beamed with happiness as she tucked her doll into a chair and settled into the small table that Kendra had set up for her just outside the kitchen door, out of sight of almost everyone.

"It wouldn't be," Kendra said with confidence. "As long as I have her, I have everything I need. If I get some great kissing along the way, even better."

"Wait, there was kissing?" Tina grinned. "Tell us more."

Kendra filled them in on the details from the night before, laughing when she had to deny three times that nothing more happened. Recounting it with her friends brought back the feelings she had woken up with that morning, and the goosebumps on her arms raised at the thought of more with Dan. It had been a long time since she had even considered any kind of physical relationship with a man, and trusting Dan with that would be a big step. She just wished she knew if it were a step in the right direction or off a cliff.

Chapter 13

Dan was up early on Saturday morning, loading up on coffee and Stella's homemade breakfast casserole before a full day of skiing. His skis were already secured on the roof of his SUV, and his gear was in a bag by the door. Although the weather was cool, it wasn't as cold as it would get later in the winter, so he had opted for a long sleeve t-shirt, a hoodie, and a down vest. The heavy ski parka in his closet would only make him sweat, and he wanted to have more range of movement with less padding, in case he needed to catch Calle.

"Morning," his dad said, coming into the kitchen from the back door and crossing to the coffee pot.

"Morning."

"Where are you off to this morning?"

"Skiing. Just about ready to go."

"Your brothers going along?"

"No, Charlie has a game at ten so he might meet us later. Patrick can't afford to get hurt, so he can't go, and Jake is still worried about the shoulder."

"You're going alone? Make sure you have your cell phone and stay off any dangerous trails when you're by yourself."

"I will, but I'm not going alone. I'm taking Calle."

His dad's eyes met his, looking surprised. "How did that come about?"

"She had asked Kendra just before I picked her up for dinner, and she couldn't take her. When I got there that night, Calle asked me to take her, and I said yes." He shrugged. "Not a big deal, I wanted to ski anyway."

"It's a big deal to a little girl."

"I know."

"Do you, though? Be careful, Danny. Someone could get very hurt in this situation."

"I will, Dad." He stood from the island and placed his dishes in the dishwasher. "I'll see you later."

"Be safe," his dad called down the hall just before he closed the door.

When he arrived at Kendra's apartment, he found a pink snowball with a grin on its face waiting for him. "Hi Dan," she yelled, diving at him. "I'm so excited."

"Hey Calle. Does your mom know you're out here?" He looked around but didn't see Kendra.

"She's getting my skis out of the garage." She pointed to the structure set back on the property.

"Should we help her?"

"Sure. Mom said I have to be careful and that I shouldn't trick you into taking me on any slopes that I shouldn't be on. She said green only but then I told her that we did blue last time, and she remembered. So maybe blue if you say that's okay." The words were fired at him at a faster rate than he was used to, and he felt his head spin.

"Let me talk to her and see, okay? I think we should start with some green and then we can move up to blue if we both think we're ready." He smiled at her and tugged on her snowcap. "You never know, you might think I'm not capable of a blue run."

"Dan." She stopped walking and put her hands on her hips. "You do the double black diamonds. I know you do."

"Guilty. But we're not going near those today."

Kendra emerged before they could enter the garage, carrying a pair of tiny skis and boots, with a helmet dangling from her wrist. He hurried over and took the gear, resisting the urge to kiss her at the same time.

"Morning," he greeted her. "I'll load this in the car."

"Thanks, Dan." She looked exhausted, and he felt bad that they were up so early.

"Late night last night?"

"I had a server call out sick, so we were short. I couldn't sneak out early as much as I wanted to." She yawned and covered her mouth with a hand. "I didn't get to bed until after two."

"That's crazy. It's seven." He looked at his watch and then back at her.

She shrugged. "That's the life of a single mom and a bar owner. No sleep for the wicked."

"Why don't you go back to bed now?" He urged her.

"I really shouldn't, I have so much to do." She yawned again. "But I might have to."

"Please, I'll feel better knowing you're in bed." He leaned closer and whispered in her ear. "It will keep my spirits up, thinking about it."

She slapped him on the arm and laughed. "Dream on, buddy."

"Ouch. At least pretend there is a chance one day."

"I'm too tired to think. Let me get her booster seat into your car." He grabbed it from her and followed the instructions on how to buckle it in, and then stepped back with a laugh when she wanted to double check it. She called Calle over and got her strapped in, then closed the door and met him behind the car. "Thanks for this, she's so excited."

"I'm too. And I'm excited about this," he said, lowering his mouth to kiss her in what he planned to be a quick peck. However, his lips had minds of their own, and he had to finally force himself to take a step backwards, steadying her as she nearly stumbled without his weight to lean against.

"We shouldn't be doing this with her right there," Kendra whispered. "And when I'm too tired to resist."

"I'm sorry, I've been thinking of nothing but that since the other night. But I'll behave now, I promise. Now please, go back to bed for a few hours." He placed a hand on the small of her back, urging her towards the stairs.

She was waving to them as he pulled out of the small parking lot, and he tuned into the chatter from the back seat. "Are you and mom special friends? Did you just kiss her? That looked like how my friend's dad kisses her mom. Is that how you kiss my mom? Does that mean you love her?"

"Do you always have so many questions this early in the morning?" He asked, signaling to take the turn to the mountain.

"Mom says I have a very busy mind. And mouth."

"Let's say one question now, and then more later, deal?" He looked in the mirror and saw her serious expression as she thought.

"Do you love my mommy?"

"I always have." He responded, hearing his voice catch as he did. "Want a donut before we get to the mountain?"

"That was a question, you know. And you said only one question now. But yes, I like the one with the sprinkles."

Dan drove the rest of the way, Calle happily eating her donut and chatting about school in the backseat. Once they arrived at the mountain, he gathered all their gear and led her to the lodge, where he traded the confirmations for the three season passes out for cards that went into lanyards they would wear under their jackets, making it easy to show at the ski lift. Kendra would get hers later, he was determined to make sure she had time to enjoy some time on the mountain with her daughter this winter.

"This is good for all winter, so you have to be careful not to lose it." Dan fastened the lanyard around her neck and made the loop smaller so it would hang just below her collarbone. "We'll have to show them at the ski lift, so leave it outside your jacket for now. I'll help you get it tucked away once we're on the lift."

"All winter? I could ski every day?"

"You could, but you'll need a ski buddy. I got the same pass, and I got your mom one too, so either of us can take you. We can surprise your mom with it later."

"Does Charlie have one?"

He laughed at her childhood crush on his nephew. "Yes, he does."

Calle stepped into her skis with little help, and Dan strapped the buckle of the helmet under her chin before doing the same. He held his poles in one hand as they made their way to the lift in case she needed help, but she was fine on her own. They boarded a chair headed for a blue slope at her insistence, and he couldn't help but grin at her confidence. He would make sure they got down the slope even if he had to hold her between his legs, as he had needed to do when he worked as a ski instructor on this mountain.

However, when they got to the top, Calle waved and then zipped down the slope faster than he could blink. A blur of pink headed straight down, with a giggle trailing behind her. He quickly pushed off and headed after her, surprised at the speed she had gathered already. Had he ever been that young and fearless?

Chapter 14

Kendra slept until after nine, something she hadn't done since having a child. It felt decadent to lay in bed when she woke up, scrolling through her phone and not having to jump right into action. She debated getting coffee to bring back in with her but resisted the urge, wanting a few more minutes in the cozy space before starting her day. Once she got up, she knew she wouldn't allow herself to return to lounge in bed. There was always too much to do, and just her to do it.

A text came in from Dan, a picture of him and Calle on the chairlift, both with big grins on their faces. The bubbles at the bottom showed he was still typing, so she waited for the next text to come in. It looked like they were having fun, and she hoped Calle wasn't too much for Dan to handle. He hadn't spent much time around kids, other than Charlie, and Calle was still young enough to need supervision.

His text came through before she could worry much. *Having a blast, wish you were here.*

She smiled before responding. *I wish I was too. I hope she's not too much to handle.*

She's not, but I can't say that Calle would say the same about me.

She tossed the phone aside and forced herself to get out of bed and into the shower, needing to get started on her day. Saturdays were always busy at the restaurant, but fall weekends were the busiest. Between the fresh snow on the mountain and the colored leaves still clinging to the trees, they were bound to be swamped with tourists, so there was no more time to waste.

***

It was four o'clock before she had a chance to even look at her phone again, and other than a few pictures from Dan, she hadn't heard much from them. She sent off a quick text, asking how they were doing, before heading to the kitchen to check in on Zoe. The lunch rush had been busy, and dinner would likely be even worse.

"How's it going?" She asked her chef, who was busy cleaning the workstation.

"It's going," Zoe responded. "That was busy for a lunch."

"Dinner will be worse. When we have a busy lunch that means even more people will come in after skiing or exploring, so we should be prepared."

"I'm on it. I already prepped for dinner and did everything I could to be ahead of schedule. Don't worry about me." Zoe smiled at her, no sign of the temperamental chef Kendra had been expecting when reviewing her resume.

"Great, thanks Zoe. The bar is ready too, and all the staff turned up tonight."

"Well, that's a relief. Last night was crazy. You can't be running around like that." She tsked quietly, shaking her head.

"I know, it was worse than usual."

"No, I mean you're the boss. You should be relaxing and counting the money, not running around serving tables and tending bar. Hire a manager so you can take some time off." Zoe hit her with a look. "Enjoy some time with that handsome man of yours."

"He's not my man, but I'll look into hiring someone. I just wanted to save as much money as possible. Buying the business has made money tight, and if I can pay myself as the manager as well as my piece as owner, it helps." Kendra chewed on her lip, knowing Zoe was right. Having a manager would make her life a lot easier.

"Money can't buy happiness. You know this."

"I do. You're right. I'll see if I can at least find someone for part time."

"Good. Now tell me about the man. This is the one you were talking about, who you loved as children?"

"Yes. Dan."

"And what is happening with him?"

"Right now, he's skiing with Calle. But I went to dinner with him the other night. And had dinner with his family the night before that. He refuses to give up and has worked his way into my life."

"This is a good thing. You need a love. And some sex." Zoe said it in a matter-of-fact manner, even though they had only known each other for a short time.

"Zoe! You don't know that."

"I hear things," she said, tapping her ear. "The other staff, they say you don't do anything but work and take care of Calle. No man in your life for a very long time. It's good to let yourself have this now. Does Calle like him?"

She smiled, thinking of her daughters face that morning as she got ready to leave with Dan. "I'm afraid she might like him too much, if anything. I was nervous about sending them off to ski together today, that she would get too attached to him and then he would leave."

"Is he supposed to leave?"

"I don't know. He lives in New York; he's been here for a few months now. But I don't know what his long-term plans are. I can't see him staying here."

"Why not? This is a great place to live."

"After being in New York for the last few years, I'm afraid it might feel small for him."

"I was in Paris, which many would say is the greatest city in the world. And I left there to go to a little French town near Germany, where I learned more as a chef that I ever would have learned under the tyrants in the Parisian kitchens. Sometimes it's not where you are that matters, but who you're with."

It was the most that Zoe had ever said about her personal history, and as much as Kendra wanted to dig deeper, she refrained. She knew what it was like to have people pry into her past, and she didn't want to do that to someone else. Zoe's resume had been way more qualified than what she needed, but when she insisted she wanted the challenge of running her own kitchen, Kendra had happily hired her. The customers were thrilled with the food coming out, and the specials sold out every night.

"You should have more control over the menu." The words were out before Kendra even processed them as a thought, but it felt right.

"Yes," Zoe nodded, confident as always. "I should, I have many ideas. We can discuss after the weekend, if you would like."

"Perfect." Kendra turned to leave the kitchen.

"Keep me up to date on this man situation, please. I need love in my life even if it's not my own."

"Maybe we should work on your own love life," Kendra called back to her, laughing as Zoe held up her hands and shook her head.

When she emerged from the kitchen, she was thrilled to see Calle and Dan coming in the front door. Her daughter ran to her, hugging her tight around the legs. "Hi Mama! I had so much fun. Can we go tomorrow?"

"I'm glad you had fun. I think we might have to wait a few days, but we can go soon, okay?" Her eyes met Dans, and she smiled at the way he was looking at her. "How did it go?"

"It was great, we had a blast. I'm exhausted and probably won't be able to walk tomorrow, but Calle could have kept going for hours." He winked at Calle, and she beamed back at him. "Want to give your mom her surprise?"

"Yes," she yelled, running back to Dan to get something that he pulled out of his pocket. She ran back and presented it to Kendra, looking thrilled. "We got you a ski pass like ours, it's good for the whole entire winter."

"Dan," she said, looking at him. "I can't accept this."

"Please. Let me do this. You work so hard; you deserve to go have some fun with your daughter."

She felt tears prickling at the back of her eyes at his thoughtfulness. "Thank you," she whispered, hugging Calle to her.

"Can I have a cheeseburger? I'm super-duper hungry." Calle bounced on her heels as she asked.

"I'm also super-duper hungry, so maybe we can sit together and eat. It's starting to get busy for your mom, so let's grab a table. I'll text Charlie and let him know we're here."

Kendra watched as Dan led Calle to a table not far from the bar, where she would still be able to talk to them as she passed. She wasn't sure whether she should be thrilled or nervous at how quickly he was settling into her life, and noticing little things like where she would be during her work shift. Seeing her daughter laugh and hand him a crayon, sharing her coloring page, she knew she had to make a decision sooner than later about how far to let him in.

****

Charlie came into the restaurant a few minutes later, followed by Jake and Shea, and joined the table. When Patrick came in, they all shuffled so he could sit with his back to the door, allowing him some privacy.

"No Ben and Stella?" Kendra asked as she passed by.

"They are on their way," Jake replied. "How are you?"

"I'm good, thanks." She smiled back at Shea and the rest of the group before moving on, keeping the bar running smoothly and an eye on her staff. The phone behind the bar rang and was answered by the other bartender, who held it up and pointed at Kendra.

"For you," she yelled.

"Thanks." Kendra went behind the bar and picked up the cordless phone, plugging one finger into her other ear to hear. "Hello?"

Silence met her ear, then a slight crackling noise that indicated someone was on the other end of the line. "Hello? Is someone there?" A faint sound of laughter rang through the phone, followed by the sound of her own voice, pleading to be left alone. Ice ran through her veins as she realized who must be on the other end of the phone, as no one else could possibly have a recording of her like that. "Brad? What do you want?"

Silence again, and she thought he had hung up. Then suddenly his voice grated in her ear, whispering one word. "Everything."

She dropped the phone like it was on fire, startling the people sitting at the bar. Her hand shaking, she stooped to pick it up and struggled to get it back into the phone holder.

"You okay?" Her bartender asked as she walked behind her, and Kendra was able to nod.

"Taking five," she responded. Pushing her way out of the bar and into the safety of her office, she sat and dropped her head to her knees, gasping for breath.

"What are you—" Zoe's voice came through the fog, and she felt her hand on her back. "What can I do?"

"Dan."

"You want me to get him?"

"Please."

The door opened and closed, and mere seconds later she felt the air change as Dan rushed in and dropped to his knees beside her. "What happened?"

"Brad just called."

"What? Where? Give me your phone, I'll call him back myself." He reached for the phone she had tucked in her pocket.

She shook her head. "No, on the bar phone. Not my cell."

"What did he say?"

"Nothing, really. He had a recording of me, from when we were together. He must have taken it as he was hitting me one day." She shuddered, suddenly back in that fearful spot. "And then I asked what he wanted."

"Did he tell you?"

She met his gaze, seeing the fire and his need to protect her. "He said everything."

"Well, it will be a cold day in hell before he gets anything." Dan's jaw clenched, and she saw the anger simmering beneath the surface. "We should call the sheriff."

"And say what? That I got essentially a crank call?" She stood up, her legs still feeling like Jello beneath her.

"They need a record of this. It's harassment, and a threat. You need to have them record it so that if anything happens, you can get a restraining order."

"Could you just hold me for a minute instead of going full lawyer?"

He grabbed her and pulled her to his chest, wrapping her up in his strong arms. "I can do both." He dropped a kiss on the top of her head and then just held on until she felt strong enough to step back. "You and Calle are going to spend the night at the house with us tonight."

"No, Dan—" She was cut off by the look on his face.

"Either you come stay there, or I stay on your couch. Those are the only two options. I figure its less questions from Calle if you have another sleepover." He waited until she nodded reluctantly. "If you're okay with it, we can send her home with my family. I'll give Jake and Patrick enough information that they won't let Calle out of their sight, and I'll wait here for you to close up."

It had been years since she could trust someone enough to make decisions for her, and to be looking out for her best interest. Putting her faith in Dan, allowing him to save her from this terrible moment, was both freeing and worrying. She chose to enjoy the sense of being cared for and pushed aside the worry about what would happen next time. Brad was enough to stress about, no sense in adding to her trouble.

Chapter 15

"Hey," Dan said as he leaned down between Patrick and Jake. "I'm going to send Calle home with you guys for the night. I'll bring Kendra up when she closes."

"Ohhhh," Patrick dragged the word out. "Interesting. Going back to your childhood bedroom, just like when you were in high school."

Dan slapped him on the back of his head. "Grow up. It's not like that."

"What's it like?" Jake asked.

"Her ex-husband just called and scared her. I don't want them to be alone tonight, and I sure don't want her closing the bar alone." He leaned close to his brother and spoke softly so that Calle wouldn't overhear.

"What did he say?" Jake was all business, ready to jump into action.

"Not a lot, but she hasn't heard from him in six years. Now he just called and scared her. Something is up, or brewing. I don't know the guy, but I've heard stories, and none are good."

"You think there is a threat tonight?" Jake surveyed the room. "Want me to keep watch?"

"No, I don't think that's necessary. If they are in the house with all of us, he would be a fool to try."

"I'll grab a gun out of the safe just in case."

"I don't know if that's a good idea, with a six-year-old in the house." Dan frowned, thinking about the risks.

Jake nodded. "You're right, but I have a smaller safe that I can put in my bedside table. I'll just put one in there, just in case. It's that or sleep in dad's office with the big safe, and Shea won't love that."

"Okay, that sounds good. Thanks." Having a trained operative in the family was turning out to be a good thing, Dan realized. As long as Jake was able to keep his PTSD at bay, but having Shea at the house would help with that.

Patrick went back to eating before turning back to Dan. "You going to fill Dad in? He and Stella are out back in the cottage alone, might be good if they know in case they hear or see anything."

"Yeah, you're right. I'll talk to him." Dan went back to his seat, where he had Calle to his right and his father to his left. Leaning close to his dad, he filled him in quickly on the situation with Brad.

"I think we should call the Sherriff." Ben started to stand from his chair, but Dan stopped him.

"I will. Once you all head back to the house I will fill him in, so don't worry. I don't want Calle's attention on this, and I don't want Kendra to be more stressed than she's right now. As soon as it quiets down in here a bit, I'll call and have him come over."

"Good. I never liked that husband of hers, she could do much better." Ben cocked an eyebrow at Dan. "Maybe even better than you, if you keep acting a fool."

"I'm not," Dan protested.

"Not now, but it's been a lot of years. I hate to think of what that girl has been through."

"I know. I blame myself."

Ben shook his head. "You can't know what would have happened. And we can't rewrite history. Take what was good from your past to dwell on and learn from the bad. That's all we can do."

"And fix what I broke."

"That too. You'd be a lucky man if you had them in your life." Ben nodded at Calle. "She's quite a kid."

"She is. I can't believe how much fun I had with her today. If you had told me three months ago that I would be spending a Saturday skiing with a six-year-old instead of working, I would have said you were crazy."

"I'm glad your life is slowing down a little. No one can keep that pace up and not fall apart." Ben held up his hand to stop his son from speaking. "Not that I think you fell apart. I don't know what happened with your work, but I'm here if you want to talk about it. I just know that we need lawyers in Windsor Peak, and it's a lot less pressure than Manhattan."

"As a matter of fact, I did sign a lease on an office right across the street."

"You did? Well, how about that." Ben turned to Stella, who was talking to Shea. "Danny boy signed an office lease here."

"That's wonderful news," Stella enthused. "Does that mean you're staying?"

"For the short term, at least. I needed to get set up on my own for the clients who need me, and then I'll go from there."

"About time," Patrick grumbled. "I'm so sick of the texts asking me when you'll be available. Everyone hates that guy in the New York office who keeps trying to call them. Three people had to get their agent to call him and tell him to lose their cell numbers, he was getting so persistent."

Dan felt his blood boiling but tried to keep his cool. "I'll be in touch with all of them Monday."

Patrick nodded. "I told them that already."

"I hope you stay," Shea said with a smile. "It's so nice having all three of you here."

"Patrick won't be here forever," Dan pointed out.

"I have to leave for filming, but I'll be back." Patrick winked at Calle as he spoke.

"This will be your home base now? Is that your plan?" Dan didn't know why he was turning the spotlight to Patrick, but it was more comfortable than on himself.

Patrick shrugged. "Why not? Plenty to do, nice people, and most of the time I can go relatively unnoticed. And I can breathe here, unlike Los Angeles or New York."

Jake put his arm around the back of Shea's chair, fiddling with her hair. "Nice to have you both here since I'm sticking around."

"You bet you are," Shea said as she smiled at him.

"You give any more thought to moving out to the cottage?" Stella asked Jake.

He glanced at Shea and then back to Ben and Stella. "If you guys really are okay with it, I think we would like to do that. I'm hoping to start building in the spring, but it would be nice to be under the same roof before the holidays. Shea has a new teacher in her school that's looking for a house, they already talked about the possibility of her buying Shea's. The new teacher is staying at the Inn, so she could rent the house while they are going through the purchase process."

Stella clapped her hands together. "Oh, this is wonderful news. Yes, let's get organized and make it happen."

Ben grinned at her. "Good thing we have all these strong men to help us. We can move back to the house tomorrow, so why don't you two decide what furniture you want to keep and what you want us to move out?"

"We can bring Shea's furniture over, whatever will fit. Everything else we can put into storage."

"Are you saying you don't want to sleep in the same bed dad and Stella have been honeymooning in?" Patrick asked, blinking innocently at his brother.

"Shut it, Patty." Jake tried to sound menacing but was too busy smiling at Shea to pull it off.

"I can help too," Calle piped in. "I know how to pack."

"Perfect, we will put you to work tomorrow." Stella beamed at the little girl.

Charlie reached over and squeezed Calle's bicep gently. "How strong are you? Think you could move a couch?"

"Yes, feel how strong!' She held up both arms in a flex and they all laughed.

Patrick excused himself and left the table, leaving the others to plan out the move. Dan was happy for his brother, after all he had been through, finding happiness again had helped him heal. Settling down with Shea would help him through the last few steps he needed to adapt to civilian life.

"You okay with me living out back?" Jake leaned over to ask Charlie.

Charlie nodded. "Yeah, lot closer than you were in Afghanistan. And I'm glad I don't have to move anywhere; I don't want to pack all my stuff up. Plus, grandpa has the highest speed Wi-Fi."

Jake laughed. "Good priorities, bud."

Patrick came back and stood behind his chair, looking around at his family. "Ready to get out of here?"

"We just need the check," Ben said as he looked around for their waitress.

"All set, I just took care of it." Patrick pulled on his jacket as he spoke.

"Son, you didn't have to do that."

"I didn't want Kendra to think she had to comp it, so easier to just hit the waitress up. You can get the next one."

Ben grumbled as he put his wallet back into his pocket but smiled at his son. "I would have ordered more if I had known. But thank you."

Patrick leaned down so he was level with Calle. "Want to come for a sleepover?"

"Yes," she yelled excitedly, before looking towards Kendra. "My mom too?"

"She will come up after she finishes, but you can come with us now," Patrick explained.

Calle bounced from her seat and took Charlie's hand. "Can I ride with you?"

"I don't drive yet, but you can sit next to me in the car if you want."

"Yes, that's what I want." She ran to her mother, hugging her around the waist. "I'm going with Charlie, mama."

"I'll see you in the morning, okay? You go to bed like last time, and I will be right in the next room when you wake up." Kendra ran a hand down her daughter's hair, seeming reluctant to let her go.

Stella stepped forward, encouraging Calle to take her hand. "You just come right down to the kitchen when you wake up. I'll be there, and Jake is always up early. Your mama probably hasn't been able to sleep in on a Sunday in a very long time, so let's make tomorrow a special day."

Dan watched his family leave, with Calle in tow, confident that she would be safe with them. There was no one he would trust more to keep something safe than Jake, and having Patrick and his dad there made him feel even more secure.

"You okay?" He asked Kendra.

She let out a long sigh. "I think so. That really shook me."

"I know. We'll figure out what he wants, or what game he's playing." He spotted Tina and Julie coming into the bar and winced, knowing they wouldn't be happy to see him. "Your friends just came in."

"I'll tell them to play nice." She headed behind the bar, so he found a barstool and was promptly joined by her two best friends.

"You really are becoming a regular," Tina said.

"Just had dinner with the family after skiing with Calle today," he explained.

"Where is Calle?" Julie looked around the room.

"She went home with my family for the night."

"Oh?" Julie's cocked eyebrow asked a lot of questions.

"It's not like that," he said quickly. "I'd rather let Kendra explain when she has a second."

They waited for a few minutes as Kendra filled drink orders, then come over with her friend's drink choices in hand. "Hi," she said as she placed the drinks down. "I'll fill you in really quickly, but I can't start crying."

Julie glared at Dan. "If he made you cry, I'll deal with him."

"No, not Dan." She took a deep breath. "Brad. He called the bar. Didn't say much, but enough to rattle me. Calle and I are going to spend the night at the Burrows' house, so we have some extra people around."

"Did you call the sheriff?"

"Not yet," Dan replied before Kendra could deny the need for it.

She shot him a look. "I don't know that it's worth reporting."

"Of course, it is," Tina insisted. "You need to have official documentation of everything in case he comes back and tries something."

"We're going to call once things quiet down a bit," Dan told her.

"What can we do?" Julie asked Kendra.

"Just be here, that's all. I appreciate you guys." She turned away before anyone could say more, wiping at her eyes.

The two women spoke quietly, heads close together, before turning to Dan with serious looks on their faces. "Listen," Julie said. "We're placing a huge amount of trust in you right now, and I don't think you deserve it. But if Calle is already at your house, Kendra won't go anywhere else, even if we try and convince her to come home with one of us. Are you able to stick around long enough to get her through this?"

"I'm not leaving," he replied, meeting Julie's stare. "And I know it's hard for you guys to trust me, but I would hope that my actions over the last few months have done a little to prove I'm trying hard to do better."

"We do see that." Tina tapped Julie's arm, prompting her to nod.

"I know how dumb I was. I was eighteen and had never really been out of Windsor Peak. Everything that happened between she and the summer after graduation rattled me, and I handled it very badly."

"Must still be a pretty shitty boyfriend if you're still single," Julie muttered.

"Or I was waiting for the right woman." He watched Kendra as she poured drinks and chatted with customers. "And always knew where to find her, I just had to get the courage up."

"We should go," Tina announced.

"What? Why?"

"It's rattling her to see us and know that we are worrying over her. We can talk to her tomorrow; Dan will make sure she calls us." She turned to face him again. "Right?"

"First thing," he promised.

"Come on. You can come to my house; we can watch a movie. You can sleep over, since both of our husbands are out of town." Tina led Julie out of the bar, waving to Kendra as she went.

Dan sipped a soda and watched Kendra work, relieved when the majority of the crowd dwindled down by ten. The band that had been playing on the small stage had started packing up their instruments, and most customers were paying their bills. The advantage of ski season, he realized, was that most people wanted to get to bed early.

Kendra stepped out from behind the bar, leaving the other bartender to deal with the last few customers, and waved for him to join her. He crossed to where she stood near the kitchen door, relieved to see she looked less shaken than she had hours before.

"I just need to run upstairs and pack a few things for Calle and me. Will you come with me?"

"Sure." He followed her up the stairs, waiting for her to unlock the door at the top. Once they crossed into the apartment, he held up a finger indicating that she should wait where she was and quickly searched the apartment. The door from the kitchen to the porch was securely locked, with a small alarm door stopper under the door for extra measure. The place was clean and undisturbed, putting his mind at ease as he went back to where she stood. "All clear."

"I do have a pretty intense alarm system, but thank you for checking." She smiled at him. "Did you learn that from Jake?"

"No, the movies." They laughed, and she headed into Calle's room, pulling a small bag out of the closet. He watched as she packed a few items of clothes, a book, and a few toys.

"I just need to grab some of my things. Want to take this and wait for me on the couch?"

"Don't trust me in your bedroom?" He teased quietly.

She considered him, and he felt the heat rise through his body. "I don't trust me with you in my bedroom."

He groaned and sank to the couch. "Don't toy with my emotions."

Her laughter rang out from the bedroom, a welcome sound after the events of the night.

Chapter 16

Kendra packed a bag quickly, throwing in the essentials for sleep and the next morning. She debated slightly when looking at her pajamas, her hand trailing over a silk slip before coming to rest on a worn pair of flannels. There would be no seduction tonight, she reminded herself. Her focus should be entirely on Brad and what she could do to be free from him forever, but Dan was a welcome distraction from those worrying thoughts. Maybe she could convince her mind to fantasize about Dan when she lay in bed tonight, rather than relive the phone call.

"Ready." She carried her bag out to where Dan was looking at his phone on the couch. His hair was messy, unlike the perfect presentation he usually had. He still wore the jeans and long sleeve Henley that he had worn when he took her daughter skiing this morning, which seemed like a lifetime ago. Had it really only been this morning that her life had seemed like it had brightness and the possibility of love again?

Without making the conscious decision, she crossed suddenly to where Dan sat and straddled his lap, pressing her lips to his. The urgency she felt suddenly overtook her, and his immediate response pulled her into a deeper kiss. She pushed her hands into his hair, seeking comfort only he could give her.

When the realization hit her what she was doing, she almost fell off the couch in her haste to move. "I'm sorry."

"Why? That was the second-best thing that has happened to me today." At her confused look he smiled at her. "The kiss this morning was the first."

"Oh," she sighed. "I'm a bit of a mess right now emotionally. I shouldn't be climbing you like a tree to take my mind off things."

"Please, climb away." He grinned at her again and then got a serious look on his face. "In all seriousness, know that not one minute of the day goes by where I don't want you. But I just texted the Sheriff and he is waiting for us downstairs to get a statement on the phone call. I know you don't want to think about it, but we have to get it documented. I'm happy to distract you after you talk to him, but when we land in bed together again, I want your entire focus on me."

"Sure of yourself that I'll be in your bed again, are you?" She sobered at the thought of the deputy waiting for her downstairs. "We should go talk to him, I guess."

"Says the girl who just almost had her way with me on the couch," he laughed.

"I'm giving the restaurant staff lots to talk about tonight," she groused as they headed down the stairs. "First I almost lose it while working, and now have the police coming."

"I asked him to wait for us outside," Dan said. "I wasn't sure you would want to talk to him inside, so he's on the back patio."

"You're a smart man after all."

"The law degree does suggest that," Dan laughed. "Why don't you go out, I'll grab him a cup of coffee and be right there."

Kendra went out through the kitchen, happy to see that only Zoe and one other staff member were still there cleaning. Zoe rarely left before the kitchen was up to her standards and didn't trust that anyone else would do as good a job as she did. A sentiment that Kendra not only understood but appreciated.

John Jenson, known to most of the town as JJ, was sitting at a table watching as she walked over. JJ was a few years younger than she and Dan, a large man with blond hair and kind blue eyes. She knew he had served in the Marines for a few years after school, but knew little else about him other than that he was a good cop.

"Hey, JJ. Thanks for coming by."

"No problem, Kendra. Your chef was nice enough to sneak me out a sandwich, which was amazing. I can see why you hired her."

"I will tell her you said so, she'll be happy to hear that."

"Dan tells me that you had a complaint to file. Do you want to wait for him to come out?" JJ asked, pushing the plate in front of him away.

"He's not my lawyer, he's just here as a friend. He'll be out in a minute, but I'll give you the quick update." She recounted the phone call from Brad, as JJ took careful notes.

"Is this the first you've heard from him in six years?"

She hesitated as Dan came and sat back down next to her. "No. He got in touch with me when Calle was two, threatened to sue me for custody, saying I was an unfit mother. Said he would go away if I wired ten thousand dollars to him."

"And did you?"

"Yes." She hung her head, ashamed that she had let him extort her.

"Anything since then?" JJ asked patiently.

Kendra fiddled with her watch. "A few thousand here and there over the years, all after the same threat. I hadn't heard anything from him in a year or two and thought he had found someone else to torture. But my accountant was in this week and told me that someone has been siphoning money from my account for a couple of months."

"What's your accountants name?" JJ wrote down the name and phone number that she recited to him. "Did you change your passwords, let the bank know?"

She nodded. "Yes. I can't believe I was dumb enough to let this happen."

"You aren't to blame here," JJ said as he closed his notepad. "There are bad people in the world, and they'll find a way to get what they want. Nothing you could have done would have changed the outcome."

"Maybe if I had said no to money the first time—"

JJ held up a hand to stop her. "Nothing you could have done would have changed this. Don't beat yourself up."

"Is it enough to get a restraining order?" Dan asked.

JJ rubbed his chin. "I don't know for sure; some judges would say yes. I can call one right now and get an emergency order, but it would only be good for two weeks. Then you would have to go into court and get it extended. Where he didn't outright threaten you, I don't honestly know which way it would go."

"But extortion and theft, is that enough for a warrant? If he were to come around, at least that could put her mind at ease that he would be arrested?"

"I need to speak to the accountant and get some files from the bank for the theft. Unfortunately, it's her word against his as to why she sent him the money to begin with. So, the latest transactions going out without her knowledge are what I'll focus on, as well as documenting this call." JJ started to stand. "I apologize that I'm not much more help. If you see him around, call me. I'll come by and have a chat with him, make sure he knows he's not welcome around you."

Dan shook JJ's hand. "Appreciate it. I'll see you at the rink."

Kendra turned to Dan after shaking JJ's hand and watching him walk back to his cruiser. "See, nothing will come of it." She let out a frustrated sigh.

"But he knows about it now. And he'll keep an eye out. He's a solid cop, and he's as big as a house. If he told me not to come around, I would think twice about it."

"Good to know," Kendra laughed. "Let me tell the staff I'm leaving; they can lock up when the last group finally heads out."

They placed the bags in Dan's SUV, after a brief argument about whether she should bring her car to his house or ride with him, and then went into to say goodnight to the staff. Once they finally got into the car and started driving up the mountain, Kendra felt some of the tension leaving her body. Once they arrived at the house, Dan carried the bags in, and they followed the sound of laughter to the kitchen. Jake, Shea and Patrick sat at the kitchen table.

"All is quiet here," Jake said quickly when he saw them. "Calle is up in bed with the dogs, Stella got her settled and Charlie read her about fifteen books. We have checked on her regularly, she's sound asleep. Everything is secure."

"Thanks, Jake." Dan clapped a hand on his brother's shoulder and indicated a chair for Kendra to take. "More wine around?"

"I'm just going to run up and check on Calle," Kendra told them. "I'll feel better once I see her with my own eyes."

"Go ahead, I'll grab glasses and have a glass of wine ready for you when you come back down." Shea smiled at Kendra as she ducked out of the kitchen.

Opening the door slowly, she smiled as she saw Calle tucked into bed with the dogs on either side of her. Twix was snoring softly, and Reese raised her head to look at her before putting it back down on Calle's leg. The relief she felt at seeing her daughter safe and unaffected by anything going on was palpable, and she took a second after closing the door to compose herself before going back to the kitchen table.

"You doing okay?" Patrick looked at Kendra with concern.

"I am, thank you. It was quite the night."

"That's an understatement." Dan passed her a glass of wine before turning to Jake. "We spoke to JJ, and he is making a report. He's going to look into a few things, see what we can do to keep Brad away from them."

"What can we do?" Jake asked.

Kendra shook her head as Dan spoke. "Probably not a lot right now but other than keeping your eyes open. I'll show you a picture of him later, if you see him around, let JJ know."

"We were thinking of playing cards," Shea said. "Any interest?"

Kendra checked her watch and was surprised to see it was just after ten. She was a night owl, usually up well past midnight for the bar, and she had gotten the extra sleep this morning. "Sure, that sounds fun."

They played cards as a group for an hour, before Jake stood and pulled Shea from her chair. "We're going to bed."

"Very caveman of you to not ask me if I'm tired," Shea laughed.

"Oh, I'm not tired." He chased her out of the kitchen, both yelling good night to everyone as they went.

"Well, that makes me very happy my room is down the hall. I think I'll head up; I have a few things to read before I go to bed." Patrick stood and stretched. "Yell if you need anything."

They said goodnight and watched him head down the hall before Dan turned to Kendra. "Want to finish our wine by the fire?"

She nodded and followed him in, taking a seat on the couch next to him this time. Being close to him gave her a sense of safety and comfort, and she was enjoying the heat that existed between them. Their teenage exploits seemed tame in comparison to what happened with a simple kiss now, so the temptation to explore further was strong.

Dan rested his arm behind her on the couch, turning to face her slightly. "How are you really? Doing okay?"

"Yes," she sighed. "It already feels like a lifetime ago when I got that call. Your brothers and Shea were nice to stay up to take my mind off it."

"I don't think that's what they were doing."

"Dan, do you play cards late at night on a regular basis?" She cocked an eyebrow at him and took a sip of her wine as she waited for him to answer.

"Huh," Dan replied. "Those sneaky bastards."

"Sneaky, thoughtful bastards."

"True, but don't tell them I said anything nice about them. Being the oldest means I have to keep them in check."

"Which you always did well."

"Imagine how wild they would have been without me." She laughed as he fake shuddered.

"I feel badly that Calle is an only child," she confessed.

"Why? She doesn't seem to mind."

"No, but she talks about it sometimes, how she doesn't have anyone to play with at home. And she's obsessed with babies, so she's always telling me what a good big sister she would be."

"I'm happy to help with that if you're—"

She slapped his chest lightly. "Be serious."

"In all seriousness, do you want more kids?"

She considered the question. When she had Calle, the idea of making another baby with Brad in the last few months they were together had made her stomach revolt. To say there was a lack of intimacy was an understatement, although it was part of why he felt it was alright to treat her badly, because she was denying him what he considered his right. However, she had a difficult delivery and had been in pain for a long time, and even when she felt better, she had no interest in him. "I always wanted to have a few. But I knew when I was pregnant with Calle that I couldn't have more with him, I just didn't know how I would get away from him."

"If you remarried, then maybe more kids?"

"Dan," she said slowly. "Do you want kids? Is that the conversation we're having here?"

He sighed, looking unsure of himself. "Maybe that thought has crossed my mind. Spending the day with Calle today really got me thinking about it, and the only person I have ever pictured having a baby with is you. Granted, we were eighteen, but that's the truth."

"You haven't seriously dated anyone since then?" She found it hard to believe that a man as good looking as Dan would remain single in Manhattan.

"How do I answer this without getting into trouble?" He smiled at her. "Yes, I have dated. A lot. But no, I never let anyone get too close. I had a few regular dates who I could bank on being presentable and handling themselves well at client dinners or work events, they were usually successful and had no interest in a relationship. Then there were the women who dated me because I had money, or my brother is a movie star, or I could get a table at a hot new spot. Those were over pretty quick."

"Lot's of one-night stands?" she asked with a teasing smile, hiding the pain it gave her heart.

"Not quite that fast. I'm still a Vermont boy at heart, the whole New York City playboy persona didn't fit the way it should have." Dan placed his glass down next to hers on the table and took her hand in his. "I firmly believe that I never stopped loving you, even when I didn't let myself see that. And I know you're not ready to hear that, but I want you to know that I'm determined to see if we can be as good together now as we were back then. I'm not going to tell you I love you because you don't trust me yet, and you shouldn't. But when I do tell you, you'll believe me."

She stared into his eyes, mesmerized. This man was the boy who had taken her to prom, had taken her virginity, and had promised to love her forever when they were still children. She wanted so badly to fall into his arms and let him fix what was broken inside her, but she couldn't fully trust that he wouldn't leave again.

"I should go to bed," she said softly.

"Yes, you should."

Before she knew what happened, they were in each other's arms again. She felt like a teenager again, making out on his dad's sofa, but he also made her feel like a desirable woman for the first time in years. She hadn't been involved with a man since Brad and had made efforts to make herself almost invisible to the men at the bar. Working without makeup, and with her hair pulled back and simple clothes, she had tried to hide in plain sight so she wouldn't catch anyone's attention. In these last six years, and even in the years she spent with Brad, no one had made her feel more wanted than Dan over the last few days.

It was much later when she slid into her bed, a smile on her face. Although they had simply acted like teenagers, with Dan being the one refusing to go any further on the couch, he had made her feel better than she had in a long time. The worry she had earlier about not sleeping due to the phone call was long gone, she knew that Dan had just guaranteed her a night of dreaming about him instead.

Chapter 17

The next few days passed in a blur, with the town filling up with tourists who would spend their Thanksgiving weekend skiing and looking at the last few colored leaves. The surge of families visiting for the holiday and old classmates suddenly in town kept the restaurant busy, and Dan was lucky to catch a few minutes with Kendra each day. Arriving earlier in the day helped, when Calle was in school and she was just starting to open, but she was still usually too busy to sit with him for long. When he got a text from her early Wednesday morning asking him to come to her apartment, he wasted no time throwing clothes on and rushing out.

When he pulled in and saw the sheriff's car out back, his heart went into triple time, and he ran up the stairs to her apartment. Walking in without hesitating to knock, he was relieved to see her sitting on the couch with JJ across from her, both sipping on coffee.

"Hey, Dan." JJ nodded to him.

"Hi. You okay?" He crossed to where Kendra was and dropped down beside her.

"Yes, I just wanted you to hear what JJ had to say."

"I was just telling Kendra that I spoke to Pete and the bank, and we're trying to trace where those wires were sent, but it doesn't look like we will be able to recover those funds. The bank is denying all responsibility, since it was sent from Kendra's log in, and the account that it went to isn't likely to share much." JJ consulted his notepad. "I was able to pull the phone number that called Kendra that night. It was a burner phone, with a New Hampshire area code. Doesn't mean he's in New Hampshire, but that's likely where he bought it. The State Police there are going to look into where it was purchased, but without any real threat or crime, they really aren't going to put much effort in."

"That leaves us where? Just waiting for him to make his next move?" Dan heard the frustration in his voice and shot an apologetic look at JJ. "Sorry, I know it's not your fault."

"Don't worry, I get it. Yes, we have to wait. I alerted everyone on our staff and most of the local business owners to keep an eye out, report in if they spot him in town. It would be very hard for him to come into Windsor Peak and not be seen." JJ turned his focus to Kendra. "Nothing more has happened since we last talked?"

She shook her head. "No, I changed all my passwords and Pete is going to change the account numbers. I haven't gotten any more phone calls, nothing out of the ordinary."

"I wish I could do more. I'm here, call me anytime if something seems even a little off. You can call my cell, even if I'm not on duty and I'll come right over."

"I appreciate that, JJ." She stood to walk him out, and Dan followed, shaking the officer's hand before he left.

"That's frustrating." Dan leaned against the counter, watching as she rinsed out their coffee mugs.

"I have to think that he just got bored and wanted to scare me. I don't know why he acts like he does, but he thinks he's the most important person in the world and probably just needed some attention." Kendra dried her hands on a towel before hanging it back up. "I really don't want to spend Thanksgiving thinking about him."

"Speaking of, Stella asked if you wanted to spend the night tonight. She can watch Calle while you're working, and I'll bring you back home with me."

Kendra looked thoughtful before shaking her head. "It would be easier to have Calle there, since it will be such a late night for me. But I always have the restaurant open for the Turkey Trot, serving coffee and pastries and just having a bathroom available. I should stay here."

He gathered her in his arms, pressing her back lightly against the counter. "What if Calle stayed with them, and I stayed with you?"

"It's going to be a late night and an early morning," she replied. "Not a lot of sleep to be had."

"I don't think I said anything about sleeping."

She laughed softly and kissed him, warming him from the inside out. "Then I say yes, that sounds like a good plan."

"We could get an early start—" Dan whispered, nuzzling her neck before she laughed and stepped away from him.

"I have to get downstairs; Zoe is already there waiting for me." She glanced out the window at where her chef would be parked. "And JJ is still here, so he must be charming her into making him an early lunch."

He reached for her, pulling her back to him. Spending the next few minutes trying to change her mind was fun, and he enjoyed the dazed look in her eyes when she pulled away again. "I guess I can wait a few more hours," he said, planting a kiss on her forehead.

"You're going to make me crazy, Danny." She pulled open the door to her porch, waiting for him to join her before stepping down the stairs. "I'll get my revenge later."

He laughed as he followed her down the stairs, watching her black ponytail bounce with each step. At the bottom they saw JJ leaving the kitchen, hands full with a wrapped plate and a to-go cup of coffee. He held them both up and shrugged sheepishly before heading over to his cruiser.

"I should go too," Dan said, catching her before she went inside. "I promised Stella I would help her today. I'll be back later, call me if you need anything."

***

"How are things with you and Kendra?" Stella asked from the stove, where she could keep an eye on his washing dishes while she baked.

"Really good." Dan knew better than to give too much away to Stella, although he knew she would find out everything with or without his cooperation. His teenage years she had always been one step ahead of him, keeping him out of trouble or helping him to make the right decisions. But if she got the sense that he and Kendra were getting serious again, there would be no stopping her efforts to see them live happily ever after together.

"You've been spending a lot of time together."

"Yes, we have. It's been amazing."

Stella checked on the pie in the oven and then turned to face him again. "You're not planning to break her heart again, are you?"

"I didn't plan it the first time," he sighed. "But no, I have no intention of hurting her."

"So, what are your intentions?" she walked right through the door he had opened with his statement.

He weighed his answer, knowing that what he said could come back to bite him tomorrow, or in the days coming forward. But he also knew the value in having Stella on his team, and needed some help to get all the way into Kendra's life. "My intention," he said slowly. "Is to win her back. Forever this time."

"Do you think you're still compatible?"

He thought about the heat between them and felt his cheeks blush, so he tried to hide by ducking his head as he rinsed a bowl. "Yes. Very much so."

"I'm not talking physically, Dan. Anyone can have physical chemistry. I mean do your goals line up with hers? Does she want more kids? Do you want kids? Do you plan to stay here forever, or is she willing to move?" She fired the questions at him quickly.

"I guess I don't know the answers to all of those," he admitted. "But I do think that where she is, I should be. And if I need to make changes in my life to have her in it, I'm willing to do that."

"When all the sacrifice is on one side, it can create bitterness."

"Are we talking about us now, or you and Dad?" Stella had lived in the back guest house helping raise the three boys after their mom died giving birth to Patrick, and Dan had no idea whether she and his dad were romantic during those years.

"Don't try and spin this," she shook a finger at him. "To answer your question, I wasn't the only one who sacrificed. Yes, I probably could have gotten married to someone else and had my own family. But your dad needed me, and I was his best friend, so I did it without thinking. Your dad, he lost the wife he loved and then he had to live by my crazy rules for years. But I got you three, and your dad, so I don't consider any of it a sacrifice."

"You didn't want kids of your own?"

"I did," she admitted. "But then I had you guys suddenly. I went from thinking I might live my life alone, and lonely at that, to having three little boys who needed me desperately. I slept in your room for weeks, with you and Jake, helping you when you wanted your mama. Never had I felt so important, so needed, than I did in those first few weeks. And then it turned into years."

"Did you always love him?" Dan dared to ask quietly, since she was sharing so much.

"Since the day I sat next to him in kindergarten, I think. It just took him a bit longer."

"I don't think I want to know, but we're all curious. Were you guys hiding a romance from us?"

"Not hiding it, really. We spent all our free time together, had dinner together every night, took vacations together. You boys just didn't want to see it, and I didn't want you to if I'm being honest. I don't know if you three would have trusted me as much if you knew I was involved with your dad, especially when you were young. But a lot of people knew."

"You're saying everyone else in town knew? People at church?"

"Most," she nodded. "Your dad was an eligible bachelor. The woman would have been lining up outside if word hadn't gotten around. I may have dropped a hint or two when we started up the year after your mom passed."

"I think that's probably where I should stop asking questions," Dan laughed.

"What questions are we asking?" Patrick asked as he came into the kitchen.

"About your dad and my—"

Dan cut Stella off with a loud laugh. "I'll tell you later. Get over here and help."

"I'm just heading out; I have a session booked at the gym. Want to come?"

"I promised I would help Stella get ready for tomorrow," Dan added a sad note to his voice and turned sad eyes to her.

"Oh, get out of here, you. I know what you're doing, go with your brother already." She swatted him with the kitchen towel as he dropped the bowl in his hands into the sink.

***

After a workout that would normally leave him sapped for energy, Dan hurried his brothers to get ready for a night out at Windsor Peak Palace. The night before Thanksgiving was always a pseudo high school reunion for everyone who had come home for the holiday, and he wanted to get a seat at the bar before the room filled. Patrick had debated all afternoon about whether to go, and finally decided to risk it when Jake assured him that he could take the car home if it was overwhelming. Jake would spend the night at Shea's, and Dan planned to stay at Kendra's, so Patrick was the only one returning to the house.

"Babysitting duty," Patrick mused as he buckled his seatbelt. "Who knew this is where my career would land?"

"I think your career is going just fine," Dan assured him. "I saw the contract for the next three films in the series, don't forget."

"How much?" Jake asked from the driver's seat.

Dan started to speak but Patrick cut him off. "You can read about it in the magazines like everyone else."

"That's rude. Dan knows," Jake pointed out.

"He's my lawyer. He is bound by confidentiality."

"I'm going to start keeping secrets from you guys," Jake promised.

"Like getting shot?" Dan cocked an eyebrow at his brother and then laughed.

"You guys have to move past that at some point."

"Technically, we don't have to do anything. Other than give you shit, which we enjoy." Patrick slapped Jake's shoulder with the baseball hat he held in his hand.

"Things must be moving along with Kendra?" Jake asked Dan as he drove. "Unless you're spending the night on her couch?"

"Not if I can help it. Yes, things are progressing."

"Never thought she would come around. When I first came home, she wanted nothing to do with you." Jake referred to when Kendra had avoided him for weeks.

"I wore her down with my charm," Dan told him.

Patrick laughed. "That and she had to free up that barstool for a customer. It was date you or deal with you in her face forever."

Dan shrugged. "It worked, didn't it?"

"I hope you guys can last this time," Jake told him. "Don't screw up."

"Why does everyone assume I'm going to mess this up?"

"History?" Jake said at the same time Patrick voiced, "You're an idiot?"

"You guys are the best. I can't tell you how much I like spending time with you," Dan said drolly. "Maybe we could talk about why our movie star brother is single one of these days."

"I'll pass, thank you very much," Patrick said. "I much prefer to focus on torturing you two."

"It's a little weird," Jake said to Dan. "He's the sexiest man alive and hasn't gotten any action in months."

Patrick laughed from the backseat. "That you know of."

Dan turned to look at him. "You holding out on us?"

"We haven't talked about things like that since high school. I highly doubt you two are going to come home and give me a play by play while I eat pancakes with Calle and Charlie," Patrick pointed out. "Let's just say I'm doing fine and leave it at that."

"Groupies?" Jake asked, looking at him in the mirror.

"I don't need to sleep with groupies, Jake."

They both waited, but clearly Patrick was done sharing. Jake parked and they all headed inside, seeing Shea at the end of the bar holding three more seats, including Jake's favorite in the corner. She waved to them as she talked to Kendra, the two woman smiling as they watched them walk in. Patrick, with his hat down low, was able to make it to where they sat with little notice, and Kendra slid a new standing bar menu so that it blocked his face from most customers.

"Thanks," Patrick grinned at her. "That was smart."

"It was that or put in a VIP section, but I didn't think you would want that." Kendra smiled at Patrick before her eyes met Dan's. "It will be crowded tonight, if Patrick needs to escape you can show him the way through the kitchen."

They settled in, enjoying seeing old classmates and teammates, before Jake and Shea begged off just after ten. As they left, Dan noticed Patrick becoming increasingly busier as a younger crowd was taking over the bar.

"Want to get out?" He asked him quietly when he was able to sit for a minute.

Patrick took a sip of water from the glass in front of him and then nodded. "Yeah, I think it would be best. People are driving here from other towns now, so the crowds will thin out if I leave."

Dan pointed to his chair when Kendra was looking, indicating he would be right back, and saw her nod. He led his brother through the door that was just behind where they sat, and Patrick sighed with relief when they got into the kitchen.

"Man, that was exhausting." He took the hat off and ran his hand through his hair.

"You would never know it from how you interact with fans. No wonder they love you."

"I try my best," Patrick said as Zoe spotted them.

"Hello, boys. Are you going to cook tonight?"

"No, just showing Patrick the exit," Dan explained.

"Did you eat?" She asked him as she plated some appetizers to send out to the bar.

"I did earlier, but that looks amazing."

Dan laughed. "Patrick is always hungry."

"You sit here in the kitchen at that table, and I will make you something," Zoe directed. "Dan, you can go, Patrick will tell me stories and I will tell him about life in France."

Suitably dismissed, he made his way back to the bar, seeing the disappointed faces of a young female crowd when he came back alone. He heard the whisperings of several, who decided they could probably catch Patrick outside before bolting to the door. It was probably a good thing Patrick was safe in Zoe's domain, if anyone dared breach her kitchen, she would take care of them.

"How are you doing?" Kendra asked as she passed by, clearing empty glasses.

"I'm good," he replied. "Looks like it's starting to slow down."

"Eleven is usually when the crowd leaves, I thought the younger kids would push it, but I guess someone is having a big party by the lake. Makes my life easier," she gave him a tired smile. "Want to get out of here soon?"

"Yes."

She laughed at his quick answer. "Give me a half hour, and I'll be done."

He waited, the people from his town swirling around him in a happy cloud, his thoughts jumping between their past and their future. The years apart felt shorter somehow, as if they hadn't existed. What felt like hours later, she walked toward him with a smile, taking his hand and leading him from the bar. Unfortunately for him, the time that followed passed much faster than the time he had spent waiting, but he enjoyed every minute.

Chapter 18

Waking in Dan's arms had to be the most surreal experience of Kendra's life so far. She had only done so a handful of times in the past, when a parent was out of town and they could claim they were sleeping at a friend's house. As an adult, it was a different sensation, where she was less worried about her bedhead and breath, and very aware of the man next to her. And he was a man now, she thought as her eyes trailed down his fit body. The teenager who had struggled to put muscle on had made up for that and then some.

He woke up slower, the result of their very late-night antics, and a sleepy smile crossed his face as he reached for her. "Good morning," he whispered as he kissed wrapped her in his arms.

She soaked in his warmth for a moment before kissing his chest and rolling back. "Good morning. Sorry I have to get up and be out so early, you can sleep more."

"No, I'll come with you. You sure you don't have an extra five minutes?"

"Five?" She cocked an eyebrow at him and then slid from the bed, walking confidently to her closet where she pretended to search for clothes.

"You're doing that on purpose," he said from the bed. "Now you have no choice but to come back."

She laughed, shooting a look at him over her shoulder. "I wish I could, trust me. But I really am running late. If you stay there, I'll come back when the Trot is over."

He groaned, pushing his face into the pillow. "I'll come with you under one condition."

"What's that?" She stopped grabbing clothes long enough to look at him.

"We both come straight back here."

"Don't forget we have to be at your house by one," she warned him.

"And I plan to take full advantage of every possible moment until then," he promised as he stood.

It was her turn to moan as he walked across the room to use her bathroom before she quickly turned away and grabbed a towel for after her shower. When Dan followed her promising he only wanted to wash her hair, she pushed him out of the bathroom and clicked the door lock.

"Charlie and his team are running," he called from the other side of the bathroom door. "I think Jake is as well. Shea said she's not a runner, but she would be there to cheer them on. Patrick was on the fence about it, he wants to do it but doesn't want to make it harder for everyone else."

"It's usually just the people from town who come," she responded. "I think he would be okay."

"I feel a little bad that I forgot my sneakers, but it just means I get to spend the time with you instead of racing. Because you know my brothers and I wouldn't be able to resist racing each other."

"It's supposed to be fun," she pointed out. She opened the bathroom door after getting dressed so he could finish what he needed before they left.

"What about that doesn't sound fun?"

She laughed at the expression of innocence he was trying to portray in the bathroom mirror they were sharing. Grabbing her toothbrush and doing the task next to Dan was a new experience, and yet felt perfectly natural. The ease she felt with him was unmatched in her marriage, where she had always been on edge. Even when she had begun dating Brad and when married, she had never felt fully comfortable with him. It bothered her the most, that she was able to get pushed into marrying someone she wasn't at ease with, but somehow it happened.

In her counseling sessions, the therapist had explained that Brad had known what he was doing. She had been struggling in her self-confidence after Dan left, and Brad had preyed on that. In addition, he had caused issues with her family and friends, so no one was able to step in and see that it wasn't the right match for her. Thankfully she had been able to repair the damage he had done to those relationships, but it had taken a long time. Seeing how she had hurt her parents was the worst, and she was glad every day that she was able to fix it before she never had the chance.

"Where did you go?" Dan asked, studying her in the mirror.

"Sorry, just thinking." She put her toothbrush back in the holder and shooed him from the bathroom.

She wasn't afraid to discuss the thoughts with Dan, she knew she was safe with him and could share anything. But bringing the ugliness of her marriage into the light after the night they had spent together was not the right time. She needed to focus her thoughts on Dan, the Thanksgiving day they were going to spend with Calle and his family, and her busy morning. Resolute, she left the bathroom and meant to march past him to the door, but he swiped her at the last minute, pulling her into his arms.

Their mouths met, and before she knew it, he had turned her so her legs were pressing against her mattress. "Dan, I have to go." She laughed as he dropped his head to her shoulder. "Later, I promise." She kissed him once more softly before starting out of the room, screeching as he made like he would chase her. They ran down the stairs like kids, laughing and teasing each other, coming to a quick stop when they found Zoe at the bottom.

"Well good morning to you two," she teased. "Looks like a fun sleepover."

"Morning, Zoe." Dan nodded and crossed the kitchen to go into the restaurant, leaving Kendra blushing in front of her chef.

"Things are moving along, I see," Zoe said.

"They are."

"I'm happy for you. He makes you smile." With her simple endorsement, Zoe went back to plating pastries and snacks, freeing Kendra to join Dan by the bar.

The staff the night before had done a good job of cleaning up, so the remnants of the busy night were washed away. She directed Dan to the kitchen to bring out the fancy espresso maker and made sure the glass mugs were on hand for Irish coffees. Satisfied, she went to the kitchen to get the hot water, cocoa and coffees Zoe had already prepped and put into large carafes.

Once everything was in place and she was satisfied, she unlocked the door and stepped out into the fresh morning on Main Street. The shops along the street were doing the same, propping open doors to the cold morning air, flipping signs to open and turning lights on. She waved to those closest to her before stepping back inside, startled to realize that JJ had come in from the kitchen while she was out front.

"Morning, JJ." She crossed to the coffee. "Coffee?"

"Please." He sat on a barstool, waiting until Dan came in with the last jug of cocoa and placed it with the others before he spoke again. "I wanted to come first thing to let you know that we have a report that Brad was in Burlington last night. A hotel clerk is dating a police officer up there, and the officer was in the lobby when the man came in. The names don't match up, but he said if it's not Brad, he has a twin."

Kendra felt the blood leave her cheeks and was glad that Dan had come to stand next to her to lean on. He gently placed her in a chair before pulling his phone out and texting quickly. "Is he still there?"

"No," JJ responded. "The night clerk said he came back around eleven, when her shift started. Then he dropped his key off around five this morning."

"He could be anywhere. He could be here."

"No one has reported seeing him," JJ told her.

"But most people don't know it's an issue," she pointed out. "Other than you and the other cops, and a few other people."

"True. If we get a sighting of him in town, I'm going to help you get a restraining order."

She choked out a laugh. "Forgive me for not feeling like that would keep me safe. Or Calle." Her breath caught as she thought of her daughter, and she jumped from her seat only to have Dan put a reassuring hand on her arm.

"She's fine. I just texted my dad, Calle is still sleeping and has both dogs with her. I asked him to go up and check on her, if anything is wrong, he'll call me. He said he was going to get a rifle out and sit on the porch, and he hopes that Brad will show up." He rubbed her back as he spoke. "I'm going to call Jake as soon as I feel like you're okay."

She nodded, trying to slow her breathing. All the joy she had felt that morning had been washed away in one moment, and she was struggling not to completely break down. She tried to focus on Dan's hand, and finally stood to be wrapped entirely in his arms, pulling support from him. When she finally felt under control, she stepped back.

"Can someone else manage here?" Dan asked, looking around. "Zoe, or one of the staff? That way I can take you up to the house and we can forget about him. He wouldn't dare come up there."

"That might solve today, but it doesn't explain why he's coming around suddenly. Plus, I do want to be here, I'm always here for Turkey Trot and I don't want him to take that away from me. Everyone picked up their Thanksgiving meals already, and Zoe will stick around for a bit just in case anyone comes looking for a meal, so I don't need to stay after the race." She took a deep breath, forcing herself to stand up straight and say the words her therapist had encouraged speaking out loud when scared. "I'm not afraid."

"I won't let anything happen to you," Dan said. "Or Calle."

JJ stood, placing his coffee mug on the counter. "I'm really sorry, Kendra. I hated to give you this news today, but the more information you have, the better prepared you can be. Call me if anything at all happens out of the ordinary. I'll be down here all morning, and if I see anything I'll touch base. I hope you have a Happy Thanksgiving."

They wished him the same and watched him disappear through the kitchen doors again. "He's a good man," Dan said finally.

"He is. And a good cop." She went behind the bar, forcing herself to tidy up the already straight bottles, just to keep her hands busy. "Let's try to forget about this for now, focus on the race and the holiday."

As the door started opening and her friends and neighbors filled the room with laughter and chatter, she forced herself to relax. She had no reason to believe that Brad had been nearby because of her, and she wouldn't allow him to ruin her day. Dan stayed close, keeping an eye on her and telling everyone who asked that he wasn't running that year.

Jake and Shea came in shortly after Dan's brief conversation with his brother, and Shea immediately went to Kendra and hugged her. "I'm sorry you're going through this," she whispered so no one else could hear. "I hope you don't mind that Jake shared with me."

"Of course not," she responded, choking back sudden tears. "I appreciate the support."

"I'm going to stay right here with you," Shea asserted. "Jake is going to run and keep his eye on the crowd. We all figured he was the best person to do it, Brad wouldn't know who he is, and he's trained in this kind of thing. If Brad is in town, Jake will sniff him out."

Jake came to where they stood and gave her a crushing hug. "We've got your back."

"Patrick is going to stay at the house," Shea explained. "He was going to come meet us, but Calle was determined to come down to watch Charlie race. Patrick got her to agree to a horseback ride instead, so he'll take her for a quick one."

"Oh, she'll love that. But do you think—"

Jake shook his head. "Dad has trail cameras everywhere, they checked and there was only the normal animal activity overnight. No sign of anyone being around the house, and Brad has no reason to think that she's up there. Patrick will bring a pistol just in case, and he knows how to use it."

She knew all three of the Burrows had been taught gun safety and how to shoot at an early age, and that Patrick was more than capable of keeping her daughter safe. Calle would have a fun morning and have no idea the fuss that was going on around her, which is exactly what Kendra wanted.

"You're staying at our house tonight," Dan added. "No debate over that. We'll all be drinking, so safer to stay. Plus, we're all going to chop down the tree tomorrow, don't forget."

"I'm staying too," Shea said, squeezing her arm. "It will be fun."

She smiled at Shea, not wanting her to see how nervous and upset she was over the idea of Brad. Fun seemed to be the furthest thing from her mind, despite her best efforts to pretend otherwise. There had to be a reason he was close by, there was no such thing as a coincidence with Brad. Now she had to wait like a sitting duck to see what his next move would be, and she didn't like that one bit.

Chapter 19

Dan paced in front of the restaurant in the limited space allowed by the crowd standing on the front porch. Seeing the fear on Kendra's face made him want to do something, but there was nothing he could do. The single most frustrating feeling for him was ineptitude, and that's what he was experiencing now. Jake had gone to run the race, and Shea was helping Kendra inside and keeping an eye on everything. There was no imminent threat to her, but he wanted this guy out of their lives for good.

Zoe stepped out onto the porch, greeting him with a nod. "I've never seen a Turkey Trot before, I don't even think I know what it is."

"It's just a fun road race, people dress up in costumes and get some exercise before eating all day," he explained.

"Ah, that explains it." She leaned onto the rail next to him, leaning forward to see more of the runners before turning to him. "Your Thanksgiving is new for me."

"That's right, you're Canadian."

"We celebrate as well, but on a different day. Almost the same traditions, other than this, I think."

"Did you go home for yours this year?"

She shook her head. "There is no one in Canada anymore, and I was working here."

"You're welcome to join us today if you'd like," Dan offered.

"Thank you, that's very kind. I'm looking forward to a day of lounging and watching movies on the TV. I don't take many days off, so a forced day of rest when the restaurant is closed, I need to enjoy."

"The offer stands if you change your mind." He watched as Jake ran by, at a slower pace than he would have expected from his brother. Clearly the focus was on surveying the crowd and not winning.

"I hope you're good to her," Zoe said. "Her heart is very fragile. She looks tough, but I see it."

He turned to face her, touched that she was out here in an effort to protect Kendra. "I plan to be. I hope I have been so far. All I want is for her to be happy."

"What if her being happy is living without you? Or without any man?"

He struggled with an answer, wanting to tell her that it wasn't possible, since he would make her happy. The idea that he could cause Kendra any unhappiness like he saw on her face this morning caused the acid in his stomach to boil in a way it hadn't since his early law career. "If I thought I was causing her any unhappiness, I would have to walk away," he finally responded.

She stared at him, considering his words. "Make sure you put her feelings first. I know yours matter too, but you're strong, she's not. This can't just be about you winning, or what you want. It has to be what she wants." With that, she turned and went back into the restaurant.

He was speechless for the first time in his life, unsure what to think or do. Was there a risk that he could hurt Kendra again, cause her pain like what she was feeling today? No, he admitted. He would never scare her, never upset her the way that Brad did. But no couple could go without their speedbumps, and they were bound to encounter some. There was no way to promise that he could keep her happy constantly, that was ridiculous. Even Jake and Shea had moments of struggle, and his dad and Stella bickered. If Kendra was invested in them together, he would do everything he could to progress the relationship, he decided. He had come on strong for a while now, so letting her take the lead might be a smart thing to do.

Resolute, he turned back to the street to see Jake making his way back towards the restaurant. He shook his head when he saw Dan looking and came to stand with him on the porch.

"Nothing," he said. "Sorry, I was hoping I would spot him so we would know where he was."

"Damn. Where is this guy? What's his game?"

"Could be just this. Cause her some turmoil, make her worried enough that when he calls looking for some cash, she's more likely to hand it over so he'll go away."

"He's not getting any more money from her," Dan vowed.

"Maybe it's a way to flush him out," Jake suggested. "If he does come looking for money, she should tell him it has to be cash because her accountant is suspicious. Then JJ can nab him when he comes to get the money. Extortion is a crime, so that would hold him up for a while."

"Not a bad idea. I'll talk to her about it." Dan started to push away and was stopped by Jake's hand on his arm.

"Before you go in, I've been wanting to talk to you, and it's been hard to pin you down."

"What's up?"

"I'm proposing to Shea tomorrow at the tree farm. She told me some of her happiest memories as a child were going there to cut down the Christmas tree, and it's her favorite season. Makes sense to add to her good memories, right?" Jake looked as unsure about himself as Dan had ever seen.

"That's great," Dan slapped him on the back. "I'm so happy for you, congrats."

"Thanks," Jake grinned. "Stella has been working on a celebration bag, with champagne and things for everyone to have after. I'll probably try and sneak away with her, but knowing Stella, she'll make it so you all can witness, so I'm not banking on any privacy. Just wanted you to know so you don't start yelling at me if I'm walking too slow for you."

"Or throw a snowball at you right before you go down on one knee," Dan laughed.

"Yeah, let's skip that if we can." He looked through the window to where Shea stood talking to Kendra. "She's everything to me, I can't wait to make her mine. I want to move into the cottage with her, but she's hesitant to do it before we're married, says she wants to make sure we are both all in. And what if something goes wrong and we break up, and we put Charlie through that. I'm hoping that this will prove that I have no intention of ever breaking up and I'm fully committed. If she can put up with my nightmares and occasional mood swings, she can have me forever."

"I think that's exactly what she wants," Dan said. "I'm happy for you."

"Thanks. I hope you'll get there one day too. I like seeing the way you are with Kendra, and the way you are here in general. This is a much better version of Dan."

"New York Dan had his good qualities."

"Name one." Jake dared as they went to walk into the restaurant.

Dan laughed. "Okay, you're right. I'm better here."

They joined Kendra and Shea, Jake telling them he hadn't spotted anything out of the ordinary.

"He's probably long gone," Shea assured Kendra. "Any chance you can put it out of your mind for the day?"

Kendra nodded slowly. "I'll try. I'm sick of him ruining things for me."

Dan met her gaze, and he saw the determination in her eyes. It wasn't just about the day, he realized. She didn't want Brad to ruin what they had just started, and that relieved a good part of the tension he was feeling. As long as she wanted him as much as he wanted her, he had nothing to worry about.

***

When they entered the house an hour later, the smells of Thanksgiving hit first, then the sound of Calle's giggle. Dan could see the instant relief on Kendra's face as she realized her daughter was not impacted by Brad's antics, and watched as she rushed down the hall towards the sound. Following her, he found his brother on all fours, Calle perched on his back.

"What do we have here?" Kendra asked as Dan burst into laughter.

"He's my horse," Calle declared. "It got cold outside so we couldn't ride any more, but he said we could have fun inside. Charlie was playing for a little while but he had an urgency on the computer, so he had to go."

"An emergency," Patrick helped. "Some of his friends were gaming and he wasn't there, so that's catastrophic."

"Let's give Patrick a break and see if Stella can use help in the kitchen." Kendra lifted her daughter off and led her from the room.

Dan started to follow but stopped at Patrick's look.

"Everything okay?"

"Yes," Dan nodded. "We didn't see Brad anywhere, even Jake when he did the course. All signs point to him being gone. I'm starting to wonder if he just came to rattle her, see what he could shake out. Jake had an idea about that, I'll talk to JJ about it some more tomorrow."

"If it's a money thing—"

Dan stopped his brother with a look. "If it were just a money thing I would take care of it, assuming Kendra's pride allowed it. But I also don't think it would solve the problem, because he would just keep coming back." He softened at the hurt look on Patrick's face. "I appreciate how generous you are, trust me."

"We can't just give him a couple mil and be done with it? Make him sign something to leave them alone?"

Dan shook his head. "Not only do I not think that would stop him, but I don't want your hard-earned money going to that guy."

"If you change your mind, the offer stands."

"Did you help Jake with his purchase for tomorrow?"

"No," Patrick said. "I offered, but he said he had plenty of money saved from all the years he spent overseas, and it had to come from him. Did you see it?"

"No, did you?"

Patrick nodded. "It's nice. Not too much, perfect for Shea, I think. He did a good job."

Dan glanced toward the kitchen, where Kendra had disappeared with Calle. "I should head in there."

"Thinking about what kind of ring you should get?" Patrick teased as they headed out of the living room.

Dan stopped walking and then laughed. "Yeah, I kind of was."

Patrick looked at him, stunned. "I was only kidding. Are you serious?"

"Not right now, I need to make sure this is what she wants. But yeah, she's everything I've ever wanted."

"Wow. If you two get married quickly and start popping out babies, that will keep Stella off my back."

"Don't get ahead of yourself," Dan warned. "Nothing will satisfy her until we're all married and have a few babies running around."

Patrick shuddered and laughed as they joined the family, but Dan couldn't shake the idea from his head. Once so quick to dismiss settling down, and having chosen career over family, now it was all he could think about. As long as the woman currently slicing carrots was willing to have a future with him.

The day passed quickly, filled with good food, wine and conversation. Dan stayed by Kendra's side as much as possible, relishing in celebrating their first holiday together in years, even if she didn't want to showcase their budding relationship in front of his family and Calle. She allowed him to pull her closer and drape an arm across her chair when they were nibbling on desserts, so he took that as a small victory. Before he knew it, he was following her up the stairs to the bedrooms, stopping her when she tried to go into the guest room. Leading her by the hand to his room, he felt like a teenager again, sneaking his girlfriend into his room. And he loved every second of it.

Chapter 20

Kendra woke up early the next morning, just as the sun was starting to light the room from behind the curtains. Slipping from under Dan's arm, she grabbed the robe he had lying across a chair and pulled it on before checking that the hallway was empty. Satisfied she wouldn't be caught, she darted down the hall the guest room, where she slipped her pajamas on and got into bed. Best if Calle didn't realize she had slept anywhere else, and it would give her a little time to reflect on the previous day.

The highs and lows she had experienced over the last twenty-four hours were remarkable. The happiness she had felt after the night with Dan, followed by the crushing fear brought on by the news of Brad. Only to be followed by a beautiful, relaxing evening with the Burrows, where she and Calle had been folded into the family dynamic with ease. Fortunately, her daughter had no idea that Brad was causing issues and had the time of her life yesterday. Not to mention, she was looking forward to the trip to the tree farm today, it had been all she could talk about at bedtime.

Dan had let her know of Jake's plans to propose during the excursion, and she was thrilled for the other couple. A tiny part of her heart panged at the thought that she had always expected to receive a ring from Dan, and here they were all these years later just starting a new relationship. If that's what it was, since they hadn't confirmed any feelings or intentions for the future. For all she knew, he planned to return to New York or conquer a new city and she was a good distraction from his workplace difficulties. A salve to his ego, maybe, since it had to grate on him that someone had gotten the upper hand on him.

The door from the adjoining bathroom creaked open, and her daughters little face peered through at her before sleepily crossing the room and sliding under the covers. Kendra snuggled her close, loving that she still enjoyed a morning cuddle before fully waking up.

"Good morning, love bug." She kissed the brown curls head tucked onto her shoulder.

"Morning, mama." A minute passed before her head popped up again. "Christmas tree today, right?"

"Yes," she said. "Stella said we would all head out after a big breakfast."

"I ate so much yesterday, there might not be any room for more food."

"When your belly smells Stella's French toast, I bet it will make room."

"I like it here," Calle declared. "Yesterday was fun, it's like having a bunch of aunts and uncles like my friends do."

"I like it here too," she agreed. Her heart squeezed at the thought that Calle was falling in love with the Burrows family just as she had when she was younger. She needed to make sure that anything that happened between her and Dan wouldn't tear Calle away from the people she was growing close to. It was time they had a talk about where they were headed, and if they should even continue whatever it was they had started.

Tomorrow, she resolved, since today was going to be filled with the joy she needed to infuse her heart and soul with.

***

Satisfied and full after a huge breakfast put out by Stella, they all split into cars to drive the short distance to the tree farm. Ben drove the truck, Stella at his side. Jake, Shea and Patrick all climbed into Jake's SUV, leaving Dan to drive Kendra, Calle and Charlie. Calle chattered the entire ride to Charlie, loving having her favorite person in the backseat with her. When Dan reached over and took her hand, she cast a quick glance back and realized Calle only had eyes for Charlie, so she enjoyed the warmth he provided.

They came out of the cars in the parking lot with a lot of noise and holiday cheer. Stella had passed out Santa hats for all the men to wear, and they all pulled them on while the women put on reindeer headbands. New scarves and gloves were a gift from Ben, in bright reds and greens. They were a walking Christmas card, and she loved that the family threw themselves into the holiday with such gusto.

After pulling on her gloves she reached for Calle's hand, only to have her fly by on Charlie's back. She laughed, looking at Dan. "I thought it would be a few years before she so clearly preferred boys to my company."

"Oh, don't be sad. I'll hold your hand." He took hers and pulled her closer, so she could feel his body heat through her jacket.

They all walked across the field, pointing to the various trees and laughing as Ben continually tried to steer them toward a smaller tree. Patrick, who carried the ax, always shook his head no and kept moving. Soon they were the only ones around in a field of Christmas trees, a soft snow falling. When Dan pulled her behind a tree for what was meant to be a quick kiss, she giggled and went along, grabbing his scarf to pull him back down when he tried to end it.

"Who knew a Christmas tree farm would get you feeling all romantic," he teased before kissing her again.

She tipped her head back, so the snowflakes landed on her eyelashes. "It's the whole day, really. And last night." Tossing him a wink she headed back to where everyone was gathered, realizing that Jake had pulled Shea slightly ahead and everyone was watching silently.

Shea looked around, probably confused that the noise had stopped so abruptly, and saw the family gathered watching. Kendra saw tears pop into her eyes quickly as she turned to Jake, as if the realization of the moment had just hit her. Sure enough, when Jake went down on his knee, the tears flowed freely down Shea's cheeks. And her own, she realized as she felt the tracks.

"Shea Kerrigan, I have been in love with you for years without even realizing it. You kept me grounded in the chaos of war, and never quit on me. Coming home to you was never in my plans, but it turned out to be everything I needed. The last few months I've found myself again, and you've helped me in so many ways. I want to be the man that you see when you look at me with so much love, the dad to Charlie and to our babies that you bring out in me. I love your kindness, your heart, your loyalty, and your unwavering support. I love how you are with Charlie, and how special you make him feel. I want to have a family with you, grow old with you, and never spend another day apart. Will you marry me?"

"Yes!" Her response could be heard clear across the field, and the entire family erupted in cheers as the happy couple clung to each other. Charlie raced across to join them, the three of them huddled together.

Dan pulled her closer, kissing her in front of everyone to celebrate in the joy. Ben and Stella were standing with their arms linked together, smiling. Even Patrick, the ax slung over his shoulder and looking every bit the movie star that he was, beamed at his brother. After all Jake had gone through, to see him find his happiness and to be a witness to this was almost too much for Kendra's emotions.

Ben pulled out a bottle of champagne from the bag Jake had dropped on the ground, and soon the adults were toasting with it while the kid's held glasses of apple juice. They celebrated until Calle shivered, and the men jumped into action, subtly directing her to the biggest, fullest tree on the lot so she could be the one who found it.

"This one," she declared, pointing at it. "That's the tree I like."

"On it, princess." Patrick hoisted the ax, chopping the tree in quick fashion.

"I thought you would let me show off my manliness for my new fiancée?" Jake called out from where he stood with Shea.

"Next year your shoulder will be up for it," Patrick responded.

"And we will have to get our own tree next year." Shea smiled at him.

"Should we get one for the cottage? We're moving in this weekend, like it or not," Jake told her.

"Oh, I like it. Yes, let's get a smaller one."

"We need one too," Calle called out. She turned to Dan; her little face scrunched up." Remember?"

"Of course, I remember. Let's find the perfect one. It can't be as tall as that one," he warned her. The two of them set off holding hands before Kendra could move, and the sight captivated her. What would it be like for Calle to grow up with Dan to count on?

Soon they had three trees stacked in the back of the truck and had purchased two additional stands from the small shack where the owner sat. Stella helped Calle pick out an ornament to remember the day by, and Kendra watched as she chose an elaborate snowflake. Stella then added a heart shaped one to the pile, no doubt to commemorate the engagement. Not that Shea and Jake would ever forget this, everything had been so perfect, but it was a nice gesture from Stella. The couple hadn't let go of each other since Jake slipped the ring on her finger, and Shea had refused to put her gloves back on so she could admire the ring.

"Ready?" Dan called over from where he and Patrick had finished tying down the trees. "Patrick and Charlie, ride with us.

We can drop off Kendra and Calle's tree first, then all go home. That will give the happy couple a little alone time, if they need it."

"Ewww," Charlie gagged. "That's my dad."

"Get your mind out of the gutter," Patrick said. "We meant in case they wanted to call Shea's parents. Teenagers, always with the dirty thoughts."

Charlie shook his head and got into the car, preventing any further discussion. Kendra indicated that Patrick should take the front, and she squeezed into the back. They drove the short distance to her apartment and made quick work of carrying the tree in and placing it in the stand.

"It's nice up here," Patrick said as he looked around the apartment. "You have way more space than I thought, and what a commute."

"I know, it makes life easier. Especially with Calle, I can put her to bed and run up to check on her every half hour. I had an alarm system installed so that I would know if a door or window opened, and put some cameras up." She laughed self-consciously. "A little paranoid for Vermont, I think."

"Not at all, that was smart." Patrick opened the door to the porch. "Ready to go?"

They all headed down the stairs, and waited a minute while Kendra stuck her head into the kitchen to make sure all was well. She had scheduled another bartender to do the lunch shift and supervise so she could take the afternoon off, and it was a relief.

Making a mental note yet again to speak to her staff about a manager position, she joined the others in the car.

"Who's in the mood for some Christmas carols?" Patrick switched the station on the radio and started singing along at the top of his voice, Calle joining in with equal enthusiasm.

***

Kendra found herself sitting with Shea on the couch as the men wrangled the tree into the stand, giving her a chance to admire the ring further. The diamond was a large princess cut, surrounded by diamonds. The band looked to be white gold and was embedded with diamonds all around. It sparkled as light danced off it from every direction, and suited Shea perfectly. "It's beautiful," she smiled at Shea. "Were you surprised?"

"That he did it today, yes. But overall, we talk about getting married all the time, so I figured it was coming." Shea smiled as she watched Jake with his brothers. "He's everything that I could have ever dreamed of, I'm the luckiest woman alive."

"I think he's equally lucky, you seem so well suited for each other."

"We are, it's amazing how quickly our lives have come together. To think that a few months ago he was in another country and I wasn't sure I would ever see him, and now this."

"It's amazing how quickly things can change," Kendra agreed. "Jake mentioned having babies, is that something you've talked about too?"

Shea nodded with a grin. "Yes. I have always wanted to have a family, and we want to start as soon as possible."

"Do you think you'll do a big wedding?"

"No," Shea shook her head. "That would take too long to plan. What Ben and Stella did might work for us, if I can talk Jake into it."

"Like in a week?"

Shea shrugged. "Why wait? We know what we want, so the faster the better."

"Let me know what I can do to help in that case," Kendra offered.

"I will," Shea beamed at her. "I imagine I'll need lots of help, especially if we do it quickly."

"Do what quickly?" Jake sat on Shea's other side, pulling her close to him.

"Make this official," she said with a kiss. "The sooner I have you officially off the market, the better."

"I'm game. Want to do it today?"

She laughed. "I need my parents to get here, and maybe to not be wearing jeans."

"Name the time and place, and I'm there."

"How are you planning to choose between your amazing brothers for who will be best man?" Patrick asked from where he held the tree in the stand.

"Easy," Jake responded. "It will be Charlie, if he's willing."

"Really?" The teen looked shocked, then grinned at his dad. "Absolutely."

"Are we really sure he's the best *man*," Patrick teased. "Maybe we could rename it. Best boy?"

Charlie scowled at his uncle and started to play wrestle, causing Dan to yell at them from where he was lying under the tree. "You guys are going to make this fall if you don't let me get it screwed in."

Patrick laughed, pointing at his nephew. "Don't say screwed, you'll get his dirty mind all worked up."

"I'm going to live among this?" Shea questioned, looking to Kendra for support.

"You'll never have a dull moment, that's for sure." Kendra secretly loved the constant chaos and loving banter that took place among the family, especially when their teasing wasn't directed at her. But even when they did turn it her way, they were always gentle and never unkind, so it never bothered her. Instead, it made her feel loved and a part of this special group of people who meant so much to her.

Watching as Dan slid out from under the tree, shaking the needles from his hair and clothes, she couldn't stop her heart from wanting to be in Shea's shoes. Be a part of his life, his family, and be planning to have his babies. The fears she felt about future heartbreak seemed far away in this moment, and she allowed herself to dream. Meeting his gaze, seeing how his eyes flickered to the ring on Shea's finger, she wondered if they were finally on the same page about their future.

Chapter 21

The next few days passed in a blur, and Dan was discouraged by his inability to spend any time with Kendra by the time Monday came around. Making the decision to let her lead where their relationship grew was getting frustrating, because she was too busy to prioritize time with him. The holiday weekend had made the restaurant busier than usual, and she had been out straight. He snuck in through the kitchen door early, armed with coffee and an almond croissant that he knew she loved, hoping to grab her before the day got away from them. As he approached the office he heard a second voice, so he busied himself with his cell phone until the door opened.

"Hey, Dan." Pete came through the open door, carrying his laptop bag. "How are you?"

"Great Pete. You?"

"Doing good. Back at it after the long weekend." He looked toward the office door and opened his mouth as if he was going to say more, and then thought better of it. "Have a great day."

Dan pushed the door open all the way, seeing Kendra hunched over her desk. "What's wrong?"

"Oh, nothing. I'm just exhausted." She ran a hand over her eyes and looked everywhere but at him.

"Why do I feel like you're lying to me?" He placed the coffee and pastry bag on the desk and then sat across from her.

"Nothing's wrong, Dan," she said with a warning in her voice.

"This is you telling me to mind my own business, I guess."

"Yeah, I guess so. It is my business, after all."

"Kendra, what's going on?"

She met his eyes finally, and he saw the heat in them. "How long are you staying here?"

"In this office, or town," he challenged.

"Town."

"I told you before, I'm not sure. I really haven't thought that far ahead."

"And that's a problem for me. You want to get all involved in my life, and what's going on here, but you may not be here in a week."

"I haven't said anything about leaving," Dan said.

"You also haven't said anything about staying."

"Is this really about me? Or did you get news from Pete that you're upset about," he pushed.

"Don't lawyer me. I can be mad at you and have something else be wrong."

"But we have been fine. I just brought you coffee and was going to see if I could take you and Calle to dinner. Can we start again?"

She stared at him for so long he was sure she had fallen asleep with her eyes open, but then she laughed softly. "Start again seems to be a theme with you."

He sighed, letting the frustration seep into the sound. "I'm trying to be patient here, but I really have no idea what the fuck is happening. I haven't seen you all weekend, we were fine on Friday. Either I did something that has been bothering you, or Pete just said something that pissed you off and it's being taken out on me. Either way, you can tell me, or I can leave."

"You should leave."

"Are you serious?"

"Yes. I don't have time for this right now. When you figure your life out, let me know."

"Me figure my life out? You're lashing out at me, and I didn't do anything."

"No, you didn't." She stared at him for a minute before turning to her computer. "I have work to do."

He waited, but when she continued to type and not turn back to him, he finally pushed to his feet and left, his head spinning. What had just happened? Things had been great between then last week, and now she was pushing him out. It had to be something that Pete discussed with her, it was the only explanation.

Texting Patrick and Jake as he walked, he decided that a good workout would help clear his head. And maybe his two brothers would have some idea about what he should do, because he was stumped.

***

"Flowers seem like a good start." Patrick suggested after Dan filled them in on his morning.

"I don't think flowers will cut it," Jake said. "If she's that mad, he obviously did something really bad."

"I didn't! Things were great between us last week."

"You spent two nights together?" Patrick asked with an eyebrow cocked.

"So?"

"Maybe you're bad—"

"Don't try to be funny right now, Patty."

"Okay, *Danny*."

"You two are brutal," Jake sighed. "Did you talk over the weekend? Maybe she thought you blew her off after that."

"Stella had suggested I let her choose the direction the relationship is headed rather than come on so strong," he said. "I obviously find it difficult to let anyone else be in control, but I've tried to just make sure she knows I want to be together and waited for her to make a move. I texted her all weekend, talked to her at bedtime. Offered to take Calle skiing, and then picked her up to go to Charlies' game. Nothing was wrong."

"I think we need to call in the experts," Jake said. "Let me text Shea."

"I don't need to talk to the whole family about this. I figured you two have screwed up with more women than me, you would know what to do."

Patrick snorted. "Yeah, I've got women mad all over the world. That would be all over Instagram if I was a jerk."

"And I barely dated," Jake pointed out. "Shea doesn't get mad, even when I'm an idiot."

Dan sighed, frustrated with his lack of insight. He had texted Kendra a few times since they arrived at the gym, and there was no answer. Feeling this confused was not normal for him, and he didn't enjoy it.

"Shea said to be home at five to discuss," Jake read from his cell phone. "We'll be there too, of course."

"You two get all settled into the cottage?" Patrick asked as he changed out weights.

"Still have some unpacking to do, but for the most part. Her new tenant was anxious to get moved in and was happy with whatever furniture we could leave behind, so we just had to move her personal stuff," Jake told them. "And the bed, because we weren't using the bed that dad and Stella had."

"Much better to use the one she had with her ex-boyfriend," Patrick responded.

"I really don't know why I like you."

"Most people say that." Patrick tussled Jakes hair, which resulted in a pseudo-head lock.

Dan groaned and stalked out of the weight room, preferring to stew in the sauna while his brothers acted like children. Maybe the heat would help him figure out what was going on.

***

Shea poured him a glass of wine and directed him to the couch, where her best friend Christine was already sitting with her own drink.

"Hi, Christine." He sat on the opposite end and smiled at her, unsure why she was there.

"I thought you needed both of us," Shea explained. "We stopped into Windsor Palace after school and had a drink."

"Oh," he perked up. "Did you find out anything?"

The two exchanged a look that he couldn't interpret before Christine spoke. "You really have no idea what she could be upset over?"

"None."

Shea sat on Jake's lap in a chair across from them, Patrick occupying the only other chair in the small living room. Jake draped an arm across her lap and kissed the back of her neck, making Dan's desire to hit someone more profound. He was miserable, and his brother couldn't be happier.

"When we went in," Christine started. "The first thing she looked at was Shea's ring, and she got a little teary."

"Did she? I didn't notice that. But she was definitely fixated on it," Shea nodded.

"She's upset that you guys got engaged? But she was happy for you on Friday," Dan said.

"She's not unhappy that we got engaged," Shea said slowly. "But I do think it's made her wonder about you guys."

"I think her biggest objection to dating you was that you were going to head back to the city at some point. She was always saying there was no way you could leave that life behind," Christine shared. "When we would get together for open mike nights, or when she joined our book club these last few months and someone would ask about you, she always talked about how you wouldn't be here for long."

"I could stay," Dan objected. "For her, I could."

"Did you tell her that?" Patrick asked, deflecting the pillow Dan threw at him.

"Let them talk," Dan warned his brother. "But kind of."

"Kind of isn't the reassurance a single mom wants," Christine said.

"Especially a single mom who had her relationship experience," Shea added. "Not just with you, but Brad. She's been hurt a lot. When we talked on Friday, she said that she's always wanted more kids. I think this has really pushed it all into her mind. She feels insecure with you, because she doesn't know your plans. But she's falling back into the old routine, and the idea of a future together is probably pretty appealing."

"No idea why," Jake added. "You're pretty miserable to live with."

"Honestly, do you two need to be here?" Dan rolled his eyes before turning back to Christine and Shea. "What do I do to fix this."

"Propose." They said it at the same time and then laughed.

Christine sipped her wine and then continued. "We're joking, of course. You've been on two dates, so that's ridiculous. But you need to reassure her that you're here for the long haul, and that you won't choose the city over her again."

"I didn't the first time."

"Really," Jake chimed in. "You took off and never told us what was happening between you two and never looked back."

"There was some stuff, it freaked me out."

"What stuff?" Jake pushed.

"I'd rather not share with the group, if that's alright."

"But you want their help," Jake nodded to Shea and Christine. "Maybe if they knew everything they could help more."

He pushed a hand in his hair, sure he would go bald from the action today alone if he didn't stop. His brothers knew how to push his buttons like no one else, and the worst was when they were right. "She thought she was pregnant," he finally said. "Just before graduation. Started talking about how I could go to college here, we could get married, it would be great. All of a sudden, my dreams were up in smoke."

"And her dreams freaked you out," Shea said softly.

"I might have, uh—"

"Whatever it is, just spit it out." Patrick waved a hand in a move-along gesture.

"Suggested that she had done it on purpose."

The two women gasped, and he hung his head with shame. Even this many years later, he knew he was wrong.

"Was she pregnant at the time?" Christine asked.

"No," he shook his head. "Or she told me she wasn't. When I left, I didn't feel confident either way, and we were barely speaking. She was angry over my accusation, and she finally kind of spit it out at me."

"She was probably devastated," Shea suggested.

"I left for New York thinking there was a good chance I could come home and find her clearly pregnant. Instead of trying to touch base with her, I just hid in my books. I did miss her, and I did plan to make things right when I came home. But I think a little part of me was afraid that if I called from school and we made up, she would tell me she was pregnant, and I would have to move back."

"So, her dreams went up in smoke and you were also gone. That's rough." Christine sent him a look he couldn't quite read, but it wasn't approving.

"I don't know that her dreams had always been to get married and start a family young," he defended himself. "She always knew that I planned to leave for school. I asked her a million times to come with me, and she didn't want to, kept saying that she didn't want the school debt and the school here was fine."

"Smart of her," Jake nodded. "Always planning ahead."

"When she thought she was pregnant, it probably changed. And you looked out for your own interests, not yours together. Do you think that could be what's in her mind now? That if things get tough, you'll take off again?" Shea looked at him sympathetically. "I hate to be the one to say this, since we're just getting to know each other, but you can be a little type A. Your way or no way."

Jake and Patrick burst into laughter. "A little?"

"What do I do?" he asked Shea and Christine, ignoring his brothers.

"Put her first." Christine's tone was firm and her gaze direct. "She doesn't want any questions about where she stands with you. She needs security for herself and her daughter. If you can't provide that, you need to walk away."

"I don't want to walk away," he objected.

"You're still only thinking of yourself," she pointed out. "Put her first. What's best for her?"

He sank back into the couch, his mind whirling. New York seemed like a lifetime ago, and he honestly didn't know that he ever wanted to go back to it. But he hadn't made that clear to her, or even allowed himself to really make a firm decision. It wasn't fair to her that he could up and leave at any moment, when she had a business and a daughter here. The longer he was here in Windsor Peak, the happier he was, and the less he wanted to leave. Why not commit to staying?

He already had a lease and had locals making appointments for legal help. Things he never would have touched in New York, like creating wills and helping small businesses. Every time he saw the gratitude and relief on the client's face, it reminded him why he went into law to begin with. His entertainment clients had always thanked him and made him feel needed, but the corporate giants he worked himself to exhaustion for barely knew he existed. Somehow, he had gotten lost in the shuffle, and he felt like he was finding himself again in Vermont.

"I need to tell her I'm staying," he declared. "Screw letting her lead, if she doesn't know what the future holds, she's never going to push for us to be together."

"Be positive before you tell her," Shea advised. "I know you signed the lease on your office, but maybe you need to completely break things off from New York so she's confident you won't change your mind."

"I'll go back and list my apartment, pack everything up and settle things with the firm there once and for all." He checked his watch, calculating the drive time. "Maybe I'll head there now, and then I can tell her when I get back.".

"Nope," Jake shook his head. "Take it from me, tell her first. If she just thinks you've left, it will create more problems."

"Why don't you take her with you?" Patrick suggested. "Calle could stay here for a day or two while you're gone."

"I'll ask her, that's a good idea." He stood and paused before leaving the cottage. "Thank you, Christine and Shea. I appreciate the female perspective."

"Hey, we helped too." Jake yelled as he walked out of the door, tossing a wave over his shoulder.

He felt lighter than he had in months and was anxious to take the steps necessary to permanently move his life back to Windsor Peak. Hopefully Kendra would be as excited about this as he was and see that he was fully committed to spending his life here, with her. It had taken him a long time to end up back where he started, but this time he was staying home and keeping the girl he loved.

Chapter 22

The emotional strain of holding together an outward appearance for her employees and customers while falling apart inside was wearing on Kendra. She had never realized how exhausting it could be to fake happiness while also being terrified that something bad was about to happen. The idea of a couple of days off to hide in her bed and try to get some sleep was so tempting, and much needed. She wasn't sleeping well at night and found herself snapping at a vendor over a forgotten case of wine.

JJ had been by daily since the Turkey Trot to give her updates, and Brad was nowhere to be seen. In her mind, he was still nearby, she could feel his eyes on her with every breath she took. It was unlikely that he came to town for one night and then left, the possibility was greater that he wanted to be seen so she would be a panic-stricken mess by the time he finally made whatever move he had planned.

Pete coming by in the morning to go through the finances had been almost her final straw. While she appreciated all his efforts to protect her, it was going to be costly to pay for all the time he had put in to counteract Brad's embezzlement. He had handled setting up the new account number, switching all the vendor payments to the correct account so she wouldn't miss a bill, and closing out the original account. All she had to do was sign a few pages for the bank, which she had stopped in to do the week before, and he had taken care of the rest of it.

To top off all her stress, she was pushing Dan away and wasn't even sure why. Going to sleep on Friday night dreaming about a future wedding with him had taken her back years, to when she was a teenager and had the same fantasy. It rattled her to have the same thoughts and yet have new fears, not only about Brad, but about Dan. She wasn't sure she could ever fully trust that he could be happy here in Windsor Peak, and there was no way she could be happy anywhere else.

Allowing herself a minute before the restaurant opened for lunch, she sank down onto a chair at a nearby table and put her head in her hands. The whole world felt off its axis, and she needed at least one thing safe and solid to grab on to while the rest of it fell apart. She just wasn't sure what that one thing was.

"You okay?" Tina's voice broke through her haze, and she looked up to see her two friends dropping into chairs at the table.

"Not really," she admitted. "I feel like I'm falling apart at the seams."

"Tell us," Julie demanded.

"I know Brad is around somewhere, waiting. I don't know why, or what his end game is, but I just know it. He probably gambled away the money he stole, or spent it all on drugs, but I'm guessing Pete shutting down his access to my accounts has triggered this."

"Well, you can't let him continue to steal from your accounts just to keep him away," Tina reasoned.

"No, I can't. But I'm worried about Calle, I'm nervous about my own safety." She took a deep breath and looked at her friend's concerned faces, deciding to plunge into her biggest fear. "I need you guys to promise me something."

"Anything," Tina responded while Julie nodded.

"If something happens to me—"

"Nothing is going to happen," Julie said forcefully.

"But if it does, I need you to promise me that Calle will be okay. No foster care, no strangers raising her."

"Of course," Tina grabbed her hand. "She has so many of us who love her, it would be a fight to see who gets to keep her. But we're not letting that happen."

"I'm just so scared," she whispered. "And I pushed Dan away, more out of sheer exhaustion and terror, but also because I'm that tiny bit uncertain about him and I can't have anything else to stress over."

"He'll be fine," Julie waved her hand. "Dan is nothing but resilient. You can't push him away and expect him to stay gone again. Even I see that, and I'm still mad at him for what he did last time."

"I just don't know what to do," she admitted. "I'm exhausted and emotionally drained, and everything just seems like too much. I want to take Calle and stay behind locked doors, but that won't work."

"First things first," Tina commanded. "You need a manager for the restaurant. You're running yourself ragged. Who do you trust the most among your staff?"

Kendra considered the question, thinking back over the last few years. "Linda. She has worked here for years, and I know she could use the extra money."

"Talk to her today," Julie instructed. "That will help. Then you need to talk to JJ about a restraining order. And talk to Dan about whatever it is going on between you two."

"I don't think I can get a restraining order if no one has seen Brad, and if he hasn't made any threats. JJ didn't see confident that it would be awarded," she told them.

"Let's forget Brad for a minute," Tina suggested. "He may be trying to scare you, but you have the upper hand right now. You're established here in town, and people will protect you. JJ and the police are watching for him, as is the entire Burrows family and us. Lots of eyes that he would have to sneak by, and he doesn't have the resources to stay hidden long. It's too cold to be living in the woods, and he wouldn't have the money for a hotel long term."

"That's true. Maybe he did skulk back to whatever hole he crawled out of," Julie said. "I know this is not what you want to hear, but the only option you have right now is to push him out of your head. If you let him affect your mood, your life, your work, then he's winning. Forcing yourself to stop thinking about him and go about your life is the best thing you can do."

Kendra nodded slowly, knowing that Julie made sense. Brad was impacting her life without any action, and if she continued to spiral who knew how bad it could get. She took a deep breath and stood, indicating the bar. "Why don't you come sit over there, I'll get your lunch orders in. When Linda comes in, I'll talk to her about stepping into a management role, and I'll deal with Dan later. I feel better having a plan at least."

As her friends ate, she filled them in on the details of Jake's proposal to Shea, and the subsequent wedding talk. Although she had shared the news via text over the weekend, they had been waiting for the full scoop. Everyone in town knew Jake's tragic past and hoped for a happy future for him.

The lunch shift flew by, and after a quick meeting with Linda, she had a new restaurant manager. The idea of being able to take a day off, or to spend an evening with Calle not worrying about the business, brought her some joy. For years her entire focus had been the business and Calle, and although it may mean pinching pennies to afford Linda's salary, it would be worth it. Once she fully paid off the Holmes' for the restaurant, the money situation would improve, so it was worth it.

When she ran to get a fancy coffee across the street in the mid-afternoon, she was surprised to run into Patrick, who was seated in the corner with a script in front of him. She sat across from him and tried to peek at the page, but he quickly covered it.

"NDA," he said, smiling at her. "How are you?"

"I'm good. Surprised to find you out in public like this," she replied.

He shrugged and looked around. "It's quiet in here in the afternoon, before school gets out at least. It's a nice change of scenery for me, and I can focus on reading."

"I should let you get back to it," she said as she started to stand.

"No, sit for a minute. I need a break." He stretched then flipped the pages over on the table. "What's going on?"

"I just hired a manager for the restaurant, so that's a big relief. I still need to sit down with Pete to figure out how I'm going to pay her, but if it means I get a little less, it will be worth it."

"Can you afford to take less?" He looked concerned, and she was touched.

"I don't have rent or a mortgage to pay, so that's a relief. If I have to pinch some pennies I will, but it may not come to that. I only have a couple more years of paying the Holmes' back, and then I can give myself a raise again." She sipped her coffee, before deciding it was still too hot to drink. "Plus, Zoe is bringing in customers from other towns, so profits are up a bit. That will help."

Patrick nodded, a look on his face that she couldn't place. "Sounds like a good plan."

"I think so. More time with Calle, less late nights. I'll still do a lot, but it will be nice to take a day off now and then."

"I know a thing or two about that," he said as he grinned at her.

"You still work hard; you don't fool me. Hours in the gym, studying scripts, and probably way more than any of us see."

He shrugged. "It's not a bad way to make a living."

"Are you still planning to stay here long term?"

"Yes," he said. "I really didn't tell anyone, so don't repeat this until I can tell my dad and Stella. But I bought the Smith property next to dad's a few months ago. It needed total renovation, so I've been waiting for that to happen, then I can move in over there. Close to everyone but my own space."

"Oh, it's beautiful there. I haven't been up in a while, but I always loved it."

"It's been empty for a while, but I don't want to tear it down and put up a Hollywood mansion. It should be done right around when I finish filming this, so I'll be able to move in then."

"I can't wait to see it." She stood up, grabbing her coffee. "I'll let you get back to your script, I've distracted you long enough."

"See you later," he called as she headed out.

Shea had stopped by after work with her friend Christine, an unusual event for a weeknight, but she had enjoyed visiting with them. She always enjoyed Shea's company, and they had really grown close over the last few months without even realizing it. Normally it would take Kendra a long time to grow so close to someone but being together so often with the Burrows had helped her get to know and like the other woman.

When Dan walked in a few hours later, looking determined, she asked the other bartender to cover for her so she could pull him into her office. "I'm sorry about this morning," she said quickly. "I had a lot on my mind."

"I understand," he said. "And I know I haven't done enough to earn your trust. I'm going to head to New York—"

She took a step back, stunned. Here she had tried to take the steps to free up her mind and her time to be with him, and he was leaving. "Oh. Okay, then."

"No, not like that." He gripped her by the arms when she tried to turn from him. "To sell my apartment and get my belongings. Finalize things with the firm. I want to be here, with you. And Calle."

"How long are you going for?"

"A day or two at most. I'll hire a moving company to take care of everything, an agent to sell the apartment. Should be quick." He rubbed her arms lightly as he spoke, helping her relax. "I was going to ask if you could sneak away with me? Calle could stay with my family, or she could come if you would rather. We can be tourists in New York for a couple of days."

"Are you really all in on this? On us?" She studied his face, seeing nothing that made her think he was only trying to appease her. "Before I really involve Calle in this more than she already is, we need to be sure."

"I'm sure. I've never been more sure of anything in my life," he said convincingly. "I have a list of arguments that I prepared if needed."

"Lawyer Dan to the rescue?"

"Something like that," he smiled at her. "I want you to know I'm here for the long haul. Whatever I need to do to prove that to you, I will. I'm enjoying my work here; I love the slower pace of life. Being around my family can be a bit much, but overall, I'm glad to be getting this time with them. And the most important thing, I love what we could be together."

"And you're really read to leave New York?"

"If I go there and make memories with you two, there's no going back alone, I promise you that. Skating with you at Rockefeller Center, seeing the tree lit up, going to see the Rockettes; all of the things I've never taken the time to do, I want to do with you and Calle."

"Oh, she would love that," Kendra said. "I know you would probably prefer a romantic couple of days alone, but if she can come, then we would like that very much."

"Really? Just like that?"

She laughed, finally feeling light. "Just like that. I spoke to an employee earlier today about taking over management duties, which she's ready to step right into. I'll talk to her and see if she thinks she can handle me being away, with Zoe's help. When do you want to go?"

"Tomorrow? I'm ready to start my life here, with you."

He kissed her while pushing the door closed, making her laugh again. "Dan, I need to get back out there."

"I'm sure you have a few minutes," he pleaded.

"Why don't you go upstairs and hang out with Calle? Nora can't come today, so I was going to make her come down for dinner in an hour. You can talk to her about New York."

"Using me for my body and my babysitting skills, I see how it is." He opened the door as he teased her, then kissed her once more before jogging up the stairs to her apartment.

The day had taken another unexpected turn, and her head was spinning a bit as she went back to the bar. At least this time, it was moving in the right direction. She might not have solved the Brad problem but getting out of town for a few days would be perfect, and spending the time with Dan would hopefully make her feel even more confident about their future. Things were looking up.

Showing Kendra and Calle around New York had been even more fun than Dan could have imagined. Both reacted with childlike joy to everything he introduced them to, thrilling him each time. The doorman had greeted him as Mr. Burrows when they arrived in the lobby from the parking garage below, and Calle's eyes had bugged.

"He knows you," she whispered to Dan, while smiling shyly at the man in uniform.

"He's worked here a long time," Dan replied. He shook the man's hand before they boarded the elevator, making a mental note to put together some gifts for the staff before he headed back to Vermont. He always gave healthy cash gifts at the holiday's anyway, so this would kick off the season and say thank you for years of looking after him.

Kendra's eyes had gone round when she entered his apartment, walking around slowly before crossing to step out on the balcony. "This is impressive," she said. The large kitchen was open to the living room, and both were filled with all the modern conveniences and comforts. Bedrooms were off either side of the living room, each with their own private bathroom. A third bathroom was tucked near the entrance behind the kitchen. It was clean, beautiful, and lacked any personality, he realized as he saw it through their eyes.

Calle had found the second bedroom and was making herself at home, so he wrapped his arms around her and enjoyed the moment. "Seeing it now, with you two here, makes me realize all that it was missing."

"What's that?"

"It's pretty sterile, a woman's touch and a little girl to make a mess now and then would have been good." She stiffened at his words, and he quickly added more to his statement. "Not that I'm asking you to move here. I'm just realizing that I prefer your place in Vermont, or my dad's house, places that are warm and lived in. This was good for a landing pad for me, but a lot of money for something so cold."

She had softened, eyes darting around the living room again. "It is plain," she said. "How's the bedroom?"

"Oh, you're not sharing with Calle?" He'd teased her but had once again put his foot in his mouth.

"I didn't think of that. She might wonder why I'm in your room." She chewed on a fingernail as she spoke.

"She's going to have to get used to it, because I'm not planning on sleeping alone anytime soon. If we don't make a big deal out of it, I doubt she'll even notice."

"She notices everything," she replied, rolling her eyes.

Sure enough, Calle had a million questions about the sleeping arrangements, and if he was her mom's boyfriend. He had let Kendra answer most of the questions, happy to take a back seat, but also thrilled when she had replied "kind of" to the boyfriend question. He would take that over a flat-out no, and hoped by the time they headed back to Vermont it was a solid yes.

He had pushed going into his old office until the final day they were in the city, knowing they were ending their day at the Rockette's show and seeing the Christmas tree would get him through the unpleasantness. When he entered, he was surprised that he was asked to wait in the lobby, not go directly to a conference room where he expected to meet with a partner to discuss his departure.

Ten minutes later, when he was about to walk out the door and go home to his girls, a senior partner finally arrived. "Dan," he said as he crossed to shake hands. "Come with me."

He followed Sam Snyder into the conference room closest to the lobby, realizing they were trying to limit the number of people he encountered while he was there. Sam had a pile of papers on the table at two spots, so Dan took the empty seat across from him and started flipping through.

"I'll have to read through all of this," he said. "I asked for it to be sent to me in advance and it never came."

"I thought it was best if we met face to face," the older man explained. "I understand you're angry and frustrated, and to be frank, I don't blame you."

Dan sat back in his chair, a little surprised to find an ally in Sam. They had never worked closely together and had rarely socialized. "Why do you say that?"

"I've been around for a while, and I know a snake when I see one. What Jeb did was wrong, plain and simple. He offered to help while you were busy with your brother, and no one realized the offer came with the contingency that he would be trying to poach your clients." He flipped through the papers before meeting Dan's eyes again. "I voted to let him go. I was outvoted, but it's only because those clients had already signed with him. I have no doubt that he'll make a fatal error one day, and I will be watching very carefully for that to happen."

"I appreciate the support," Dan replied gruffly.

"You're a good man and a great lawyer. You did the right thing, focusing on your brother. I lost my brother in Vietnam," he said sadly. "If I had the chance to spend time with him, or to help him, I would give up everything. I'm glad that didn't happen in this case. You have a buyout offer there that I negotiated for you, and an agreement that the clients who have left with you will be let go without a fuss. They do want you to sign a non-disclosure agreement, and to agree not to approach the clients who chose to switch to Jeb. However, if they approach you, there's nothing we can do about that."

"Honestly, I don't think I want the big corporations anymore," Dan admitted. "I enjoy the entertainment work, which will pay the bills, and I have been doing some smaller things for the people in my hometown. It's oddly fulfilling, more than I would have imagined."

Sam laughed. "Don't say that too loud, we will have people running for the mountains. But I'm happy for you, and I wish you well. I'll let you read through everything, and if we need to make any changes, I can take care of it."

Dan read quickly, realizing that the older partner really had gone to bat for him. He and his clients would be able to walk away from this firm without incident, and he would have a healthy amount to add to his savings account. He picked up his pen and started signing, looking up to see the surprised look on Sam's face.

"I thought you would have at least a few small changes," he admitted.

"No," Dan shook his head. "I appreciate all you have done for me here; I can't imagine this was easy. All I want is to keep my clients and get back to my quieter life."

When he finished signing, they both stood and shook hands. "I wish you the best," Sam said.

"If you ever find yourself in Vermont, please give me a call so I can take you to dinner."

"Will do. The wife enjoys road trips, so we may take you up on that."

Sam left the room while Dan gathered his belongings and copies of the papers. He looked up as he tucked the last page into his bag, finding his old friend Jeb standing outside the glass.

"Dan." Jeb moved to the open doorway, sticking his hands into his pockets.

"Jeb." Dan started to brush past him and was surprised when the other man wouldn't move. "You should step aside now."

"I don't know why you took it personally. You would have done the same."

"No, I wouldn't have. I respect my colleagues, especially those that I considered friends. If you had a family emergency, I would have covered for you and respected the client boundaries. I wouldn't have used your sibling's mental health to gain an upper hand in a client relationship."

"I didn't do that."

"Really? Every single client that I spoke to told me the same thing, that you inferred that instability could run in the family and suggested I could have a breakdown like my brother. No mention of the fact that my brother had served in war zones for the better part of fourteen years. Or that he lost his wife in a terrorist attack when they had an infant at home. He sacrificed for his country, and you were spineless enough to twist that into something you could use against me." Dan's voice was getting louder, and he was aware of the audience they now had. "My brother is a better man than you could ever dream of being, and I'd say he's more mentally stable than you. He knows the difference between right and wrong, and you clearly don't. There is nothing mentally unstable about me or my family, and I can't say the same about you. Anyone who would stab a friend in the back and lie like this has their own issues to contend with."

"I, uh—"

"Stop talking. Did you really think the Hollywood elite that my brother Patrick runs with would believe your lies, or not tell me what you were saying? Maybe some corporate people would just go with the easy choice, but you tarnished this firm's name with all our entertainment clients. And I will laugh my way right to the bank thanks to that mistake." Dan bumped his shoulder as he pushed past him, and then walked to the elevator without looking back.

This part of his life was over. He wanted to wash this encounter out of his mind and get back to the two people who were his future.

***

Sitting in Radio City Music Hall that evening with Calle and Kendra looking beautiful in the special holiday dresses he had arranged to be sent to the apartment, he couldn't think of a time he had been happier. The squeals when they had opened the boxes from Bergdorf Goodman had made him look forward to Christmas morning, when he planned to spoil them both. Calle had declared that she was never taking the dress off but was finally convinced it was for special occasions but that the bracelet Dan had included could be worn daily.

"You can't spoil her too much," Kendra whispered to Dan. "She won't ever want to go home."

"It's her first trip to New York, I want to make sure she remembers it."

"Trust me, she'll never forget it. Just like I'll never forget that frozen hot chocolate, I need to get Zoe to figure that recipe out as soon as we get home."

"I don't know why I didn't think of your sweet tooth before, when I was trying to win you back," he said.

"It probably would have saved us both a lot of time and tears if you had just shown up with that to begin with," she teased.

The curtain rose, and they spent the next ninety minutes enraptured with the Rockette's before spilling back out to the sidewalk and the short walk to Rockefeller Center to view the Christmas tree. He tied skates for Calle before putting on his own rentals, so they could spin around the synthetic ice under the tree. Skating slowly, holding Kendra's hand, they watched Calle make her way around.

"She's a natural. We might have to get her a hockey stick."

"I'm surprised she hasn't asked yet, honestly. Watching Charlie all these years, she loves it. Maybe when we get home I'll ask her," she said.

"Are you looking forward to it?"

"To what?" She nearly stumbled as she looked up at him, and he helped her right herself.

"Going home."

"Yes. I have really enjoyed these few days, but I'm not made for the city life," she replied. "How are you feeling?"

"Excited. The meeting this morning went better than I could have possibly imagined. Not only did I get more than what I expected, but I got to say my piece to the guy who stabbed me in the back."

"What exactly happened?"

"I'll tell you tonight, I promise. I don't want to put a damper on this moment," he said. "But to answer your question, I'm ready to go home. I'm ready to plan a future with you, and with Calle. I know that's fast, and I'm not going to push too hard, but I'll warn you right now that I don't plan to wait long."

"Are you planning to find another girl if I drag my feet too long?" She squeezed his hand, confident enough in his feelings to tease him.

"There is no one else," he said as he pulled her closer. "There never will be anyone else.

They kissed under the Christmas lights, skaters swirling around them, until Calle crashed into them and almost sent all three to the ground. Laughing, he led them off the rink to remove the skates, before convincing them he had one more treat before they left the next morning. The horse drawn carriage ride through the park to his apartment building was the perfect way for him to say goodbye to this city he had called home.

Chapter 24

JJ was in the kitchen with a plate of food in front of him when Kendra came out of her office midway through the week. She realized she hadn't thought of Brad in days, since before they went to New York. The last few days had been blissful as she decorated the restaurant for the holidays and spent time with Dan and Calle. They had barely been apart since returning from the city, and Calle hadn't thought it was odd when she woke up and found Dan at the kitchen table drinking his coffee. Kendra was still getting used to it, but at least it hadn't affected her daughter at all.

"Hey, JJ."

"Kendra," he wiped his mouth with a napkin. "Sorry, every time I walk in here Zoe feels the need to feed me. I have to do extra workouts now that she's in town."

"You have nothing to worry about," Zoe replied from where she was prepping the kitchen.

"Is everything okay?" Kendra asked, worried he was there with news for her.

"Yes," he nodded. "Nothing new. No sign of him anywhere, so I think he must have gone back to where he came from. Maybe it wasn't even him in Burlington, or he had some other business he was doing that had nothing to do with you. I think you can relax now. You fixed the bank, and nothing came of it, so I don't see any reason for you to be on alert any longer."

She nodded, thinking back over the last few weeks. Brad would have known by now that his money siphoning game was over, and he hadn't reacted at all. She had changed all of her passwords to obscure things, to the point that she could only remember them thanks to the note app on her phone. There had been no strange calls or calls from Brad period. Wherever he was and whatever he was doing, she had to hope it kept him busy for the rest of his life.

"Alright, I hope that's the case. Thanks, JJ."

She crossed into the restaurant and unlocked the front door, ready for the lunch rush. The Holiday Festival was taking place over the upcoming weekend, so the town had already started filling up with tourists who came each year. They enjoyed skiing on the mountain and taking part in the Christmas themed shopping and activities on the town green, since it was still early enough in the season to hold outside. A few more feet of snow and they would have needed to move the entire thing to the high school gymnasium, which drew foot traffic away from the downtown businesses, so she was glad the weather had held.

Kendra had helped organize many of the festivals the town held over the course of the year, seeing the impact they had on many of her fellow small business owners. Although she got regular business from the locals, many of the small stores survived off tourists, and finding new ways to bring them to town had been a fun task. It was becoming a lot of work, and she had to speak to the mayor about finding a full-time coordinator for the task sooner than later. Juggling Calle, her business, all the festivals and now Dan was just too much. Hopefully this would be the last one that she felt responsible for, it would be nice to pass the tasks off and simply be an attendee one day.

Her cell phone rang in her pocket, and she smiled when she saw the name on the screen. Janet Holmes, who had sold her the restaurant when she and her husband retired, had become like family to her over the years. They spoke regularly, when Janet could find the time between her beach days and pickleball games and the Holmes' visited frequently.

"Hi, Janet. How are you?"

"Great, honey, just wanted to check in. Things on track for the festival this weekend?"

"They are, I was just looking at all the decorations on Main Street as I opened up for lunch." Kendra waved as a couple came in for lunch, choosing a table by the window. "Looks like we're in good shape."

"That's great. I wish we could make it, but Ron signed us up for a golf tournament this weekend not realizing it was the same date."

"Don't worry, you shouldn't leave paradise to come be cold here," Kendra joked.

"You know we love it there, but it is so nice to be warm every day." Janet whispered something that Kendra couldn't hear, likely to Ron. "We wanted to talk to you quickly about something, I know you're busy for lunch so we will get right to it."

"Hi, doll." Ron's voice came over the line as Janet switched over to speaker.

"Hi, Ron. Miss you guys," she said, hoping whatever was coming wasn't bad news.

"We sent you an overnight package and wanted to talk to you before you got it," Ron explained.

"It's good news," Janet interjected.

"I was getting there," Rob grumbled. "Your loan is paid off, so we sent you the signed paperwork so you can file for the deed. We did everything down here with a lawyer yesterday, so it's all being filed on our end, you just need to go sign a few papers."

"What do you mean? I still have a few years of payments left."

"Well, we can't say much," Janet said. "But someone wanted to take care of it."

"Was it Dan?" she asked breathlessly, unable to wrap her brain around the news.

"Dan? Is he back?" Janet sounded shocked, and Kendra realized she hadn't filled her in on the news.

"He is, I'll tell you all about it later. So, it wasn't him?"

"We really promised not to say anything at all about this. Sorry, but this is a good example of not looking a gift horse in the mouth," Ron stated.

Kendra's stomach sank. "Please tell me at least that it wasn't Brad."

"Brad," Ron spit the name out. "Why would you think that? I wouldn't take a flyer from the man on the street, never mind a dollar."

"Is he back too?" Janet's worried voice came across the phone.

"No, I don't think so. Sorry, my head is just spinning."

"Spin away, and then celebrate. You worked so hard for this, and we couldn't be happier for you." Janet cleared her throat, sounding near tears. "We have to run now; we have a game to get to. Love you, and we will talk soon."

"Love you too," she said as the phone disconnected. She stood in place, stunned by the news, until new customers came in and she realized she had to do her job. After the lunch rush, she could sit and dwell over this news, but for now, she had drinks to pour.

***

"Did you pay off my loan?" she blurted out as soon as Dan opened the door to his new office. She clutched the paperwork she had just received from FedEx, showing the restaurant was now hers free and clear, but it was still hard to believe.

"What loan? And hi," he said as he dropped a kiss on her lips.

"Hi, sorry. This just came, and the Holmes' called earlier to tell me that someone had paid off the rest of my loan with them." She handed him the envelope, watching as he flipped through the pages.

"Looks like everything is in order. Did they file these, or do you need to file everything after you've signed?"

"I have no idea. But first, Dan, who would have done this?" She paced in front of his desk, unable to sit.

"You say it like it's a criminal act," Dan laughed. "It's a shock, but not a bad one."

"Did you do it?" She stared at him, knowing if he lied she would pick up on it.

"No," he answered simply. "I would have, if I had thought of it. But I don't even think it processed in my head that you were still paying it off."

"Who could have done this?"

"One of your friends?"

"No," she shook her head. "Julie and Tina are good friends but would never get involved in my financial affairs. And I wouldn't want them to put up that kind of money. Plus, why now? It doesn't make sense."

He stood and crossed to where she was wearing a path on his carpet, stopping her by enfolding her into his arms. "It's an amazing gift, whoever did it. One less thing for you to worry about, so don't bring on new stress by overthinking it. Maybe the Holmes' decided to give it to you now and are just using this excuse to not make you feel indebted to them."

She sagged against him. "That makes perfect sense."

"See, that's why you come to me. For all my wisdom," he smiled down at her.

"Yes, that must be it," she rolled her eyes.

"Listen, if you want to use me for my body, I'm game."

"I'll keep that in mind," she said with a laugh. "I should get back to the restaurant."

"Come over for dinner tonight? We're talking wedding, it's the only focus of the whole house right now, but I think they are ready to make some decisions."

"Sure, Linda is working tonight so I can head up around five."

"I can come pick you up?" he suggested, walking with her to the door.

"I'll bring a bag," she smiled at him. "Just in case I overdo it with the wine."

"Solid plan." He gave her a big kiss and she headed across the street, a walk she took slowly knowing he was watching from his office window.

***

Kendra pulled in behind Shea's car that evening, having followed her friend up the windy mountain road to the driveway. Calle leaned forward, eyeing the car. "Is Charlie in there?"

"No, honey, I think it's only Shea."

"Okay, I'm going to find him." She disappeared into the house as Kendra gathered her purse and a bottle of wine from the passenger seat. As she closed her door, she saw Shea waiting with a smile.

"Hi," Shea gave her a quick hug. "I'm so glad you could come. I have a million ideas and the boys are sick of talking about it."

"Between Stella and I, we can help." Kendra linked arms with Shea as they walked across the icy walkway to the porch. "And I'm sure Christine is ready to pitch in."

"She is, but I think she's maybe keeping a little secret from me," Shea confided.

"Really? What?"

"The tiniest little one," she smiled. "I think she might be pregnant. I'm not even sure she suspects it yet, but she looks exhausted, and she got sick yesterday when someone in the teachers' lounge had a tuna fish sandwich."

"Oh, that's exciting. I bet she is." Kendra thought back to her own morning sickness and felt a wave of sympathy for the other woman. "I hope she has an easy time of it."

"Knowing her, even if it's awful, she'll do it with a smile. They are going to be amazing parents." They both hung their coats on the hook by the door, where Shea swapped out her boots for a pair of slippers. "I'm still getting used to coming home here, seeing my things right next to everyone else's. Jake and I end up having breakfast in here almost every morning, because we can't get out of our own way to make something in the cottage. I always go out this way regardless, since Charlie rides with me to school for now. My slippers sitting here probably drive them crazy here all day."

"It's nice that you're getting settled in, and I'm sure if they were driving Stella or Ben crazy, you would hear about it. Neither is the type to bite their tongue," Kendra laughed.

She followed Shea into the kitchen, where controlled chaos was underway. Stella was at the stove stirring something, Ben at her side. Charlie and Patrick looked to be setting the table, but seemed to have some kind of race going at the same time that Calle was giggling over. Jake was in the adjoining room lighting a fire, Dan leaning on the wall next to him, the two locked in a conversation. Only the two dogs were quiet, lying peacefully next to the giant Christmas tree that still needed decorations.

"We're going to need a bigger table," Patrick called over to Ben as he placed the last plate.

"Is that a Jaws line?" Charlie nudged him with an elbow, moving him out of the way so he could place the last silverware.

"Yes, genius. They were sailing around the Cape Cod Bay on a table." Patrick rolled his eyes. "Shea, do something. Make him go back to elementary school and start all over again."

She laughed as she handed Kendra a glass of wine. "I'll stay out of that, thanks. Do you want a glass of this?"

"I'll get it, you two can go see your men," Patrick offered.

"We really need to find him a girlfriend," Charlie stage whispered. "He's so cranky."

"I do just fine, thanks. We can discuss your love life in great detail at the table though," Patrick teased. "I heard some stories about Homecoming."

Charlie's face turned a blazing shade of red before he darted to the hall. "Forgot some homework, be right back."

"Does Charlie have a girlfriend?" Calle pouted to Patrick.

"No, he's way too smelly for that," Patrick said as he patted her on the head.

"He is not!"

"Calle, come help me with this cake," Stella called, shooting Patrick a warning glance.

"Let's go say hi to the guys," Shea suggested.

Kendra watched as Jake popped up from the couch to greet his future wife, seeing the happiness on his face. Dan turned to her with a similar look, and her heart was simply gone in that simple moment. A normal weeknight, nothing special going on, and with one smile she realized she was fully back in love with this man. She hadn't been away from him for more than a few hours, and yet realized she had missed him. It was shocking how quickly things had changed, and yet she wasn't resistant to it any longer. Focus on the happy, she told herself, accepting a kiss from him.

"Stella wants us to decorate the tree after dinner," Jake told them. "The two bozos are going to put the lights on now while we talk wedding."

"Which two bozos?" Shea asked innocently.

"Bozo one," he pointed at Dan. "And two." Patrick was pointed at as he came into the room.

"I'm only here because I'm the tallest," Patrick stated. "Short stuff over here can't reach the top of this tree."

Jake rolled his eyes. "Enough with the short jokes. I'm not that much shorter, and you can't reach the top of this either. It has to be twelve feet tall, at least."

"What did you say down there? It's hard to hear," Patrick cupped a hand to his ear.

Jake slapped his brother on the head while Dan went to set up the step ladder, which they then tussled over who would climb up and who would untangle the lights and hand them up. Quickly deciding they needed another ladder, they left for the garage to find one, leaving the other three in front of the fire.

"Finally, some peace." Jake leaned back on the couch, draping an arm around Shea. "Should we talk wedding?"

"What are you thinking?" Kendra asked.

"Next weekend," they responded in unison.

"Like in a few days?"

Shea laughed. "No, the weekend after that. We don't want to interfere with the Christmas Festival in town, but the weekend after is pretty slow all around."

"The church can do the ceremony on Saturday night, so we just have to decide the rest of it. It's short notice for you, so we can call the Inn or come back here if you're already swamped at the restaurant," Jake explained.

"Never too busy for you guys," she responded. "I'm happy to have it there. Most of the town will probably attend anyway, so it's just the skiers who will have to eat elsewhere."

"Ok, one thing checked off the list. Let us know what we should do about the food," Shea told her.

"If you don't mind, I'll have Zoe text you. She knows what they can handle and what will work best, and I try not to step on her toes."

"That's perfect," Shea smiled at her. "I called the florist today; they can do a simple bouquet."

"Don't do simple if that's not what you want," Jake said with a frown. "I want it to be perfect for you. Fast, but perfect."

"I could say 'I do' right here and now and it would be perfect, because it's to you." She kissed him, and Kendra smiled at the couple.

"But since we're doing this, we need music." Jake looked at the list on her phone. "And a photographer."

"I can take care of the music," Patrick offered as he came back into the room. "Photographer too, if you want."

"Really?"

He shrugged. "Sure, not a problem. I'll take care of it tomorrow, consider it done."

"That just leaves us with a few smaller details," Shea said.

"Did you find a dress?" Kendra asked.

Shea shook her head and frowned. "Not yet. I'm starting to get nervous about that."

"I can take care of that too," Patrick offered.

"You learn how to sew?" Dan asked from the other side of the tree.

"No, but I might know a few people in costuming and the fashion industry," Patrick replied dryly. "Shea, if you want to send me a picture of what you like, I can see what they can do."

"Patrick, that's so nice of you," Shea gushed.

"Not a problem. Just remember it when this guy decides he wants a private plane to a private island for the honeymoon," he teased.

"Now that you mention it, that sounds really nice," Jake said.

Kendra watched them interact, shooting glances over to where Dan was hanging off the ladder to get the lights just right. What more could she ask for than this?

Chapter 25

Dan finished stringing lights just as they were called to the table for dinner, so he rushed to wash his hands and then found he was stuck across the table from Kendra. Calle sat on one side of her, Stella on the other, so there was no moving either of them so he could sit closer. A few weeks ago, he wouldn't have even noticed, now he wanted to always as close as possible to her. It had become a distraction when he should be working, and instead found himself staring across the street, trying to catch a glimpse of her through the window. A few times he almost packed his laptop up and went to work out of the bar, but he didn't want a reputation for being a drinking lawyer as he was starting up his practice.

She smiled at him from across the table, as if she could read his thoughts, and she probably could. No one in the world knew him or understood him as well as she did, he realized. Even his brothers, who he also considered to be his two closest friends, didn't see the vulnerable side that he allowed her to see.

"Did you get the plans all worked out?" Ben asked from the head of the table.

"I think so," Jake nodded. "Patrick offered to help with a few big items, so that will give him something to do."

"About time he earned his keep," Dan joked.

"I do plenty around here," Patrick argued.

"Not as much as me," Charlie said, earning looks from all the adults at the table. "What?"

"You barely pick up your own towels off the floor, champ. I wouldn't be asking for more chores." Ben reached over to squeeze his grandson's shoulder, taking the sting from the words.

"Besides, you have school. Poor Patrick is just sitting around lonely all the time," Jake said to his son.

"Who said I'm lonely? Or sitting around?"

"We don't think that," Stella soothed.

"It's weird you don't have a girlfriend," Dan said.

"You think it's easy to meet girls who like me for who I am?" Patrick challenged him, eyes blazing. "All I get are women who want to be on the red carpet or want their shot in the movies. They want me to introduce them to directors or my agent. Or they want to get pictures so they can go viral and be an influencer. Not one single woman has spent time with me in at least five years who wants doesn't want something from me."

"I'm sorry," Dan replied quietly. "I know it's hard."

"It's stupid, that's all." Patrick let out a frustrated sigh. "I have the perfect life; I have nothing to complain about. If it's hard to find a friend or a date, I can deal with it."

"Maybe we could fix you up with someone?" Shea offered.

He shook his head. "Please, no. That never goes well, and then whoever it is will be bugging you. I'm not hard up, if you know what I mean. I just don't have a future wife like you two. But I'm also much, much younger, so we can let this go."

"Maybe you should elaborate in great detail about what it means to not be hard up, especially for Stella and Calle's sake," Jake teased him.

"I take back all I offered for the wedding," Patrick declared.

"No, he's sorry," Shea said quickly. "Aren't you sorry?"

"Not even a little," Jake said with a laugh. "Did we talk about the cake?"

The conversation shifted to the cake, and then to a first dance song. Everyone seemed to have an opinion about what they should dance to, and the constant demands for Alexa to play a song had everyone laughing as they finished dinner.

"I have a dessert, but do you want to decorate the tree first or have cake?" Stella asked as Charlie and Calle carefully cleared plates from the table.

"Decorate first, I'm stuffed." Ben leaned back and patted his belly.

They all jumped in to clear the table before spilling into the living room where the tree stood waiting, and the fire blazed. Calle's eyes shone as she stared up at the tree, seeing it with the lights on for the first time. "We should turn them off until we decorate," she declared. "That way when we're done it can look extra pretty."

"Off it is," Dan declared as he pulled the plug on the lights.

"Charlie and Patrick brought all the ornaments in today," Stella explained, pointing to the boxes on the wall. "Why don't we let Calle hang the first and then we can all start filling in."

The little girl took careful consideration of where she wanted her ornament to go, having chosen to hang the one Stella had purchased for her at the tree farm. Finally settling on a spot out of reach, she turned trustingly to Dan. "Will you help me?"

His heart constricted as he picked her up, waiting patiently for her to hang it with her small fingers. He had never given much thought to how he would be as a stepfather, but he realized now he was all in. He would move the moon if she asked, without complaint. She had him wrapped fully around her little finger, along with the rest of his family, who all looked on adoringly.

Calle spent the next hour directing where every ornament would be hung, much to Kendra's dismay. The family had repeatedly told her not to worry, they were enjoying her input. And if all the ornaments ended up in one section of the tree, they would have that memory to laugh at for years. Plus, Dan knew Stella had another stash of ornaments that she would break out later, making his dad hang them to even things out. She had done it for years when they were kids and had each decorated one small section of the tree heavily, leaving the rest empty.

They would wake the next day to find a perfectly decorated tree, with their section still intact.

After they hung the last ornament, Charlie helped Calle set up the train that would run under the tree while the adults went to the kitchen to start coffee and cut the cake Stella had made. This time, Dan made sure to claim the seat next to Kendra before anyone else sat down.

"I'm making cocoa and coffee," Stella announced. "Patrick, you know where the Irish whiskey is if anyone wants to add a little flavor."

"I'm hoping you'll take her up on that," Dan whispered in Kendra's ear. "I wouldn't want you driving after that."

"Oh, I'm clearly way too far gone to drive," she replied. "And it has nothing to do with alcohol and everything to do with how lightheaded I feel after seeing you and Calle together."

"I hope I didn't overstep."

"Not at all. She hasn't really had a man around to depend on since Ron moved away, it was really sweet. I just hope it wasn't too much for you."

"The opposite." He studied her face, seeing the curiosity over his statement. "Made me want to throw you over my shoulder and bring you upstairs to make one of our own. Not that I need one of my own, I think I already love her as I would any other kids."

"You do want to have kids?"

He nodded slowly. "It really had left my mind while I was in the city, I never really saw any. Just Charlie, and that was not as much as it should have been. Being here, spending time with Calle, makes me realize all I've missed out on. But if you don't want more, that's fine too."

"I always wanted more, but then my circumstances changed, so I was happy with what I had. Now they've changed again," she said, meeting his gaze.

"What are you two so serious about?" Jake asked as he and Shea joined them at the table.

"Babies." The word came out before he could stop it, and he could have slapped himself for the slip.

"Did Kendra tell you?" Shea asked with an expression he couldn't decipher.

"Are you—" Dan asked.

"No," Shea shook her head. "But I think Christine might be."

"That's exciting," Dan replied. "They've been married for a while."

"And trying for a long time. I think she had given up, honestly, so I'm not even sure if she recognizes the signs. I might have to buy a pregnancy test and present it to her, but I don't want the town to start gossiping about us."

"Have Patrick buy it," Dan suggested. "Imagine what the tabloids would say."

They all laughed as Patrick dismissed the idea. "Even if I drove to Canada, that would still make news. I'll pass."

***

Patrick shocked him the following morning when he announced that he and Jake planned to attend open mike night at the Windsor Palace that night. Patrick had been avoiding the more crowded nights at the bar, preferring to go early and have dinner, or stay outside on the patio under the heat lamps when there was a crowd inside.

"It will help her business," Patrick explained. "And a lot of people came to town hoping to see me at the festival. Maybe if I get it out of the way tonight, the weekend will be a little easier."

"You know the exact opposite is true, right?" Dan asked his brother from the weight bench he was standing behind, spotting Jake.

Patrick shrugged. "Whatever. It will be crazy no matter what, might as well enjoy a little and earn Kendra some extra dough."

"Plus, I get to feel like a celebrity," Jake added as he finished his set. "Good to have a little ego boost before my big day."

"Speaking of, do you want a bachelor party?" Dan realized they hadn't discussed it at all, and time was short.

"Absolutely not," Jake's tone was firm. "This will suffice, we'll have some beers, I'll play guitar, and I'll be home by midnight."

"You sound like dad," Patrick laughed.

"I'll deal with that," Jake said. "I have everything I need in Shea, so I don't need to go to a strip club or anything like that. I don't like to gamble. It's too cold to golf. This is perfect."

"Alright," Dan conceded. "I'll let Kendra know we're coming, let me know who else will be there."

"Probably Ryan and Christine," Jake said. "And I'm sure Julie and Tina will join us. I'll mention it to a few other people, but most will already be going anyway."

"True," Dan laughed. "Not like Windsor Peak has a lot happening after eight."

***

Dan settled into the table that Kendra had reserved for them, watching Jake and Patrick set their guitars into stands on the back of the stage. Although everyone was welcome to perform, usually when Jake and Patrick took the stage no one wanted them to leave. They always invited others to join them, so occasionally it turned into a comical karaoke-like event, but most were content to listen to them.

The restaurant was packed, and he scanned the crowd, seeing many old friends. Their trainer was there, with a group of equally fit people, and he waved across the room. Dan felt unsettled for some reason, but nothing in his line of sight could be causing the feeling. Kendra came and slid onto the chair next to him, a smile on her face.

"Hi," she said. "I can't sit for long. I had hoped I could just enjoy the show tonight, but it's way too crowded, I feel guilty if I sit for too long."

"Anything I can do to help?"

She laughed, kissing him quickly. "Thanks, but I've seen you try to carry a tray. Things will run smoothly; we have a good crew on tonight. I should get up there and open the microphone, people are getting antsy."

Patrick and Dan were sitting on two barstools on stage, waiting for Kendra to make her usual welcome statement. Christine, her husband Ryan and Shea had joined him, and he spotted Tina and Julie making their way through the crowd. A few weeks ago, sharing a table with Kendra's closest friends had been uncomfortable, but now he felt them softening toward him.

"I heard you decided to stay and set up a practice here," Ryan said. "That's great, congrats."

"Thanks, it's been going better than I could have imagined."

Ryan nodded. "Lots of people had to drive to Burlington to find a lawyer, it's nice to have you right here. My sister has been working for a firm in Plattsburgh, I can't believe the hours she works some weeks."

"I don't doubt it," he said. "Is she a lawyer?"

"No, a paralegal."

"If she ever wants to move here, have her send me a message. I need to find some help but haven't had time yet."

"Really? That's great, I'll mention it to her. She'd love to be closer to us when—" Ryan cut himself off and started fiddling with the label on his beer.

Dan grinned, noting Christine's glass of water on the table. "No problem, it would make my life easier too."

Ryan looked relieved that he hadn't pushed for the rest of the sentence, and turned as Kendra took to the stage to introduce his brothers.

The evening passed quickly, his brothers rarely leaving the stage other than a short break at Shea's insistence. A few brave people went and sang with them, but no one asked them to give up the spotlight. Dan had refused to go on stage more than once, his brothers could force his hand on karaoke nights, but the crowd was too large to make a fool of himself tonight.

Instead, he watched Kendra as she interacted with the customers at the bar, deal with a handful of people who were getting a little too intoxicated, and clear plates when people finished meals. She was in her element, and he knew that she was making each of the customers feel special just by smiling at them.

His phone buzzed in his pocket just after ten, and he pulled it out to see a text from JJ asking him to come out back for a minute. He frowned, then told the table he would be right back and headed out through the kitchen. Zoe waved as he went through, but the rest of the staff didn't react, so they were used to his presence by now.

"Hey," JJ said as Dan jogged down the steps. "Thanks, I'm sorry to interrupt."

"No problem," Dan said as they shook hands. "What's up?"

"Gas station just outside of town called in a sighting of Brad. It was the one by the highway, so good chance he just got off and got gas, then kept going. But there's also the chance that he was getting off to come this way."

"Any idea what he was driving?"

JJ shook his head. "I'm trying to get the camera footage from the manager, but apparently the ones by the pumps haven't been working great. The clerk said there were a few cars out there at the time, and she didn't pay attention to which one he went back to."

Dan let out a frustrated sigh. "He could be here."

"Yes, he could. I came to tell Kendra, but it's so busy in there, I didn't want to upset her."

"Mind if I tell her later, rather than disrupting her whole night right now?"

"If you want, that's fine with me. I'll keep her posted if I find out anything more."

"It might be easier to keep me updated," Dan suggested. "With the festival and everything she has going on this weekend, the stress of this could be too much. If this turns into nothing, then I'd rather not upset her for no reason."

"Sure thing," JJ said. He pushed off the cruiser he was leaning on, starting to walk toward the restaurant. "Since I'm here anyway, might as well say hi to Zoe."

"And get some food?" Dan laughed.

"I can't help it that she likes to feed me," JJ said with a grin.

"Just between us," Dan said before they entered. "Do you think this is gong to turn into something?"

JJ frowned. "I'm not sure. I never knew this guy, but everything I've heard has been bad. My gut says something is off, but for all we know, he's moved on with his life and forgotten them. At least, that's what I hope."

"Appreciate your honesty. I'll stay here with them tonight, make sure all is quiet."

They entered the kitchen, and Dan ran up the stairs to the apartment to check on Calle. He felt better after seeing her tucked in her bed, and the door locked securely to the outside. Nora had been with her earlier but usually went home after Calle fell asleep, since Kendra kept a video monitor with her downstairs and the sensors on the door and windows would make a racket if they were opened. There was no chance a stranger could make their way past the kitchen staff to go up the stairs, so he wasn't surprised that all was quiet, but it made him feel better.

"Everything okay?" Kendra asked with a concerned look when she saw him come down the stairs. "I just saw you on the monitor."

"Everything is fine," he replied. "Just wanted to make sure she was sleeping, and I figured it was less crowded to use your bathroom. Mind if I stay over tonight?"

"Of course not. Go up when you're ready, I'll be there when we close."

"I'll stay until Jake and Patrick finish; they should be just about done. Then I'll head up and get some reading done while I wait for you."

"Don't stay awake for me," she said. "I could be late."

"Oh, I have ulterior motives keeping me awake," he said with a laugh as she went back to the bar. He didn't mention the worry that would keep him awake and hoped him keeping this secret wouldn't come back to bite him. But adding stress to her busy night didn't make sense, he told himself. He could tell her after the craziness of the weekend passed, unless JJ reported a sighting that couldn't be ignored.

Chapter 26

Kendra was exhausted by the time the Holiday Festival was fully set up and ready to open on Saturday. Starting the weekend off with a busy, and late, night for open mike had been profitable but exhausting. Friday had been nonstop, running around to get the tent and portable heaters set up on the town green, then managing the installation of tables and power supplies for the vendors. Saturday morning, she had greeted all the volunteers and vendors, helping everyone find their spot, and watched as it all came together.

She sagged against Dan ten minutes before everything was to open, grateful that he had been with her the last two days to get everything done. He had barely left her side the last twenty-four hours, helping with any task. He had insisted that Calle stay with Stella and Ben for the night, so she had one less thing to worry about, and although she missed her daughter, it had made her morning easier. They were all on their way, and Calle would be over the moon about attending with Charlie.

"I think we're ready," she said, looking around.

"Looks that way," he dropped a kiss on her head. "Good job."

"Thanks for all your help. I don't know if I would have gotten it all done without you."

"Yes, you would have. You're a wonder woman; you can do anything."

She loved that he thought that of her, but she felt like a clown juggling too many balls most days. She was looking forward to the following week, when the crowds would slow down, and the town would be filled with more familiar faces for Jake and Shea's wedding. Glancing at all the vendors set up in the tent, she made a mental note to see if she could get some Christmas shopping done while she was here. The holiday was sneaking up on her, and she had more gifts than usual to purchase this year.

"Anything you need for Christmas?" She looked up at Dan, stumped at what to get him.

"You."

"I mean something that could be wrapped."

He grinned at her. "I don't see the problem."

"Oh, you're no help." She slapped his arm and laughed. "I'll figure it out on my own. I think I see your family coming."

They crossed the tent to meet his family, Calle refusing to let go of Charlie's hand to hug her mom fully.

"Charlie might want to spend time with his friends," she warned her daughter. "If he wants to do that, you can stay with Dan and I."

"Or us," Stella offered. "Ben has an awful sweet tooth and will need help trying all the candy and fudge."

"I'm really good at that," Calle nodded.

"This is fantastic," Ben noted. "It has really grown over the years. Good job, Kendra."

"Thanks. I'm secretly hoping this is the last one I need to run; the mayor has promised she'll budget for an event planner for next year."

"They'll miss your touch, but it must be a lot of work," Stella said.

"Are Patrick and Jake coming?" Dan asked his father.

"Jake and Shea are on the way; Patrick will be along shortly. He offered to sit at the table for the animal shelter again, helping them raise money." Patrick had done so at the Autumn Festival and raised a good amount of money for the shelter.

"I'm surprised they aren't dressing him up like Santa," Dan said with a grin.

"I have a feeling there is at least a Santa hat in his future," Ben laughed. "I think the people at the shelter decided not to push their luck and ask for the full suit."

The tent started to fill as people filed in through the entrance, paying a small entrance fee that would help the town fund playground repairs and school events over the next year. It was a small change implemented for this festival, but Kendra had made sure that no one would be denied entry if they couldn't afford it. The funds would be so helpful to the school, but she didn't want anyone to miss the fun over a few dollars.

Calle tugged on her arm, pulling her attention away from the growing crowd. "Mom, can we get some apple cider donuts for breakfast?"

"We ate breakfast," Charlie responded. "But I'm game for a donut."

Calle rolled her eyes at him. "You weren't supposed to tell her that."

"They would have gotten you one no matter what," he argued.

Kendra laughed as she and Dan followed them to the table where the fragrant donuts were being served warm. Her stomach growled and she realized she hadn't had anything to eat yet, so she accepted the warm treat from Dan with a smile. The six of them started walking slowly around the tent, eying the goods for sale and all the delicious foods they were sure to eat over the course of the weekend. When they saw Patrick enter from the side, Ben and Stella stepped away to help him get set up.

"I just saw my dad and Shea," Charlie nodded toward the entrance. "I'm going to say hi. I'll be right back."

Calle pouted as he ran off, but her attention quickly turned to a section of the space that was dedicated to crafting. "Can I make a reindeer?"

"Sure." Kendra took her daughter's hand and brought her over, helping her gather all the supplies she needed. She and Dan watched as she applied glue carefully to each piece, biting her lip in concentration. Soon a couple of girls from Calle's class joined her, and it was clear she had no intention of leaving the area for a while.

"Why don't you shop around a little," Dan suggested. "I'll keep an eye on her."

She agreed and started making her way around the space, careful to keep them in her line of sight in case Dan needed backup. A table displaying a selection of books whose covers had been replaced with artistic flair caught her attention, and she selected a beautiful Jane Austen novel that she knew Stella would love. Choosing a handmade bookmark to include before paying, she finished her purchase and turned away, tucking her wallet into her bag.

Suddenly caught in a small surge of people, she felt her breath catch as she felt trapped. Looking around for a place to step aside, her eyes locked on a red baseball cap at the edge of the tent and all the air seemed to leave her lungs. Panicked, she pushed her way out of the group and doubled over, trying to find some oxygen. Starting to feel lightheaded and nauseous, she tried to remember what her therapist had told her to do in these moments, but all rational thought escaped her.

A firm hand on her back pushed her out of the tent through a flap, and she heard Jake's calm voice through the fog. "Kendra. Listen to my voice. You're safe. I'm here. Breathe."

She was pushed down to a chair, her head between her knees with his hand firm but gentle on the back of her neck. His orders came out regularly, telling her to breathe, walking her back slowly from the panic that had taken over her entire mind and body. She was aware of Shea rubbing her back but had no idea if she had been there the whole time or had just appeared. Sitting up slowly, she felt the tears spill over her cheeks and could do nothing to stop them.

Shea embraced her from behind. "Are you okay?"

"I don't think so." Kendra rubbed her temples, where a migraine threatened to form. "That hasn't happened in so long."

"Any idea what triggered it?" Jake asked.

"Yes," she let out a shuddering sigh. "I saw a baseball hat exactly like the one Brad used to wear all the time. I was stuck in the middle of this big group of people and already feeling claustrophobic, and then I spotted that, and it just did me in."

"Do you think it was him?" Jake was already surveying the area for anyone who would fit the description.

She shook her head. "I have no idea. I couldn't see anything after that."

"I'm going to check on Calle," Shea said suddenly. Kendra watched gratefully as Shea moved back into the tent, glad she had so many people to help. Wanting to be with her daughter, she started to stand, but Jake's hand stopped her.

"Give yourself a minute. You're still really pale."

"I need to make sure—"

"Shea is doing that, and Dan was right with Calle just before we saw you go down. He didn't see you, so he has no reason to leave her side." Jake hunched down in front of her, meeting her eyes. "I know how much that rattled you. Don't try to go back in there yet, you need to let your body decompress."

"I know," she said. "I hate it so much. Why can't I just be normal?"

"Look who you're talking to," he gave her a wry grin. "At least we have each other."

"I'm so lucky you were there; I don't know what I would have done. Probably passed out right in the middle of the tent."

"You've saved me before too, don't forget. It's easy to recognize when someone else is going through it, less simple when it's about to happen to you." He glanced behind her as the tent flap opened again, Dan rushing through. "I'll go in with Shea and keep an eye on Calle until you're up for it. If you decide to go home, let us know and we'll bring her back to the house with us."

"Thanks." Dan clapped a hand on Jake's shoulder quickly before grabbing Kendra in a bone crushing embrace. "Are you okay?"

"Getting better," she admitted. "That came out of nowhere."

"Shea said you might have seen Brad?"

"It was just a hat, and it could have been a different one." She shook her head, unable to get a clear picture of what the hat had looked like now. "I was already spiraling a little, because I got swept up in a little crowd and had no space. I don't like that, it's why I'm always behind the bar, because no one can crowd me. When I saw that hat it just sent me over the edge."

"I think we should go home," Dan suggested.

"I really can't," she said. "I need to be here to oversee things, and Calle is having way too much fun to make her leave. I'll be okay, I just need a minute."

He held her, fortifying her with his strength and warmth, until she felt ready to be seen again. Holding tightly to his hand, she followed him into the tent, and breathed a sigh of relief to see the crowds had thinned out a bit. She could see Calle still at the craft section, Jake and Shea right behind her. Scanning the crowd, she saw nothing but red Santa hats and decided her mind must have been playing tricks on her. Best to put it all behind her and get through the rest of the weekend, not allow thoughts of Brad to ruin yet another occasion for her.

***

The weekend flew by, and before she knew it the tent was emptying on Sunday evening as the tourists started their drive home, and the town residents brought their weekend to an end. The festival had been a rousing success, the mayor declaring it the best to date. The animal shelter had raised thousands of dollars with Patrick's help, and the entry fee had more than exceeded their expectations.

"Ready to head home?" Dan asked her, carrying an armful of shopping bags.

"I think so," she said. "The mayor has other people assigned to clean up duty, so I'm officially done. And exhausted."

"Stella was making a feast at the house with Calle's help, football is on TV, and I'm ready for a cold beer."

She smiled and took his offered hand, letting him lead her out of the tent. They were halfway to the restaurant, where Dan had left his car, when JJ pulled up next to them.

"How was the weekend?"

"It was great, JJ. Glad you could make it by yesterday." Kendra had seen him briefly as he ate a giant gingerbread cookie, talking to some of the high school students. "Did everyone behave?"

"I think so," he rubbed his chin. "Any further sightings?"

"No, it's been a few weeks now." Kendra felt Dan tense up next to her and saw a look exchange between the two men. "What am I missing?"

"We had a report that he was seen at the gas station by the highway on Thursday," JJ said. "I thought you knew."

"No, how would I know?" She turned to Dan. "Did you know?"

"Yes," he said quickly. "JJ told me. But I didn't want it to ruin your weekend, I was going to tell you later."

"When?"

"Tomorrow, or maybe tonight. I don't know, I didn't think that far ahead."

"That wasn't your choice to make," she said to Dan. "And JJ, you should have told me, not him."

JJ nodded. "It was really busy, and I didn't want to distract you. But I'm sorry, I will in the future."

"So that might have been him in the tent."

"You think you saw him?" JJ put the cruiser in park and stepped out of the car. "When?"

"It was yesterday. Not his face, just a hat that reminded me of him, and then I had a little panic episode. It might not have even been him, or even been a baseball hat. Everyone was wearing the red Santa hats, so maybe my eyes played tricks on me." She pulled her hand from Dan's. "But I should have known."

"Agreed," Dan said quickly. "I'm sorry."

"You had no right to keep this from me."

"I know. I'm sorry."

JJ stood in front of them, looking regretful that he had even stopped. He opened the car door and started to get in before turning back. "I apologize, Kendra. I hope it was nothing, and since there haven't been any more sightings of him, I think it was a mistake. I hope this doesn't ruin your night."

They watched him drive away, and Dan tried to take her hand again. "I was trying to protect you. I know that was wrong, but I will always try to keep you safe and happy."

"This feels like you trying to control me," she said. "I think I'll take my own car and bring Calle back here for the night."

"Please don't do that. Give me a chance to make it up to you," he begged.

"I need some time and space. This weekend was exhausting, and now finding out you've been holding this from me for days really hurts. Maybe I'll feel differently tomorrow, but right now, I want to be alone." She crossed her arms, feeling lonelier than she had in months. She had known if she let down all her defenses that Dan would somehow break her heart, and she did it anyway. Now she needed to figure out if she could move past yet another betrayal by the man she loved.

Chapter 27

"Dan." Kendra sounded as if she were crying, and was struggling to get her next breath in.

"Kendra, what's wrong?"

"Calle. She's gone."

"What? What do you mean, she's gone?" Dan checked his watch, seeing that it was just after four on a Tuesday. Calle should have gotten off the school bus a half hour ago, if he had the timing right. Kendra hadn't spoken to him since Sunday, texting yesterday that she needed some time to move past his secrecy. If she was calling now, something would have happened that scared her.

"He took her. Please, just come."

"I'm on my way." He shoved his feet into sneakers and thundered down the stairs, finding a startled Jake at the bottom.

"Where's the fire?"

"Kendra just called. Something happened with Calle, I think her ex might have shown up and grabbed her. I have to go." He grabbed his jacket off the hook next to the door and his keys from the bowl below.

"Hang on, I'm coming." Jake yelled down the hall towards the kitchen. "Patrick, Charlie, let's go."

"I'm coming too." Ben stepped out of his office behind Jake, and Dan was overwhelmed with the show of support from his family, with no questions asked. Stella was pulling her coat on behind him without a word, waiting for the group to be ready. Pushing the thought aside to ponder later, he opened the door and ran to his car, the others following.

"I'll drive too, just in case we need two cars." Jake yelled as he and Charlie climbed into his SUV.

The two cars raced into town, and Dan's stomach crashed when he pulled onto Main Street and saw a police cruiser parked outside the restaurant. He was still hoping there was a mix-up of some kind, that even if Brad had Calle, it was just to toy with Kendra before returning her.

He ran into the restaurant, finding Kendra between Tina and Julie, with Zoe pacing behind the three of them. JJ was standing, notepad out, and turned as he and his family came into the building. He nodded at the Burrows before turning back to Kendra. "I'll head over to the school; another officer is there talking to the staff now. If you can think of anything at all, you have my cell. We'll keep you updated."

Kendra crumbled into herself, her sobs ripping through the empty room and his heart. As he moved toward her, Tina stood so the chair next to Kendra was open, and he slid into it. Gathering her in his arms, he pulled her onto his lap and felt her arms grab hold of him.

He heard Jake's rough voice over Kendra's sobs. "Can you fill us in?"

"Yes," Julie's voice was all business. "Calle didn't get off the bus. We were here chatting with Kendra and said we would run over to the school and get her, we thought she had missed the bus somehow. Or maybe had an activity after school that she forgot to tell Kendra about. She called the school, and the office told her that she had been picked up at ten this morning."

Dan's stomach dropped again at the words. That was over six hours ago.

"Did they say who picked her up?"

"Brad." The word was spit out by Tina, who was never known to be as venomous as she sounded with that one syllable.

"The school didn't know who he was, but he had a copy of her birth certificate and his driver's license," Julie explained. "He is listed on the paperwork as her dad, so they didn't think much of it. Kendra never even thought he would do something like this, and they don't have a custody arrangement to share with the school anyway to restrict his pickups. He just left, and she got Calle by default. Not that he would have wanted Calle anyway, but luckily, she didn't have to fight over it. She let him walk away without paying a dime in child support, just so she could ensure Calle's safety."

"I ju—" Kendra sobbed out. "Just wanted him to go away."

"Shhhh," Dan whispered in her ear. "We *will* find her."

"Don't make more promises you can't keep," Julie snapped at him.

"I'm going to head over to the school, see what is happening and how we can help. Charlie, you want to come with me?" Jake took charge, his military background helping him stay emotionally detached and organized. "Dad, why don't you gather up as many people as you can to help search. Get the word out through the mayor on the town app. Patrick, sorry bud, but we're probably going to have to use you."

Years ago, when Jake's wife had been missing following a terrorist attack, Patrick had gone on the news asking the public to report in any sightings of her. The increased attention hadn't brought Jenna back to them, but it had helped significantly in gaining public attention to those missing. Dan knew if Patrick asked for the public's help, they would be swarmed with both police resources and public help.

"I'll call my agent now, tell her what we need." Patrick stepped back as he pulled out his phone.

Once Jake and Charlie had departed, Ben and Patrick were busy on the phones, Dan focused his attention on Kendra. Her sobs had quieted but she looked pale and felt frail. "What can I do for you?"

She took a deep breath and then slid off his lap, leaving him feeling empty. "Just be here, please." She let him take her hand, helping ease the sudden detachment he felt from her moving to her own chair.

"I put the closed sign up, but people are standing outside." Zoe announced as she looked out the window.

"I'll go deal with them." Julie stood to head to the door, but Tina grabbed her arm.

"We might need their help." She turned to Kendra. "Do you mind if we let them come in? Zoe can get some snacks out, Julie and I can make coffee, and we can start getting a search party organized. If we don't need it, we can send everyone home."

"Let me just get Kendra into her office, so she has some privacy." Dan started to stand, but Kendra tugged on his hand to stay where he was.

"No," she said quietly. "I've hidden so much from my neighbors and friends; they don't need to be kept at arms distance anymore. Let them in, they aren't going to judge me for being a mess."

Soon the room was full of neighbors and local business owners, talking quietly in groups. Dan was touched at how many people came out once they heard, bringing along classmates of Calle's and teachers Shea knew from the school. Julie, Tina, Shea, Christine and Stella were managing to keep coffee and hot chocolate flowing, while Zoe and the waitstaff provided snacks from the kitchen. It appeared the entire town was in or outside of the restaurant, ready to spring into action.

"This is amazing," Kendra whispered. "All these people care about my daughter."

"And you," Dan replied. "They care about both of you."

"I don't know what I would do without her."

"You're not going to find out. We're going to find her." Dan watched as Patrick crossed the room, looking like he had news.

"I just heard from Dad; they want me to go on the news. I'm going to step outside, there is a news crew that just arrived from Burlington waiting to talk to me." He looked at Kendra quickly. "You can join if you would like, but it's not necessary if you'd rather not."

She took a deep breath and nodded. "I think I should."

Dan stood with her, still holding tight to her hand, and followed Patrick out to where a news camera was set up on the sidewalk. The darkness of night had already fallen, but the camera had a bright light and the backdrop of the holiday lights on the restaurant ensured they would be clearly seen. Dan watched as Patrick accepted a large printout of Calle's school picture from the newscaster and gestured for Kendra to join him. Letting go of Kendra's hand so she could walk over to join Patrick left him feeling even more lost, like they were each other's lifeline in this nightmare.

The interview was brief, and Kendra didn't have to speak as her swollen eyes and red cheeks clearly showed her grief. Patrick appealed to the masses to report any sightings of Calle or Brad and urged everyone to help in the search. "The people of Windsor Peak have the town under control, but we believe that Calle has been taken out of town. Please, ask your local hotels and gas stations if they have seen her. If anyone knows or recognizes the man on the screen, or sees Calle, please contact your local police. Our family deeply appreciates the support. Calle, if you're watching this, we will see you soon."

The lights turned off and Kendra returned to Dan as Patrick shook hands with the news crew.

"How will they know what Brad looks like?" Kendra asked.

"They pulled an old mug shot. Apparently, he had several to choose from." Dan indicated the door of the restaurant. "Want to go back inside?"

"I just need a minute, please. I'm trying to hold it together in there, but it's hard."

"What do you need? I can take you to our house, no one is there. Maybe you can get some rest." He rubbed her arms, trying to put some warmth back into her, but knowing nothing would do that until her daughter was back in her arms.

"I won't sleep until she's back with me," Kendra sniffled. "Just hold me for a minute, please."

He wrapped her in his arms, trying to fill her with his warmth and strength with the embrace. She had always been so strong, so capable, like him. This was beyond what either of them could possess for strength, but he was determined to be her rock until her daughter was returned. Getting Calle back was the only end to this nightmare, and he refused to think of anything else.

Patrick joined them, explaining that he was going to go live with the Today show in the morning if they hadn't found Calle yet. Kendra sagged against him at the thought, and he held her up. "JJ is coming, let's see what he has to say."

JJ approached, taking his hat off when he stepped onto the porch. "Kendra, I'll keep this short. We know he was driving a Ford F250 when he went to the school, the camera at the school caught the license plate. When we ran the plates, we found out it was stolen about ten days ago in White River Junction. That's probably what he used to get up to Burlington, when he was spotted at the hotel. State Troopers have gone to the address on the registration, it's an elderly gentleman who has been in the hospital for a few weeks. No one even knew the truck was missing, and no one has ever seen Brad before."

"By now he could be anywhere," she whispered. "You don't even have an idea of where to search."

"We know that he didn't take her on a plane, that was one of the first things the State Police checked. They are checking with bus drivers now, but that will take a little longer. He most likely has to be within driving distance whether it's the truck or a bus, and he couldn't have gone north without her passport."

"Have the other states been notified?" Dan asked.

"Yes," JJ nodded. "The state police in all of New England received the alert, and as we speak Patrick's statement is being aired across the region. It's been roughly eight hours, but that doesn't help much because for all we know, he drove to a hideout in Vermont. The FBI is going to get involved, thanks to your brothers."

"Patrick can bring a lot of attention to this," Dan remarked.

"Jake as well," JJ added. "He's got some high-powered friends in the military and the bureau; he called in a lot of favors."

"What else can be done right now?" Dan asked, seeing his family waiting for an update through the window.

JJ hesitated, his eyes flickering to Kendra before meeting Dan's again. "Pray, if you're so inclined. When the Feds get here, have as much information as possible to give them, I suggest you sit down and write down everything you can think of about Brad. Even Calle, things that could help identify her. Favorite foods that might be uncommon, anything that someone might notice at a gas station if they were to see them. I know we've already gotten a description of her jacket, backpack and sneakers, which will help. He's unlikely to buy her a new jacket or shoes, at least not tonight, so that's what we're asking people to focus on if they think they spot them."

"Her bracelet," Kendra spoke suddenly. "She's wearing the bracelet you got her in New York, there is no way she would take that off even if he tried to get her to change clothes."

"Do you have a picture of it?"

"Yes," Dan fumbled for his phone. "Let me pull up the email receipt."

He passed JJ his phone and then texted him the screen shot so they could put it on the news. The pretty snowflake bracelet that Calle was so proud of, and showed off as often as possible, just might help them bring her home.

Kendra hugged herself while Dan and JJ were looking at his phone, and Dan was grateful that Patrick stepped in and put an arm around her. He was talking quietly in her ear, and she leaned into him. When he finished with JJ, he was glad that she went straight into his arms. As much as he appreciated Patrick supporting her when he was doing something else, he wanted to be the one she turned to.

"I'm going to talk to the team, check in with the Feds, et cetera." JJ said as he stepped away. "I'll be in touch."

"She must be so scared," Kendra's voice sounded strangled.

"Hopefully she doesn't think anything is weird, just that it's an adventure. Like when we went to New York," he reassured her.

"What if he hurts her?"

Dan's eyes met Patrick's, seeing the same fire in his brothers that he felt inside. "Then he is going to have to deal with us. And it won't be pretty."

Chapter 28

Time had lost all sense of meaning, but she figured it must be late in the evening as people started to head home. Families with children in Calle's class had left hours before, and now the room held only a small crowd of close friends. And the Burrows, who had rushed in to help without a thought and hadn't left her side. Jake had been working with the state police and federal officers who had appeared after Patrick's public plea and had kept them updated with regular messages. Charlie had quickly organized his hockey team and started making stacks of flyers to hang up in neighboring towns if Calle wasn't back by morning.

Everyone seemed to have a task other than her, she realized. As she sat in a daze lost in thoughts of her daughter, the town had organized around her, with the Burrows in the center of it all. "I don't deserve any of you," she said softly to Dan. The man she had pushed away so many times, who had not left her side in the last several hours.

"You deserve all this and more."

"I've been so awful to you."

"Kendra, we don't have to do that now. And you haven't done anything other than protect yourself and Calle. I'm here, and I will always be here. Don't give that thought any room to grow, you'll never push me hard enough to make me leave."

"What would I do without her?" The words escaped, the thoughts that she was trying to keep at bay spilling out.

"That's not happening. She's coming back." He sounded so sure, she clung to that confidence with all her might.

"Can I get you anything?" Zoe appeared at the table, squatting down so she was eye level with Kendra. "You haven't eaten a thing, and you need to. What will you eat?"

"I'm not hungry," Kendra insisted.

"You need food for strength. You too." Zoe nodded at Dan before turning to the kitchen. "I will be right back."

"She's a good person." Kendra said as she watched Zoe disappear into the kitchen. "I never thought when I hired her that I would lean on her the way I have, but she has become a good friend."

"Good. I know these two are always there for you." He indicated Julie and Tina, who were walking towards them.

"How are you holding up?" Tina asked, a concerned look on her face.

"Not good," Kendra admitted.

"They are going to find them," Julie said with a confidence Kendra admired. "And then I want ten minutes alone with that bastard."

"Get in line." Dan muttered, squeezing Kendra's hand.

"I just want my baby back." The thought consumed her, made it difficult to focus on anything else. She watched as Zoe came out of the kitchen, two steaming bowls and some plates on a tray that she placed down next to them. Chicken noodle soup and half of Zoe's specialty coq a vin sandwich were placed down in front of her and Dan, along with utensils.

"Eat." Zoe commanded as she picked up the tray and walked back to her domain.

"She's right, you need to eat something." Tina pushed the bowl a little closer. "And it will warm you up."

Kendra took a few spoonsful of the soup to appease those around her, but did find the warmth and familiarity of the comfort food to be soothing. Before she knew it, the plates were empty, and the weight of exhaustion hit her. Covering a yawn with her hand she saw the room now only held those closest to her. Most had given in to the demands of sleep, and she knew even those left would need to do the same.

"We need to send everyone home for the night. Will you ask your dad and Stella? If they go, most people will follow their lead." She knew the older couple had to be running on fumes at this point and didn't want to push their limits.

"I'll try, but I don't know if they will leave. Will you be alright if I go talk to them?"

She nodded and he stood up, kissing her on the head before walking over to talk to his father.

"He's been amazing," she said quietly to her two best friends as they watched him.

"I think he loves both of you," Tina said softly. "It makes me happy to see. When Calle gets back, I doubt he'll ever let either of you out of his sight for long."

"What if —"

"Nope." Julie cut her off firmly by holding her hand up. "We're not doing that. She'll be back. That's all there is to discuss."

"But—"

Tina reached across the table and squeezed her hand. "I know he was violent, but I truly don't believe he would hurt her. He has no reason to."

"He has no reason to take her, either."

"True, but he's hurting you by doing that. He hurt you by stealing money from you." At Kendra's startled glance she nodded. "Pete told the police."

"He was here earlier," Julie interrupted. "I think he drove up to Burlington to hang flyers."

"Brad wants your attention, and he wants to hurt you. He's a sick man. He needs all the attention on him, even if it's negative. And he needs to feel like he controls you." Tina went on, drumming her fingers on the table. "I don't know what brought this up after all these years, but that's what this is. I don't believe he'll hurt her, knowing that she's missing will cause you pain is what he wants."

"What if she annoys him?" She whispered the thought. "Cries or makes too much noise, and he hits her."

"We'll find her, and hopefully find her before any of that happens. Right now, she probably thinks it's exciting, meeting her dad and going on a trip." Julie stopped talking as Dan and Patrick approached.

"Jake called," Dan said quickly. "A lady traveling on business saw Patrick on the eleven o'clock news. She's apparently a big fan so she stopped what she was doing to listen. She was checking into her hotel in Boston and swears that she saw Brad and Calle at the desk. The FBI is already on their way to the hotel."

"I called for a jet," Patrick said. "It will be ready for us in Burlington when we get there. They are clearing it so we can land in Boston right away, it should be a quick trip."

"How sure are they? What if she's not there?" Kendra wondered out loud. "What if I go to Boston and she comes here?"

Dan and Patrick exchanged a look. "We really don't know anything other than someone thinks they saw her. Jake said he and Charlie would go if you wanted them to. You can stay here, and Dan can either go or stay."

She considered the options. Having her daughter in her arms was her first priority, but the uncertainty of whether the woman had the right man and girl was holding her back. "Dan, will you go with Jake and Charlie? Patrick, you can go too. We'll stay here." She indicated her friends at the table, who nodded.

"Will you try and get some rest?" Dan circled to hug her quickly.

"Probably not, but I'll say yes if that makes you feel better."

He kissed her quickly. "I'll call you as soon as we know something. If anything changes here, call me. My dad and Stella won't leave, so they'll be here."

Tina stood up. "I'm going to see if they will go up to your place and rest, okay?"

Kendra nodded, grateful that her friend was so thoughtful.

"Dan," she grabbed his hand as he turned to leave. "Please bring her back to me."

"I'm going to." He cupped her face in his hands and looked deep into her eyes. "I will not stop until she's home with you, I give you my word on that."

She watched them leave, sitting back heavily in the chair she had been in for hours. Tina returned, Ben, Stella and Shea in tow, who had refused the comfort of the apartment to sit vigil with them. Zoe came out and quietly sent the staff home before sitting at the table with the rest of them, after refilling coffee mugs and placing a plate of cookies on the table.

"My boys will bring her home," Ben said.

"They will." Stella nodded. "I just know they will."

Kendra held on to the hand that Stella offered, praying to any god who would listen that their words would be true.

Chapter 29

The drive to the Burlington airport was done in record time, in the SUV driven by a trooper that Patrick had arranged with the state police. There was little traffic on the road to deal with, but Dan didn't want to risk having to stop for a speed trap and lose precious time. The cop dropped them at the curb and wished them luck before speeding off, and Dan raced into the terminal with Patrick behind him. Jake and Charlie were standing by a door talking to an airport official.

"Have you heard anything else?" Dan demanded of his brother as they ran up to them.

"No," Jake replied. "Let's get in the air and then I'll fill you in."

They followed the airline official to the tarmac, where a small private jet waited for them. Boarding quickly, they buckled into their seats and impatiently listened to the safety speech from the lone flight attendant before the plane started taxiing.

"We'll land at Logan airport in Boston, it's about fifteen minutes from there to the hotel. The state police called ahead and have a Massachusetts trooper waiting to drive us to save some time. The FBI is already on site at the hotel, but when I last checked, no one had eyes on Brad or Calle." Jake filled them in, leaning between the space to be heard. Charlie sat next to his father, leg bouncing from what Dan guessed was nervous energy.

"How sure is this woman that it was them?" Patrick asked Jake.

"She said ninety-five percent sure. She remembered that the little girl was wearing yellow leggings and a pink top, which is what Calle wore to school today," Jake shared. "They also showed her a picture of the sneakers that Kendra told the FBI she wore to school today, since she had gym class. The woman said they looked similar, that she knows the sneakers lit up when she walked. But most importantly, she said when the little girl waved back at her, she knew she was wearing a bracelet. It caught her eye because it's not something a little girl would normally have one, so it sounds like the one you got her."

"I can't believe she remembered all of that," Patrick marveled. "I can barely remember what shoes I have on right now."

"I know," Jake said. "But she works in fashion and has a daughter nearly Calle's age that she's missing while she's traveling. Thank God, because she paid more attention to the little girl than she did the man, so that's the five percent uncertainty. All she could say for sure was that he had a hat on, and she thought he was carrying a bag of some type. Not unheard of in a hotel lobby."

"The hotel doesn't have cameras?" Charlie asked.

"They do," Jake responded. "he kept his face down so the hat covered it, and Calle is too short to be seen. There was one outside, but they either came in a side door or somehow avoided."

Dan cursed the hotel for the faulty camera that could have told them for sure it was Calle. "Credit card?"

"The room was prepaid, booked online. Then he used a prepaid card at check in, so they only make sure it has the money and places a hold on the funds. They checked his license, and it matched the name on the reservation, but the clerk can't be sure that it wasn't stolen."

"He didn't look at the picture and the person to make sure they were the same?" Dan huffed out a breath of frustration.

Jake shrugged. "Big hotel, the room was paid for, the guy was respectful and had the card for incidentals. It didn't raise any flags."

Dan pulled out his phone, checking for texts from Kendra with any updates at home. No new messages, despite having a signal.

"How long until we land?"

Patrick checked his watch. "Should be about a half hour."

"Shit," Dan muttered. "I need to be there now. Are they waiting for us?"

Jake shook his head. "They don't want to. I told them it would be less scary for Calle, if it is Calle, if we were there but they wouldn't make any promises. They did put an agent in the room next door, they are trying to listen for anything through the connecting door. If they hear anything alarming, even her crying, they are going to knock on the door under some guise."

"I'm not waiting for her to scream," Dan insisted.

"They need to follow the rules. We don't." Jake glanced around as if checking to make sure no one could hear him before realizing they were alone. "I have a buddy on the Massachusetts State Police. He's keeping me in the loop, and I know if I put a little pressure on, he'll give me the room number. But I will not put you, me, or Calle in danger. Following the professionals is the way we're going to do this, unless we get desperate."

"I'm feeling desperate. Kendra is broken, I need to fix that."

Jake reached across and clapped a hand on his knee, squeezing quickly. "I get it, trust me. But we need to make sure we do everything right to maintain this little girl's safety. Whether it's Calle or not, that needs to be the priority."

Dan groaned and leaned forward, head in his hands. "I just need to know if it's her. And to have her safe."

The flight attendant came by with bottles of water and offers of drinks or snacks, which Charlie took advantage of.

"Bottomless pit," Jake laughed as Charlie filled up.

The father and son talked quietly; heads huddled together. Dan leaned back in his seat, wishing the plane to move faster. He sent a quick text to Kendra, letting her know they were approaching Boston, and he would update her as soon as he could. She responded quickly, thanking him.

The time on the plane dragged on, and yet before he knew it, he was running down the stairs and into a waiting SUV. The trooper greeted them with a nod before flipping the lights on and zipping out of the airport towards the hotel. They raced through the nearly empty city streets, at just after midnight on a weeknight there weren't many cars to contend with.

They all hurried from the car to the hotel ballroom in record time, led by the hotel clerk who spotted Patrick. They entered what looked like controlled chaos, with a mix of state troopers, FBI agents and hotel personnel huddled in groups around the space. Jake eyed the situation and then pointed to a group of three men and one woman who were sitting at a table in the center.

"Jake." The woman stood and shook his hand. "We met years ago in Afghanistan, congratulations on your retirement. I understand you all have a personal relationship with the missing child and I'm sure you want us to get right down to it."

"Please," Dan replied.

"The witness identified the child from the photo held on the news by your brother, Patrick." The man speaking nodded to Patrick before continuing. "She gave us a good description of her clothing, and we then verified the sneakers and that she saw a bracelet. She's from Dallas, has no connection to this case other than being the next in line at check in. We were able to pull footage from one camera near the elevator, it's a very quick glimpse, but you may be able to confirm that this is the child in question."

The man turned the laptop toward them, and they all huddled in to see the grainy video. As a luggage cart passed by the elevator, they got a quick glimpse of a man with his head down, hat hiding his face, with a small girl next to him.

"That's Calle." Charlie yelled confidently, and they all nodded in agreement.

Dan waited for Jake to speak, knowing it was best to let him take charge. "Yes, my son is correct. There is no question that is Calle."

"Then we will move on the room." They all stood, and everyone in the room got quiet and moved closer.

Before they could step forward, Jake held up a hand. "I know it's out of protocol, but I would like to be with the group that goes in. Calle knows me and will be less scared if she sees me. Agent Rodriquez can speak to my capabilities. I don't need to be armed and will wear whatever you need me to wear for protective gear. I fully understand the risk."

"Dad—" Charlie paled as he looked at his father.

"Charlie, she's six. There are going to be a lot of strangers in helmets covering their faces, holding large guns and probably shields. She's probably sound asleep, so this is what she'll wake up to. The least I can do is make sure she sees someone she knows before she's too terrified."

"I can do it." Dan stepped forward. "I know the risk. I'm not trained like my brother, but she knows me the best."

"Really, no one should." The state trooper looked to the female FBI agent waiting for her response.

"You two." She pointed at Jake and Dan. "Can be in the hallway. I will bring her out to you immediately. I don't want to make this anymore traumatic for the child than it needs to be, but I'm also not going to compromise a crime scene. You trust me, don't you?"

The question was aimed at Jake, who didn't hesitate to nod. Dan was slower to respond and reached for her arm as she turned to leave. "Please. Please bring her out safely."

"I will."

The room listened to the agent as she outlined the plan, with four people going through the hallway door and four more from the connecting room. They all suited up quickly in bullet proof vests and helmets, pulling the face shields down. Charlie shuddered as they marched out, and Dan caught sight of Patrick putting his arm around their nephew before he rushed out of the room with Jake. He didn't have time to send Kendra a text, but prayed he would be calling her in a few minutes with good news.

Tina and Julie had run up to her apartment looking for a phone charger, since Kendra was obsessively checking for updates from Boston. Two FBI agents had joined them in the restaurant, wanting to be nearby in case Kendra received a phone call from Brad, but they sat a few tables away and were so quiet she kept forgetting they were there. Shea had disappeared into the kitchen with Zoe, no doubt making even more food that no one would be able to eat. She watched as Ben stood to use the restroom, squeezing Stella's shoulder as he passed.

Stella held her rosary in her hand, Kendra noticed for the first time. She reached over and touched a bead, remembering the times her grandmother had sat with her own strand.

"I'm saying it for Calle," Stella told her. "It helps keep me calm, and in my belief it will help. I hope that's alight with you."

"Of course, it is," Kendra replied. "Thank you."

"She'll be okay."

"She has to be," Kendra whispered, tears threatening again.

Stella covered her hand with her own. "Your friends are right. He wanted to hurt you and taking her did that. I don't know him well, but I don't believe he is capable of doing more than that."

"Problem is, I don't know for sure. He changed constantly, like a chameleon. Always lying, so it was impossible to ever know what the truth was. He had me so under his spell, I didn't know which way was up. If he has enough time with her, he could turn her against me."

"That would never happen." Stella shook her head, looking resolute. "That little girl thinks the sun rises and sets on you. And she's so smart, she knows that something is off."

"Do you think she's scared?"

Stella looked thoughtful. "Probably. She's only ever slept away from you when she was at our house, and she's still very young. Being away from your regular routine is hard at that age, even in the best circumstances. She struggled to go to sleep at our house, it was only that she had been there with you before that settled her. I remember the first time Dan tried to sleep at a friend's house, Ben had to go get him at one in the morning. From then on, they tended to have kids sleep over rather than going somewhere else. Part of that was losing their mom so young, but the comforts of home are hard to shake when there's a lot of love there. But for Calle, as soon as she is back with you, she'll be okay. This will all be a distant memory soon enough."

Kendra fiddled with her phone, lighting up the screen again to see that it remained blank. "I should probably call my parents. And the Hughes."

"Let's wait until you have good news to share. Unless you want them to come, but it would be hard to get flights here so late." Stella considered the clock behind the bar. "Although if we call them now, they could be on the first flight out in the morning to be here for the celebration when the boys bring her home."

Kendra wiped a tear away, wishing she could feel the same confidence. A void was inside her where her heart and soul normally resided, and it would stay that way until her daughter was back. "Will you call them for me? I want to keep my phone line open."

"Of course. Here comes Ben now, I'll have him call Ron Hughes and I'll call your mom." She stood and left the table, talking quietly to Ben before they both dialed on their cell phones and stood across the room.

Julie came back with a long phone cord plugged in behind where Kendra sat, which she plugged into Kendra's phone. "Tina is just using the bathroom; she'll be right down."

"Do you want to get some rest?"

"No, I'm fine. I've had so much coffee I might not sleep for days. Do you want to lie down for a bit?"

"I won't be able to sleep, so better to just stay here."

"No news?"

Kendra shook her head, checking the phone again as Tina joined them. "I'm going crazy without an update."

"Who are Ben and Stella talking to?" Tina asked, indicating the couple.

"My parents and the Hughes'. Stella thought they might want to get on the first flight in the morning so it would be better to call them now."

"That was a good idea." Julie tapped her hands on the table with nervous energy. "Anyone else we should call?"

"No, not that I can think of." Kendra checked her phone again. "I wish Dan would send me some kind of update. I'm going crazy."

"What was the last you heard?" Tinas asked.

"They had landed and were in the car on the way to the hotel. That was a half hour ago, and nothing since." She looked between her friends, seeing the stress and exhaustion she felt on their faces. "Something must be happening for them to be so quiet."

Shea came out of the kitchen, carrying a pitcher of water and a tray of snacks. "We thought everyone needed a break from coffee, but it's in the kitchen if anyone would rather."

"Shea, you haven't heard anything from Jake, have you?" Julie asked as she placed everything on the table.

"No, sorry." She shook her head. "I can try to text him? But he texted from the plane last, said he would be in touch as soon as they knew anything."

Stella came back, sliding into her chair. "Your mom is booking flights right now and will text me when she has her information. Charlie's hockey coach is on standby, he said he'll do airport runs at any time and get another parent to help if needed. I'll have him get them when they land."

"Everyone has been so nice," Kendra whispered.

"You're well loved, and so good to the community. And we all love Calle. Not surprising the town would rally around you." Shea responded, squeezing Kendra's hand as she spoke.

"Ron Hughes will be in touch with his flight information. He and Janet are online now looking for options." Ben told them as he sat back down. "I told him to let me know what time they arrive."

"Now we just wait some more." Kendra let out a frustrated sigh. "I should have gone with them. Nothing is happening here."

"It's impossible to know where you'll be needed," Tina replied. "For all we know, she could walk in the front door any minute now. So don't be too hard on yourself."

"I just hate not knowing what is happening."

"I'll tell you what's happening here in town, maybe that will help." Ben leaned forward in his chair as he spoke. "Town Hall and the church are both brimming with volunteers, prepping flyers to hand out and hang up. They are ready to hit the streets searching for her as soon as the sun comes up. There are several cars ready to take people anywhere they need to go, and to do the airport pickups. And in every single house, everyone is thinking of you and Calle, praying for a good outcome."

"I thought everyone went home to bed?" Kendra questioned, shocked at what Ben said.

"No, they just didn't want to crowd you. The younger kids are sleeping, lots of sleepovers happening tonight so that more people can help and only have one parent watching a bunch of little ones. They even called off school tomorrow, so teachers can help."

"Wow. I had no idea." Kendra felt the tears again, feeling the support from this town she had always loved.

"This town is something special. More than just about organizing a festival for every possible occasion, they come together when someone needs a little help." Ben scratched his cheek. "And without question. They all just jump into action, they formed their own groups and were organized so quickly, they didn't need much direction. The mayor is overseeing everything, but it's a well-oiled machine right now."

Tina nodded, looking up from her phone. "I got a text from one of the doctors at the hospital, they are all ready to help tomorrow. They already have shifts of volunteers to set up and make sure people are healthy as they search for her, if we get to that point. They offered to come here tonight and be with us in case you needed anything, but I told them I would call if I thought you did."

Kendra shook her head. "I only need Calle."

"I know," Tina nodded. "But the offer stands if you want something to help you get some rest, or if I think you need some hydration. I know you're not eating, but at least make sure you're having some water so we can keep you ready for anything."

"I can't be dehydrated, I keep crying."

They all laughed softly, the sound warming the room somehow before a shrill ring came from the phone of one of the FBI agents in the corner. They all stilled and watched as he answered, listening intently before thanking someone and hanging up. He crossed the room in a few strides and stood facing Kendra.

"That was an agent in Boston, they believe they have her in the hotel. They are giving instructions now for breaching the room to the team that will go in." He recited the information quickly, while maintaining eye contact with Kendra. "Your friends arrived, and two of them are insisting they be included in the initial entry. They are working that out now and then going to proceed."

"And they think it's her?" Ben demanded.

"Yes." He nodded as he said the words.

"Is this dangerous?" Kendra wasn't able to form the words and was grateful that Shea had asked.

"It can be, but they are professionals."

"Jake must be trying to be a part of it," Shea said.

"And Dan," Stella said confidently. "Charlie is too young, and Patrick knows he only plays a superhero."

"They could be hurt." Shea had paled at the news, and Stella reached over to hold her hand.

"Jake knows what he's doing. I'm not worried one bit."

Stella may not be worried, but Kendra could see the look on Ben's face and knew he was. Her stomach rolled at the thought of her daughter and Dan being at the center of something so dangerous, and a sob escaped. She felt her friend's arms go around her, offering strength she couldn't find within herself.

Time seemed to stand still as they all sat, clinging to each other in one way or another. The second agent came to stand nearby, both checking their phones constantly for updates. Zoe emerged from the kitchen to stand behind Kendra, placing a hand on her shoulder to let her know that she was there. Terror ripped through her body at the thought of armed men breaking down a door to get to her baby, and at the thought that Dan was putting himself in harm's way for her. It was difficult to even breathe through the fear, it had such a vice on her.

"Slow and steady," Tina's voice encouraged in her ear. "Nice slow breaths. You're going to be okay. We have you. Focus on one small thing, we can't have you passing out now."

Her fingers found the string bracelet on her wrist that Calle had made and proudly presented her with. Pulling it out from beneath her sleeve, she forced herself to focus on the small beads her daughters' fingers had strung on. The pink and purple one that she had declared was her favorite was at the top, and she focused all her energy on that one bead, trying to force all other thoughts out of her head. Her breathing slowed so she felt like she was finally getting oxygen into her lungs, and the anxiety that threatened to overtake her was held at bay.

Then her phone rang, Dan's name showing on the screen, and everything stopped again.

Chapter 31

"Listen to me carefully, okay?" Jake said firmly as they ran to the elevator that would take them to the twelfth floor, where Brad's room was located. "You need to stay behind me at all times. I will do my best to make sure we're not in the line of fire, but things can go sideways. We're going to stay low to the ground, and you're going to listen to everything I say from here on out."

Dan nodded, then grunted agreement when Jake didn't look satisfied with the nod. "I get it."

"No, you don't. That's why you're going to be behind me the entire time." Jakes eyes met his. "Promise me."

Dan could see his brother's fear, and it had nothing to do with facing gunfire again. Jake was terrified of putting his brother in danger, or to see him as he had seen so many soldiers in his years serving. "I promise. I will do everything you tell me to. I'll stand all the way down the hall if that would make you feel better, I just need to be close enough for when she comes out."

Jake nodded. "Good. Down the hall is even better."

They exited to the floor at the same time the rest of the squad arrived on the floor in the other elevators. Hotel staff remained at the elevator doors, security inside keeping them locked on the floor. The hotel staff had moved the guests from the room next to Brad and directly across the hall earlier in the night at the FBI's urging, so they didn't need to clear any rooms before going into the one where Calle was. Dan listened impatiently as the lead agent went through the plan one last time, assigning everyone a task and telling Jake to remain in the hall.

They followed the team down the hall, watching as half disappeared into the connecting room. Jake pointed silently down the hall, and Dan half ran to the other end, then turned to look back at his brother. A hand signal indicated that Jake wanted him to be on the ground, so Dan squatted down, half inside the door to the ice room. Jake gave him a thumbs up before lowering himself against a room door diagonal from Brad's room.

Seconds later, Dan heard the thunder of the battering ram and the shouts as the room was entered. He held his breath, eyes never leaving his brother as the chaos erupted. The adrenaline was coursing through his veins, thundering in his ears, making it difficult to hear if any gunfire rang out. He startled as he saw Jake leap to his feet and run towards the room, and he called out his brother's name without even hearing it leave his lips A second later, he saw Agent Rodriguez exit the room, holding a child wrapped in a blanket and handing her to Jake. He sprinted down the hall towards them.

"I've got you, Calle. It's me, Jake. Charlie's dad. I'm right here." Dan could hear Jake reassuring Calle as he ran towards them. "Here's Dan."

Dan accepted the half-asleep child from his brother as they continued down the hall towards the elevator, tears running down his face. He pressed his face into her hair as she hugged him, crying softly. "Dan, I want my mommy."

"I know, baby, I know. She wants you too. We're going home." The agent in the elevator signaled for them to enter and hit the button for the lobby.

"That was really scary. There were so many people, and so much noise. My ears hurt," Calle's tear-streaked gaze met his absolute trust that in him.

"I know it was scary, but it's all over now."

"He said he was my dad. That we were going to spend the weekend together and that mom was happy about it. But then he wouldn't let me talk to her."

"We will have to interview her downstairs," the agent said quietly to Dan.

He nodded that he understood but kept his attention on Calle. "We'll explain it all to you. The most important thing is that you're safe and going home to your mom."

"And you'll stay with me? The whole time?" Her arms tightened around his neck as she asked.

"You won't be able to get rid of me."

"You too?" She looked at Jake as she asked.

"I'm all yours, kiddo. You're safe with us, we won't leave you." Jake looked shaken, and Dan made a note to get Patrick to check on him as soon as they got downstairs. The incident may have triggered his PTSD, and Dan didn't want him to have a major setback on his account.

They emerged from the elevator and were shuffled right into the ballroom, with hotel staff agape as they came out with the little girl. The police and agents in the ballroom allowed them to enter without being swarmed, which Dan appreciated.

Calle spotted Charlie immediately as he popped out of his chair and ran towards them. "Charlie!"

"Calle, I'm so happy to see you." He reached over and hugged her, and Dan felt her weight shift as she lunged into Charlie's arms.

Patrick was there suddenly as well, dropping a kiss on her head and patting her back. As Charlie sat down with her, the three brothers stood staring at each other.

"I can't thank you guys enough," Dan started to say.

"There is no need for that," Patrick said. "Seeing her, that's all we need."

Jake nodded silently.

"You okay?" Dan asked quietly so only Patrick could overhear.

"I will be."

"Patrick—"

"Got him. You go be with Calle, I can see them ready to swarm in." Patrick slung an arm around Jake and led him to a quiet corner, where they sat huddled together. Charlie's eyes followed his father as he went.

"Is he okay?"

"Yes, I think it just triggered a little something. Just give him a minute, I think he'll be okay." Dan pulled Calle onto his lap as he sat down, freeing Charlie to move if he wanted.

"I'll just bring him some water," the teen declared as he stood. "Be right back, Calle."

Dan held a hand up to ward off the approaching agents. "Let me call her mother, and then we can talk."

They nodded and stepped back, notepads in hand.

Calle sipped from a bottle of orange juice as he pulled his phone out, pulling up Kendra's name and hitting call before turning the speaker on and putting it on the table in front of him.

"Dan?" Kendra's voice came through the phone, sounding as frantic as he knew she felt.

"Mama, I miss you." Calle started to cry, and Dan hugged her to his chest.

"I've got her, Kendra. She's fine."

The sobs that came through the phone matched those of Calle, and he saw hotel staffers wiping their eyes. It took a few minutes of crying and reassuring noises to get Calle to settle down enough to hear what Kendra was saying through the phone.

"Oh, my baby, I can't wait to have you home. Dan is going to take good care of you and bring you straight back to me."

Calle looked at Dan with the trust only found in a child. "I know he will. I want to come right now."

"We have to just talk to these nice officers," Dan replied. "Then we can go to the airport and go home."

"On a plane?" Calle's eyes bugged slightly at the news.

"Yes, Patrick got us our very own plane to come and get you."

"Wow." She picked up a cookie, suddenly seeming much improved. "That will be okay. As long as I get to see my mama soon."

"Kendra, do you want to stay on speaker while they talk to her? Or do you trust me with this?"

"Yes, I trust you. Please just get home as soon as possible." Kendra's voice muffled for a minute and then came back. "Is Jake okay? Both of you? We heard you were insisting that you go up with the officers."

"Yes, we're good. I'll have Jake call Shea as soon as he is free." He looked to where Jake was sitting, drinking from a water bottle and looking a little less pale than he had a few minutes before.

"Call when you're on your way. We're going to meet you in Burlington," Ben's voice came through the speaker.

"Sure thing. I'll call you soon." He hesitated before disconnecting, thinking of the room full of people in front of him and those surrounding Kendra before deciding he didn't care. "Kendra, you should know I'm never letting either of you out of my sight again. I love you. I'll see you soon."

Her strangled laugh came through the phone and was a salve to his soul. "I can't wait to see you attending first grade with her. I love you too. So much. Thank you for doing this."

He hung up and signaled Agent Rodriguez, who had just come back into the room. "Can we get this taken care of so I can get her home to her mom?"

"Typically, we have to go through some steps, since you're not family. But I have my people on the ground in Windsor Peak getting her mom to sign off on you bringing her home instead of us doing it, and obviously I trust Jake." She sat at the table, shifting so the gun at her hip was out of Calle's line of sight. "I just need to talk with Calle, and I can send you home. I will likely be up to see her again tomorrow, once I get a little sleep myself."

Dan held Calle as she recounted the last fourteen hours that she had been with her father. He held his breath, fearful of any bad experiences she would share, but it all sounded innocent. A long road trip, lunch, and a visit to a department store where he had purchased her some clothes and toys before checking in to the hotel. She had thought she was on a fun weekend, and only got upset when she wanted to call Kendra to say goodnight. It broke Dan's heart to hear that she had cried herself to sleep, missing her mom, making his resolve stronger to keep her safe and away from Brad forever.

As his brothers and nephew rejoined them, ready to depart Boston, he had the chance to ask the agent a question of his own. "He's in custody?"

She paused and glanced at Calle before answering quietly. "He's down."

"Down—" Awareness popped into his head before he could elaborate on the question further, and she nodded that he was correct.

"He was prepared for us, and we had no choice. It was quick and we were able to maintain her safety and keep her from seeing anything," the agent told him. "Fortunately, he was a little slow on the uptake, so I was able to get to her first. I shielded her myself, although I know anyone in the room would have done the same."

"I can't thank you enough, Agent Rodriquez. There are no words," he stammered.

"It's the job. I'm happy this had a good outcome," she smiled at Calle. "Now, let's get you home to your mom and then we can talk tomorrow. Okay?"

"Yes," she smiled at the agent. "We have a Christmas tree, but Dan's is even bigger."

"Maybe I'll get to see it tomorrow," the agent said. She shook Dan's hand and looked across the room. "Let me just make sure the paperwork is in order and you can be on the way."

Chapter 32

Waiting for the plane to touch down on the tarmac was excruciating. Even though she knew Calle was safe with Dan, she wanted her daughter in her arms immediately. And then she was never letting go again, which might cause some problems when Calle was a teenager, but they would cross that bridge when they got there.

Ben paced behind her as they watched the lights of the plane approach, the airport having been persuaded by Patrick's team to reopen to allow the plane to land. Otherwise, they would have needed to drive back, or wait until morning, and everyone was too impatient for that to happen. The air traffic controller had been well compensated, according to Ben, as well as the ground crew that had to come in unexpectedly. Apparently, there was also a risk of a fine for landing after hours, but Stella assured Kendra that Patrick had been firm in telling them to get it done no matter the expense.

When the plane finally came to a stop in front of them, Kendra ran to where the door would open. As it lowered, she saw Dan standing in the doorway, lit from the lights in the cabin. He was holding Calle, who looked to be sound asleep on his chest. The sobs overtook her, and suddenly she couldn't stand any longer, dropping to her knees as he rushed down the stairs to her.

"She's okay. Look, Kendra, she's fine. She's sleeping."

Jake had followed Dan down the stairs and gently took the sleeping child from his brother so Dan could lift Kendra to her feet. "I was so scared," she sobbed.

"I know, but it's all over now. We can go home. She's safe."

"Are you sure she's okay?"

"Yes," he nodded. "The paramedics looked her over, offered to bring her to the hospital. But she said nothing bad happened, she just got sad she couldn't talk to you. She thought you knew where she was and had no idea anything was wrong. He didn't touch her, everyone asked in a hundred different ways to be sure."

"Where is he?"

Dan hesitated, then responded quietly. "He had reached for a gun when they went into the room, was able to get one shot off. Calle was already covered by Agent Rodriquez, who knew Jake and had promised to keep her safe. Fortunately, he fired at one of the other agents, not in Calle's direction, and only got him in the vest so he's fine. I don't think Calle even knew that he was shot, she just heard a lot of noise."

"Is he dead?"

"Yes."

"Oh." The air escaped her lungs suddenly. "I don't know how to feel about that. It feels wrong to feel so relieved, but I do."

"You're both safe now. He can't hurt you anymore." He gathered her in his arms. "It's okay to feel whatever you're feeling."

"She'll never know what it's like to have a dad," she whispered.

He pulled back and looked down at her, a frown on his face. "I know I'm not her dad, but she'll never wonder because I'll always be there."

"You're a million times better than her dad, I shouldn't have said that."

"Kendra, you don't have to edit yourself around me. Your emotions are running high. Let's get her buckled in the car and get you home. Do you mind coming to the house with us?"

"Of course not." She slid into the back of Jake's SUV, which Shea had driven to the airport. Calle was gently placed next to her, and her sleepy head found its way to Kendra's arm. She pulled her daughter in close and kissed the top of her head, burying her face in the brown curls. *Never, ever letting go.*

Dan carried a sleeping Calle into the house, and Kendra pointed to her room, indicating that he should put her in that bed. "I'm not letting her out of my sight," she whispered. He kissed both of them on the head and then left the room, closing the door quietly behind him.

Kendra spent the few hours left before sunrise sleeping sporadically, waking in a start to make sure her daughter was still next to her. She finally gave up on sleep when the sun started peeping through the curtains, content to just study Calle's face as she slept. By the time the little girl woke, every eye lash and freckle were committed to memory, and Kendra had shed more than one tear in gratitude at how it had all ended.

"Morning, mama." She stretched and yawned, eyes squinting, to look around the room. "How come I slept in your room?"

"Well, we're at the Burrows' house, so it's the guest room. But I wanted to be close to you, I missed you when you weren't here."

"I missed you too. So much. I didn't know that you weren't coming with us until I had to go to sleep. He kept telling me that he was my dad and taking me to meet you for a surprise."

"Was he nice to you?" she held her breath, scared of the answer.

Called shrugged. "He was okay, I guess. He didn't really talk to me much, but he bought me candy and the snacks I wanted. And at the hotel they brought us chicken fingers right to the room, and I got to eat them on the bed while I watched a movie."

"You weren't scared?"

"No," she studied Kendra. "Were you?"

"I was. I didn't like not having you with me."

"I'm back now," she smiled. "And it was really fun to fly with Charlie. Did you know the plane was just for us?"

"I did," she swiped away tears again. "That was really nice of Patrick to do."

"I'll make sure to say thank you to him. I think I fell asleep."

"You did, Dan carried you here when we got back."

"I don't remember that."

"It was really, really late. Way past your bedtime."

Called yawned again. "I'm still tired."

"Do you want to try and sleep some more?" Kendra pulled the blanket up a little more, covering them.

"No," Calle said finally. "I'm hungry. And I want to see the tree."

"Okay, let's get dressed and we can go down." Kendra saw the clothes that someone had put on the bureau before they got back and sent a silent thank you to Stella. She must have had the foresight to grab some things from the apartment to bring back to the house.

Ben and Stella were at the kitchen table when they came down, sipping cups of coffee.

"Good morning," Kendra greeted them. "I'm surprised you're both up so early, it was a late night."

"It was," Stella smiled at them. "But we're so used to being up early. I'm sure we will have a good nap later."

"Is anyone else up yet?" Kendra watched as Calle gave each of them a hug and then slipped into the living room to stare at the tree.

"Not yet. I was just about to start some bacon, that will get them all up." Stella stood, pausing to glance back at Kendra. "I may have heard Dan moving around, if you want to go check. She's okay here with us."

"I said I was never letting her out of my sight again," she said quietly.

Ben set his coffee mug down and looked at her. "He's gone, honey. You can relax. She's safe."

His firm tone was the reassurance she needed to slip back upstairs and into the dim light of Dan's room. He must have gone into the shower; his bed was empty, and the light was on in the bathroom. She looked at the pictures strewn around his room of him and his brothers, and some of their old pictures that Stella must have pulled out recently. Their prom picture made her laugh, and a picture of them with Jake and Jenna pulled at her heart.

She turned as the door opened, and Dan came in with a towel slung around his hips. "Oh, I didn't expect you to be up so early."

"Me neither," she admitted, enjoying the view. "I guess this just made it worthwhile."

"I know we never got a chance to talk about what happened on Thursday, but I wanted to say again that I'm sorry I didn't tell you what JJ told me. I don't know if that would have changed things yesterday, but I wasn't right to have kept that from you."

"No more secrets. Ever. Okay?"

"You have my word." He kissed her and started walking her backwards towards the bed until she laughed and ducked away from him. "Your dad and Stella know that I just came up here,

I'm not going down to breakfast and having them give us the look."

"What look?"

"The one that says they know exactly what we were just up to."

"We're consenting adults," he argued.

"Yes, but even if we were married, I would worry about them. It's still your dad's house."

"We should do that," he said.

"Do what?"

"Get married."

"Dan Burrows, you did not just say that while you're mostly naked and trying to get me into bed." She put her hands on her hips and glared at him.

"Hang on, I'll get some clothes on." He let go of her and rushed to his bureau, and she laughed as he tried to pull on boxers.

"I'm going back down to the kitchen; I just came to tell you we were awake and having coffee." She ran out of the room, not wanting him to see how rattled she was by him throwing the subject of marriage out so casually. The word yes had been right on the tip of her tongue, and she needed time to really determine if that was what she wanted or if it was an emotional hangover from the last twenty-four hours.

Stella was bustling in the kitchen, making what smelled like an amazing breakfast as Ben sipped his coffee over the newspaper. She made her way into the living room, where Calle sat on the floor by the tree, studying the presents underneath.

"Mama," she whispered. "Some of these are for me!"

"I'm not surprised, everyone here loves you a whole lot."

"They have a big chimney here too," she continued. "I think maybe it would be easier for Santa to find me here."

"We have some time to decide, so let's save that discussion for when I have more energy." They both turned as Dan came into the room, hair still wet and carrying a steaming mug.

"Do you need a refill?" he asked, pointing to her cup.

"No, I'm good for now," she replied. "I think I drank enough coffee yesterday for the whole month."

"She seems unaffected," he said quietly, looking at Calle.

"Slept fine, still doesn't really seem rattled by it at all. I'll probably still have her talk to a counselor, just to be safe."

"Good plan."

Jake and Shea entered from the back door, sending a swirl of cold air through the house. Shea called out a greeting to everyone as Jake headed straight for the pot of coffee. Kendra noticed that he seemed a little off and turned to Dan.

"Is Jake okay?"

"I think so," he nodded slowly. "It rattled him for sure, triggered his PTSD. But I think once he came down from hearing the gun shots and all of it, he was doing alright. Coming home to Shea was probably the biggest help for him. And I'm sure he'll talk to his counselor this week."

Kendra watched as Jake glanced in her direction, then tilted his head at Shea indicating he was going into the living room.

"Jake," Kendra said. "I can't possibly thank you enough. I owe you my life."

"You don't owe me anything," he said gruffly. "I know if the roles were reversed and you could help Charlie, you would, no questions asked."

"I hope it didn't cause you any issues with your PTSD," she said.

"Nothing I can't deal with. I knew what I was going in to, and if I thought it would set me back, I would have stayed here. But Patrick and Charlie helped talk me down, and my therapist will have something to work with this week," he shot her a small smile. "Plus, I never know what will trigger it. I could have been fine with this and then be in the grocery story when someone drops a box, and I'd be on the ground taking cover."

"All the more reason that I appreciate what you did." She crossed the room and hugged him quickly, fighting back tears. "And I'm so glad to call you a friend."

"Right back at you," he whispered, hugging her tight. "I'll be fine. I'm just glad she's home."

"Me too," she said. Right now, in this warm house, with the gigantic Christmas tree lit up and the smells of breakfast floating through the air, it was hard to believe what had happened in the last day. She looked at Jake and saw understanding in his eyes. "Makes you really think about what's valuable, doesn't it?"

"Sure does." He nodded in agreement before slinging an arm around her shoulder and leading her toward the kitchen. "Now let's see if we can sneak some bacon, because that's on my list of priorities."

Chapter 33

"Can we make a quick stop on the way to grab the suits for the wedding?" Dan poked his head into Patrick's room, where his brother was getting dressed.

"Sure," he replied. "Where?"

"Jewelry store."

"Wait—" Patrick yelled as Dan closed the door and jogged down the stairs. Jake was looking at his phone in the kitchen, waiting for both of his brothers.

"About time," he said as he put the phone down.

"I've been ready, it's Patrick who's late."

"You weren't down here, so you're late. This week is important," Jake reminded him.

"I know. Obviously, I'm happy for you," Dan said. "Mind if we make a quick stop on the way?"

"Why are we going to a jewelry store?" Patrick demanded as he thundered down the stairs.

"We're what?" Jake asked. "Shea and I already picked up the rings."

"I happen to need something," Dan replied.

"What?" Their voices rang together, both staring at him.

"Let's just go, I'll tell you when we get there."

He managed to get them both out the door and into the car without giving into their pestering questions. Flipping the radio on and turning the volume up, he tried to block them out.

"He must have screwed up big," Patrick said to Jake.

"You're right, but why jewelry? Kendra's not really the type."

"Maybe it's a Christmas present? Something for Calle?"

They were both trying to catch some response from him as they threw out more and more absurd guesses. Finally, Jake sighed, glancing out the window. "I guess he'll finally tell us when he's ready to propose."

Dan glanced at him quickly, and Patrick hooted from the backseat. "Oh my God, that's it. You're going to propose?"

"You two are the worst."

"You know I'm getting married in three days, right?" Jake asked.

"I do."

"No, that's his line." Patrick swatted him on the shoulder.

"You're not going to propose at my wedding, are you?"

"No, I'd never do that."

"Then when?"

"Tonight," he admitted.

"Like in a few hours?" Jake stared at him. "What the hell is going on?"

Dan shrugged. "I've lived too many years without her, I don't want to spend even one more day without being fully committed to her and Calle."

"Are you planning to get married tomorrow?" Patrick joked, and Jake grew still as he stared at Dan.

"Is this a competition? Trying to beat me to it?"

"Dude, you've already been married," Dan reminded him. "There's no way I could ever beat you in the race to get married first. I was just inspired by you, and when everything happened with Calle, it really solidified for me that I need to be with them forever. We won't get married before you, I promise."

He pulled into the parking lot and waited before turning the car off. "If you want me to wait, I will. I don't want to ruin your week or make your wedding about me."

"I appreciate that," Jake said gruffly. "Let me think about it, alright? I'm happy for you, I don't mean for it to seem like I'm not. It's been a long time coming and I'm glad you two have finally figured things out."

"Mind if I at least pick out a ring?" Dan pointed toward the store.

"As long as it's not bigger than Shea's," Jake grumbled.

"We're both screwed when Patrick finally settles down, anyway."

"True," Jake bumped Patrick with his shoulder as they walked. "But that doesn't seem like it's happening anytime soon."

"Hey, I offered to help with the ring for Shea, and I'm happy to help you too, Dan."

"We can't take a handout from our loaded brother for an engagement ring," Jake rolled his eyes.

"But we could let him pay other stuff for us," Dan suggested.

"Not a bad idea," Jake said. "I could use new skis."

"*Santa Claus is coming to town,*" Patrick started singing as they walked.

The store was quiet when they entered, being early on a weekday. The clerk immediately recognized Patrick and rushed over to help them, offering to lock the door so they could have the store to themselves. Patrick looked around the empty space and told her he didn't expect it to be a problem, and they started looking in the cases.

"What do you think she'll like?" Jake asked.

"Something simple, I think."

Shea's ring featured a large princess cut stone on a band with diamonds embedded in it, making the ring as sparkly as she was. It suited her perfectly, but Dan guessed Kendra would prefer something even simpler. He honed in on the solitaire rings, seeing the clerk's disappointed expression when Patrick indicated she should go with him.

"Anything in particular you're looking for?" she asked.

"Something unique, but simple. If that exists."

"Let me call my manager, we have something in the safe that might be perfect." She walked back to an open door and spoke to someone inside, then crossed back to Dan. "He'll be right out. Is there anything else you wanted to see?"

"She also has a daughter, and I'd like to get her something as well. But I don't know that a ring would be appropriate."

"We have some nice necklaces that might work, that way you could replace the chain as she gets older." She pulled a tray out of the case, showing him the heart shaped necklaces.

He scanned them all and stopped when he saw three hearts intertwined, embedded with small diamonds on the center heart. "This one, please," he said as he pointed.

"Do you want me to check the price?" she asked as she reached for it.

"No, that's the right one," he replied as the manager came out of the office.

"Hi," the manager greeted him. "I understand you're looking for something special for an engagement?"

"Yes, I'd like to find something that will suit her. No frills, but beautiful."

"I just had a diamond come in that I was about to set, so if you like the stone, we can look at settings to decide. The stone is three carats, which sounds like a lot, but it's a radiant diamond so they tend to be on the smaller side. It's very beautiful and extremely rare that we have something like this on hand." He stopped talking as Jake and Patrick approached.

"Nice to see you again," Jake shook his hand. "Please make sure to give my brother something that won't have my fiancée upset with me."

The manager chuckled and shook his head. "Your ring was also very unique, but it has more flair than this. I think both of your ladies would be happy, and no one would be disappointed."

"Going to make it hard on you when the time comes," Jake said, slapping Patrick on his back.

"I'll manage," he laughed.

The manager brought out the stone and Dan nodded instantly. "That's the one. It's perfect."

"Let me show you the bands that I thought would work with it," he replied, reaching into another case. "This is a solid white gold, no frills. I have another that has diamonds embedded, but I thought that might be too much. Or this last one, also white gold, but with the infinity symbol on either side to add a nice touch."

"Yes, that one." Dan was confident, seeing the band and diamond put together, he knew it was exactly what he wanted for Kendra.

"If you can give me a half hour, I can have it set for you. Feel free to browse, or if you want to come back later and get it, that's fine."

"We were about to go pick up our suits for Jake's wedding," Dan said. "Why don't we go to the tailor and then we will stop here after. Would you like my credit card information now?"

The manager shook his head. "When you get back is fine. Let's make sure you like it first, and you have my word that I won't sell it to anyone while you're gone."

As they tried on their suits for the wedding, Dan couldn't get his mind off the ring. Jake and Patrick had to yell at him twice to get his attention when they were looking at ties, and Jake finally laughed at him. "Patrick, we're just going to get what you want and he can deal with it. He's in another world right now."

"What do you want?" Patrick asked Jake, pointing to the options.

"I'm wearing my uniform, so it's really up to you."

"As much as I want to make Dan wear something crazy, let's just go with red. It will match your colors, and the Christmas decorations. Plus, our suits are navy, so we won't stand out next to you." Patrick grabbed three red ties from the display. "Charlie already tried his suit on, right?"

Jake nodded. "I had him do it when we were in town, I knew we wouldn't get back in time with his schedule."

"What if she says no," Dan blurted out.

They both turned and stared at him. "Why would she?" Jake finally asked.

"I don't know. Because I'm an idiot and walked away from her before."

"That was a long time ago, she's clearly forgiven you and moved on." Jake handed him the suit he was meant to try on. "You guys seem solid. Stop freaking yourself out when there's nothing to freak out about."

"What he said," Patrick yelled from his dressing room.

He was nervous as he entered the jewelry store for the second time, but seeing the ring made all his misgivings float away. It was perfect, and represented their past and their future, and his dedication to be with her for the rest of their lives. The necklace for Calle was placed in a silver box with pink lining, which he knew she would love. Feeling secure, he signed the credit card slip without looking, shook everyone's hands, and walked to the car excited about the future.

***

Two hours later, as he sat at the desk in his childhood bedroom staring at the ring, Jake knocked on the door. "Can I come in?"

Dan nodded, and Jake crossed to sit on the bed. "I talked to Shea," he said. "And she told me I was an idiot. Of course, your proposal has nothing to do with us, and the more love the better. Matter of fact, we should probably see if Patrick wants to propose to the girl at the gym, or Zoe, so we can just do it all at once."

They both laughed and then Dan met his brother's eyes. "Are you sure? Because I can wait."

"I'm sure. You guys are meant to be together, and I don't want to be the one holding things up. Shea asked if you could do it immediately so we can celebrate tonight, but no pressure."

"On it," he grabbed the ring box and the box containing the necklace. "Thanks."

"Good luck," Jake yelled as he ran down the stairs.

Parking behind the restaurant, he realized he hadn't thought about what to say. Shooting off the cuff had been a strength of his in law school, and he needed to hope the skill still existed. Somehow the words had to come out just right and convince her that he was worth this risk. He climbed out of the car and headed inside, resolving not to leave until he was engaged.

"Hey, Zoe. Is Kendra around?"

"She just went upstairs," the chef responded.

"Thanks," he called over his shoulder. The shower was running when he got to the apartment, so he took the time to compose himself. He had about a half hour before Calle's bus would come, and he wanted to have this moment with Kendra privately.

The shower switched off, so he crossed to the bathroom door and knocked softly. "Just wanted you to know I was out here so I wouldn't scare you."

The door came open, and she stood wrapped in a towel. "Still scared me, but thanks. What are you doing here? I thought you guys had wedding stuff to do."

"We finished a little while ago. I needed to talk to you," he explained.

Her face paled. "Is it bad news?"

"No," he shook his head. "Not at all. The opposite."

"You're going back to New York," she guessed with a flat voice.

"No, not even close. I told you I was not leaving, now or ever. Unless you want to. But I don't." He closed his eyes and told his mouth to stop talking. "Do you want to get dressed and we can start over? I don't want to do this when you're mostly naked."

"Wait, what?" She stared at him with a confused expression, and shrugged when he pushed her towards her bedroom door. "Give me a minute."

He paced in her family room waiting for her, unsure of where he should be or what he should be doing. He thought about waiting, taking her for a fancy dinner and doing it right, but the ring was burning a hole in his pocket.

"Okay, what's up?" She crossed to him, wearing jeans and a soft grey sweater, her hair wet and feet bare. Looking like the woman he wanted to see every morning for the rest of his life.

Without thinking, he dropped to a knee in front of her and took her hand. "I love you. I never thought it was true that two people could each be half of a whole, but that's what it feels like. You're my other half. You inspire me every day with your strength, and grace, and the love you give to everyone around you. I feel lucky to even be around you, never mind be man enough to be loved by you. You are everything to me, and I can only hope that one day I'll be able to give back to you a quarter of what you give to me every day.

I love Calle. I don't want to live one more second without you two as my family. The last few months have reminded me of how incredible we're together, and how lucky I'm that you even give me the time of day. Getting to know Calle, and especially what happened, has made me want to be there for her in every way possible. I know I screwed up in the past, and I'm sure I'll make mistakes again, but there is no one else for me. Please marry me."

She had her free hand over her mouth, tears brimming and love shining in her eyes. When he took the ring from his pocket she gasped, the tears falling freely as she nodded.

"Say yes, Kendra. I need to hear you say it," he whispered.

"Yes," she sobbed. "Yes, I will marry you. I love you."

He slid the ring onto her finger and caught her as she launched herself at him, and soon they were a mess of tears, kisses, and laughter. "I thought I was going to have to persuade you," he finally told her.

"Oh, I probably should have played hard to get," she replied. "This ring is amazing though, so all other thoughts went out of my head."

"Wait, so you said yes to the ring, not me?"

"It was a major selling point," she kissed him. "But mainly because you know me well enough to get something I would love."

They heard the bus horn outside the building and hurried to their feet. "Should we tell her?" Kendra asked anxiously.

"I actually have something for her, will you let me do it?"

"Sure," she said, and the absolute trust she had in him went right to his heart. They paused listening to the footsteps running up the stairs before Calle burst through the door.

"Hi! Everyone at school was talking about my trip, and I told them all about it. The police and the private plane and how I had to meet with the people yesterday. I was the most popular person today," she announced.

"That's great," Dan cleared his throat. "Calle, can you come in here for a minute? I have something to ask you."

She dropped her backpack and ran to him, looking up with curiosity. "Sure."

He knelt down so he was eye to eye with her and then cleared his throat again, glancing at Kendra to ease his nerves. Somehow this was harder than asking Kendra, and Calle was only six. "Calle, I asked your mom already, but I'd like to ask you too. I love you both a whole lot, and I want to be part of your family. Would it be okay with you if I married your mom?"

Calle studied him, and then glanced over at her mom. "I think that would be good. You make her smile, and you're really nice to me. Plus, I really like your family, it's fun to be there with all of them, and now I can be a part of it. Does this mean you'll be my dad?"

Kendra dropped down next to him and took her hand. "Well, Dan technically—"

"I'd be honored," he replied. "If you both agree, I would love to adopt Calle and officially be her dad."

"Does that mean I can call you dad now?"

"Maybe we should wait—"

"Yes," he replied over Kendra's voice. "Whenever you're ready, that would mean the world to me. And I'll work on making it official. Deal?"

"Deal," she nodded solemnly. "Daddy."

Choking back tears, he pulled the box from his pocket and handed it to her. "I got you this, it isn't a ring like your mom's, but it is something you can wear to show that we will always be together."

She pulled open the ribbon and smiled when she saw the necklace. "I love it." She hugged him tight, and then handed him the necklace. "Help me put this on, please."

He took the tiny clasp between his fingers, seeing his hands shaking. Kendra tried to take over, but he felt that it was important that he be the one to hang this around her tiny neck, so he finally pulled it together enough to close the clasp. She turned to him, beaming as she looked down at it.

"Can we go to your house and tell everyone that I'm related to them?"

"Calle, maybe we should—"

"Let's go," Dan replied.

"Is this what my future holds? You two conspiring against me?" Kendra laughed as they both looked at each other and nodded.

"I've never had a dad before, but everyone at school says that dad's let their little girls get away with anything," Calle told them as they started walking to the car.

"Maybe not everything," Dan suggested.

"But we have a lot of time to make up for," Calle told him seriously. "This is my first Christmas with a dad."

"Oh, we have created a monster," Kendra laughed. "Let's get through today, kiddo. Then we can revise the Christmas list if you feel the need."

Dan knew that whatever she put on the list, he would somehow have to find over the next week. And he couldn't wait to do so.

Chapter 34

They entered the house to find a crowd inside, delectable smells in the air, and the spirit of a party. Kendra was stunned to see Janet and Ron Holme's in the kitchen, chatting with Shea's parents. Her own parents were in the corner, talking to Ben, who was pouring glasses of champagne for everyone.

Shea caught sight of them and grinned, rushing over to Kendra. "Did you say yes?"

"What if I didn't ask yet?"

"Oh shoot." Shea shot a panicked look at Dan, who laughed.

"I said yes," Kendra replied, pulling her hand from Dan's to show the ring.

The room erupted in cheers, which doubled when Calle pulled out her necklace and announced she had also said yes. "I have a daddy now," she told the room.

When the hugging and showing off the ring died down, Kendra found herself tucked at Dan's side as Ben raised a glass for a toast. "I want to congratulate both of my sons for finding women who are able to manage them," he laughed. "But in all seriousness, witnessing Jake and Shea, and Dan and Kendra, fall in love has been a lot of fun for Stella and me. Even inspired us to finally tie the knot, so we know romance is in the air. We all wish you many years of happiness, health and love together. Jake and Shea, we can't wait to see you get married in a few days."

"Can we get married then too?" Calle's voice chimed in.

"No, honey, it's Jake and Shea's day," Kendra said quietly.

"I don't see why not," Shea shrugged. "I don't mind sharing the spotlight, and everyone we love seems to be in town already. If you guys want to double up, we don't have a problem with that."

"Shea, that is so incredibly generous, but we couldn't possibly—"

"It's not an imposition," Jake inserted. "We would be honored. Sharing the day with my brother can only make it more special."

"But it's in two days." Kendra's mind went blank at the thought of all they would need to do to prepare.

"I have a designer in town with dresses, plus a photographer and videographer on the way." Patrick told her. "And a hair stylist and makeup artist for the big day, as a gift to Shea."

"Oh, Patrick, thank you," Shea said.

"We already have suits," Jake told them. "The church and the reception are all set. I don't see a problem."

Kendra turned to stare at Dan, who shared the same shocked expression she was sure her face had. "What do you think?"

He grinned, suddenly snapping out of his daze. "If we can make it work, then let's do it. I can't wait to make you Mrs. Burrows. And start making little Burrows."

"Ewwww," Charlie yelled.

"If you're sure," Kendra looked at Shea, who beamed and nodded. "Okay, I guess we're getting married this weekend."

"We need to plan a rehearsal dinner! How could we have forgotten?" Stella fretted.

"We can do it here," Ben replied. "Friday night."

"Friday? That's not a lot of time to prepare, but I'll figure it out."

"Do something easy," Ben told her. "Just make twenty lasagnas, that will feed everyone."

"Ben Burrows, did you really just suggest that?" She put her hands on her hips and stared at him in mock outrage.

"I'm sure Zoe will be happy to help," Kendra offered.

"I will call her tomorrow. Twenty lasagnas," she said under her breath. "He's lucky I love him."

"If someone doesn't ask me soon to be their best man, I'm going to lose it," Patrick declared.

"Please be my best man, Parick," Dan grinned.

"I'll squeeze it in. Thank you for asking."

"I have Christine and my sister," Shea said. "I couldn't have decided between them. Will you have Julie and Tina?"

"I will have to ask them, but they were in my first wedding. The only person I know for sure has to be included is Calle," she smiled at her daughter. "I think flower girl might be the perfect role."

Calle jumped up and down and clapped her hands. "I get a special dress too, right?"

"You do," Dan said. "If Patrick's friends don't have something, we will figure it out."

"They can get it," Patrick responded confidently.

Wedding talk swirled around the kitchen, everyone excited to help plan. Kendra's head swirled, but every time her eyes met Dan's, she knew they were making the right decision. After wasting years, she didn't want to wait one more minute to start her life committed to him, and being able to say he was hers.

***

The next morning, Kendra and Shea dropped Calle off at school and headed to the Inn to meet Patrick's friends. "I'm so glad I was able to take a few days off," Shea said. "I never could have gotten everything done if I had to work today and tomorrow."

"I know, I'm so glad I have Linda and Zoe to manage the restaurant. Dan and I have to run to get a marriage license today, and I'm sure there are a million other things to do."

"Most of it Patrick handled. We owe him huge when he gets married," Shea laughed.

"He's so generous, and it's certainly helpful that he can just make a call and have people appear with designer gowns."

Kendra parked and they climbed from the car, looking at each other nervously before going into the Inn. "I can't believe we're doing this," Shea whispered. "Is Stella still meeting us here? It wouldn't feel right to do it with our moms and not her."

"Yes, the boys were going to drop her off on the way to the gym. Then we can all do a girl's lunch after, if we're happy," Kendra said.

"Oh good. I felt bad rushing out this morning when she wasn't ready, but I couldn't sit still one more second."

"I think she plans these things to get time alone with the boys."

"Oh, why didn't I think of that? You're right."

They entered the lobby and found their mothers, along with Janet Holmes, waiting for them. Stella entered a minute after they had finished saying good morning, and the whole group proceeded to the suite number that Patrick had given them. The door was opened by a woman dressed in black, glasses perched on her head and hair pulled into a bun. She was no more than five feet tall, and yet the group of them snapped to silence when she glared.

"Who are the brides?" She gestured for them to walk in, studying them all as they walked.

"We are," Shea linked her arm with Kendra's.

Kendra gazed around the living room, which had been transformed into a dress shop. Racks of gowns in various shades of white, cream and blush pink were in every available space, and a large mirror was set in the middle of the room in front of a small circular stage. Two younger women were steaming gowns in silence, nodding at the group as they entered.

"You all sit there," the woman commanded the older ladies in her faint Italian accent. "I'm Maria, and I will find your dress. First you." She pointed at Shea and then the stage.

Shea hopped onto the stage and Maria walked around her in a circle, then began calling out instructions to the two other women who moved quickly, pulling dresses from the racks and placing them on a smaller rack by the bedroom door.

"Let's go." Maria marched into the bedroom, Shea trotting behind her, shooting a look that crossed between laughter and fear to Kendra as she went. The door closed behind them and Kendra heard as Shea was told to take her clothes off, laughing quietly at the command.

She circled the room, attempting to touch one dress before one of the young girls shook her head quickly and caused her to pull her hand back. Finding the perfect dress seemed impossible without the ability to look at the options, but she went and perched on a chair next to Stella.

When the door opened and Shea walked out, the room gasped. She looked like a princess, wearing a dress in the lightest shade of gold that made her cheeks and eyes glow. The bodice was fitted and strapless, with small jewels encrusted along the waist and the sweetheart neckline. The dress billowed in clouds of white and gold, shimmering with each step she took. Shea stepped onto the stage and caught sight of herself in the mirror, immediately bursting into tears.

"Tissues," Maria snapped. "No tears on the dress."

"I'm sorry," Shea sniffled into a tissue. "It's amazing."

"This is your dress," Maria nodded, studying her from all angles before a kind smile crossed her face. "It was made for you."

Shea nodded happily, wiping at her cheeks. "Mom? Stella? Do you like it?"

Both were crying openly and hugging each other on the couch, nodding their approval.

"Veil?" Maria said it as a question, but it clearly wasn't directed at Shea. One of the young assistants approached with a veil that was clipped to Shea's head. The single layer of tulle was embedded with gold string and fell in a wide swarth as a train behind Shea.

"Oh, it's perfect," Shea said breathlessly.

"Pins," Maria barked. An assistant immediately came forward, dropping to her knees to pin the extra material around the hem. "That will do. Fortunately, the rest fits you perfectly, you're just a little too short."

"I'm, uh. Sorry?" Shea stammered, blushing.

"Not your fault," Maria waved a hand. "You go change now; Lila will help you. And you, come here."

Kendra took Shea's place, feeling self-conscious in her jeans and sweater when Shea had looked so beautiful in the same spot seconds before. Maria did the same slow walk around her, making noises and calling out instructions to the second assistant. When Shea emerged in her regular clothes, Maria snapped her fingers and indicated that Kendra was to follow her.

In the room, the rack of selections had been placed so only Maria could see them all. Shea's dress hung on its rack by the bathroom door, shining in the light and making Kendra question whether anyone would even see her on the wedding day, with Shea next to her. Stripping down to her bra and panties as instructed, she tried to pretend she was in a bathing suit and not uncomfortable to be wearing significantly less clothes than everyone else in the room.

"Put those on," Maria pointed to a pair of heels on the floor.

"I don't walk well in heels," Kendra dared to reply.

Maria studied her. "With your legs, that's a shame. Patrick suspected as much, though. Lila, swap the shoes."

Lila ran to the closet, grabbing a larger box off the floor and pulling out the most beautiful white cowboy boots that Kendra had ever seen. Sliding into them, she decided she could get married in anything if she had them on her feet. Maria studied her, a small smile on her face.

"Yes, this is perfect." She pulled a dress off the rack and walked toward Kendra. "Arms up."

The dress slid over her arms and head, falling in a simple sheath to the ground. She didn't have time to look at it before Maria had turned her around and steered her to the stage, but seeing the tears in her mom's eyes when she walked out had her nearly crying. Shea clapped her hands and smiled, clapping a hand over her mouth after as she seemed to battle back another round of tears.

Kendra gazed at the image in the mirror and couldn't believe it was her. The dress had small shoulder straps and then dipped low, presenting more cleavage than she thought she had. It clung to her torso and hips before spilling into a small pool around her feet. The boots showed clearly through the slit that ran up the front of the dress to mid-thigh. The entire dress was covered in embroidery that kept it from being too simple and caught the light with the different shades of thread. She had never felt more beautiful.

"This is the one," Maria announced. "I am very good at my job."

"It's amazing, thank you."

"Lila, the pearls."

Lila rushed into the other room and came back carrying an elaborate piece that Kendra couldn't see clearly. She gestured for Kendra to lean her head down, and placed it on her like a headband, then fussed with the back. Turning, Kendra realized it was a headpiece that had pearls and something sparkly mixing with her dark hair.

"The hair stylist will do your hair just right for this," Maria told her. "I will send her a picture."

Kendra smiled, happy to have one more decision out of her hands. The idea of a veil had been bothering her without even realizing it, because she wasn't the girly type. Not to mention, it would have brought back memories of her first wedding, and she didn't want any of that on this day. Pulling her thoughts back from Brad, she watched as Maria considered the hemline.

"You're tall, so this is fine. Fits perfect. This was made for you." She offered Kendra a hand to step down. "You two made this very easy for me. I'll do the alterations for the first and help you both get dressed for the big day. Now for the mothers."

Her attention turned to the four older women in the room, who all tried to object.

"I don't need anything," Stella insisted. "I can use a dress that I have."

"Nonsense," Maria said. "Patrick has had all these dresses flown in, and he wants you all to be happy. Don't turn down a gift like this. Who's first?"

They all pointed at Stella, the most likely to accept the gesture. If she refused, Kendra knew they would all do the same. However, she pushed to her feet and next thing they knew, she was sniffling into a tissue looking at herself in the mirror. All four were treated to the same experience, with Janet Hughes trying and failing to insist she wasn't a part of the wedding party before beaming in the dress that Maria had chosen. All six were on cloud nine by the time they were saying their goodbyes to Maria and her staff.

"Thank you so much," Kendra said. "Will you stay and enjoy the wedding with us?"

She shook her head. "That's very kind, but Patrick has arranged for us to fly out immediately. I may be a tyrant to work for most days, but I will get these two home to their families for Christmas and be home to terrorize mine as well. Speaking of children, I will have a dress for your flower girl on the wedding day, don't worry about that. And I have three full racks of black dresses for your wedding party, it will be easier if we don't try to get everyone in the same dress. Any alterations I will make that morning."

Kendra thanked her and the assistants before taking a last look at the dress and boots on their special rack and missing them already. As she stepped out into the living room, everyone was gathering their jackets and purses and saying their goodbyes to Maria and her helper. They all piled out of the room, heading to the dining room at the Inn to have lunch and discuss any other tasks to be accomplished.

Shea sighed, propping her chin on her hand. "I couldn't have even conjured up that dress in my dreams."

"I know what you mean. Somehow, she got me with one look. I would never have figured that out on my own," Kendra admitted.

"You both look amazing. Dan and Jake are lucky men, and they are going to have their socks knocked off," Stella smiled at the thought.

"What else do we need to do?" Kendra asked Shea.

"The florist asked if we could stop quickly now that we have seen our dresses, just to finalize the bouquets. I asked them to keep it very simple, I hope that's okay with you," Shea said.

"Of course. I don't think a big fancy bouquet would work with my dress anyway."

"And honestly, no one is going to be looking at the flowers with you two in those dresses," Kendra's mom laughed.

"I think we're ready," Shea said to Kendra. "Just need our men and the rings, that is."

"Rings," Kendra clapped a hand over her mouth. "Dan and I need to get rings."

"Easy enough," Shea assured her. "Stop there today when you get your license, they had a ton to choose from and were so helpful."

They all discussed the wedding as they ate, the older women sharing stories from their own wedding days and sharing advice for the brides-to-be. "The most important thing," Stella told them. "Is to enjoy the day. Take a moment to really soak it in, and to celebrate with your new husband. It's a day to share your love with all of us, but it's a day you'll remember forever. Savor every second."

Shea and Kendra smiled at each other, both lost in their own thoughts. After all this time, and all this heartbreak, Kendra finally got to marry the man who stole her heart all those years ago. She was so grateful that she had never fully gotten it back and had finally opened herself up to the possibility of loving him again, because now she couldn't imagine her life without him in it.

Chapter 35

Snow was falling softly outside the window when Dan woke early on his wedding day. Kendra had insisted on sleeping at her apartment that night, determined to follow tradition and not allow him to see her until the church that evening. Her parents had dropped her at home after the rehearsal dinner his dad had hosted at the house, since it was close to midnight when she left, and she was worried about the clock switching to their wedding day. He had teased her about being Cinderella before kissing her goodnight, and then gone to bed realizing that it was the last time he would kiss her as anything other than his wife.

The only dark spot on the last few days had been early Friday morning, when he had received a call from Agent Rodriquez. She had informed him that Brad's body was ready for release, but he had no family or friends who were willing to take the responsibility of burying him. Since Calle was technically the closest to a next of kin, she had wanted to give them the option to do something before he was buried by the state. Dan had made a few quick phone calls and made arrangements, not wanting the father of his soon-to-be stepdaughter to be buried anonymously. Even if she never wanted to know anything about him, Dan felt better giving the man a burial in return for the gift of Calle. As much as he disliked Brad, having Calle and her unending joy had done so much for his family, so he felt he had to do that one thing. He had debated not telling Kendra, as he didn't want to bring Brad into their wedding week, but finally determined he had to. The promise he made to not keep secrets from her was on his mind as he made the decision, and he knew he couldn't enter their marriage with that between them. Thankfully it hadn't upset her too much, and she had been grateful that he had handled it for her.

He let Patrick drag him to the gym along with Jake, and then the three of them went to Charlie's hockey game. It felt like an ordinary Saturday, except for the number of times he checked his watch.

"We have hours," Patrick reminded him.

"I know, I'm just anxious for it to get here."

"Have you heard from the girls?"

"Yes," Dan said as Jake nodded. "They are getting ready and having a blast. Thank you for arranging all of that."

"What's the point in having a favorite makeup artist if you can't spoil your new sisters?" He held up his hand. "And no jokes about the makeup, please."

"We will spare you, since you've been so helpful." Jake bumped him with a shoulder before erupting into a cheer when Charlie scored.

"Calle has her dress and apparently fought when they took it off her to do some alterations," Dan laughed. "And the other women were equally happy with the choices picked out for them by Maria. Apparently, no one is allowed to have an opinion with Maria."

"Oh, no one would dare," Patrick stated. "She's the best at what she does, and she's never wrong."

The game ended and they started filing out of the stands with the other fans. "I told Charlie to hustle so we can get home and start getting ready," Jake told them. "Stella was going to leave sandwiches for us, Dad was dropping her off to get her hair and makeup done. She's going to ride over to the church with the girls, dad will come back and go with us."

"Shit's getting real," Dan joked.

"Second thoughts?" Jake studied him as he asked.

"Not a one. You?"

"Nope." Jake shook his head after a minute. "Not sure how I got so damn lucky twice, but I'll take it."

"Me too," Dan agreed. "Now if we could just get to the altar, this waiting is killing me."

They laughed at him, and passed the time waiting for Charlie talking about who would be attending. Dan was happy for Jake that some of his friends from the Army were able to get the time off to visit Vermont and be there today, as well as many of his friends who had left the service over the years. In contrast, Dan hadn't invited anyone from his New York life other than Sam Snyder and his wife, ready to put that part of his life behind him.

***

What seemed like a lifetime later, he was finally standing in the back of the church, waiting for the cue to walk Stella down the aisle along with his brothers. He had offered to walk Kendra's mother as well, and she waited just behind Stella. Jake would then accompany Shea's mother, before they would finally take their spots waiting for their brides. Both women looked stunning and were thrilled with the pampering they had received at the hands of Maria and the hair and makeup staff. Dan had tried to catch a glimpse of Kendra or Calle when the door to the bridal room opened to let the florist in, but Patrick had stepped in the way with a wink.

Hearing *Ave Maria,* he smiled and stepped forward with Stella. Jake took her other arm, Patrick walking just behind as they escorted her to her seat next to Ben. Dan and Jake then escorted their mother-in-law before meeting at the back of the church to walk down once more.

"Ready?" Patrick eyed them both.

Charlie nodded. "I'm."

"I've never bene more ready for anything," Dan said. "Let's get this show on the road."

The doors opened, allowing Charlie to pass through as Jake's best man, followed by Jake. Patrick waited until Jake was all the way down the aisle before stepping out, and Dan followed his brother. The church was full of people from town, and he smiled and tried to store the memory away but was consumed with the thought of seeing Kendra take the same walk.

As they stood at the altar, the music changed, and Calle appeared in the doorway. It had been decided that she would go before both brides, and she took her time walking down the aisle strewing rose petals. Dan laughed when Charlie finally waved to her to move faster, and she immediately dumped the flowers out and ran to his side.

Christine followed, then the song changed to the bridal march for Shea and her father. Dan saw his stoic brother openly cry at the sight of his bride and choked back his own emotions. Shea was glowing with happiness and kissed her father before taking her spot with Jake. The crowd laughed when Jake kissed her and she laughed, telling him he jumped the gun.

The music changed and the church doors opened again, and Tina walked the aisle, followed by Julie. When the bridal march began again, he lost his battle with his emotions before the doors even opened. But when they finally did, and he saw Kendra in a body-clinging dress that accentuated every bit of her beauty, he cried even more. The cowgirl boots brought a smile to his face, and when their eyes met, he could see how radiantly happy she was. Suddenly everything inside of him settled, and he pulled it together just before shaking her father's hand and offering her his arm.

"Hi," she whispered.

"You're stunning," he whispered back. "I'm the luckiest man in the world."

"Second luckiest," Jake stage whispered from next to them, and all four burst into laughter.

The ceremony passed in a blur, first watching as Jake and Shea exchanged vows and rings and then finally being able to do so himself. Sliding the wedding band onto Kendra's finger had him flashing back through all the years to their first kiss. If someone had told that teenager that he would screw up as badly as possible but that this incredible woman would somehow not only forgive him, but be his one day, he wouldn't have believed it. But here he was, finally making his first love his forever love.

***

Dan stood on the side of the dance floor with Kendra and Calle on either side of him, watching Jake and Shea share their first dance. Dan and Kendra had wanted them to have their own moment, and then they would do their own dance. Sharing a wedding song was the one spot where they had all agreed wouldn't work, and it was nice to watch his brother revel in his happiness. He watched as Shea whispered in Jake's ear, causing him to pull back and stare at her before grinning and kissing her.

"Wonder what that's about," Dan murmured to Kendra.

"I'm sure we'll find out," Kendra squeezed his hand. "Ready to dance?"

"For you, yes." He leaned down and met Calle's eyes. "Just your mom and I first, then we'll have you come out, alright?"

"Can Charlie dance with me?" she asked hopefully.

"Next time, this one is just for us," Kendra told her.

The first strains of a Florida Georgia Line song played as Jake and Shea left the dance floor, and Dan led Kendra out to take their place.

"I love this song," Kendra smiled at him. "And I'm so glad to be growing old with you."

"I love you, Kendra Burrows." They kissed as their guests clapped, and then Dan waved for Calle to join them. Picking her up, he kissed her on the cheek. His arms around both his girls, surrounded by all the people he loved, he couldn't think of a time when he had been happier.

***

On Christmas Eve, the whole family gathered in the kitchen at the Burrows' house, ready to celebrate the holiday together. Dan had moved in with Kendra and Calle the day after the wedding, once they had returned from their suite at the Inn. Jake and Shea had barely been seen for days, and even now, Dan noticed that they didn't stray far from each other. His brother had an ease about him that had been missing for so many years, and Dan was thrilled for him. They had all agreed to stay in the main house for Christmas Eve, so that Calle could wake up with everyone together early the next morning.

When Shea joined Stella, Calle and Kendra in making cookies, Dan indicated to his brothers they should move into the living room. Settling into the couches by the fire, he grinned at them.

"Who would have thought six months ago that we would both be married?"

"It's crazy," Jake ran a hand through his hair. "And about to get crazier."

"What do you mean?" Patrick asked.

Jake leaned forward and looked around to make sure no one else could hear him. "Shea's pregnant. She told me at the reception."

"Congratulations," Dan and Patrick said in unison.

"Is that what she told you when you were dancing?" Dan thought back to the moment and the look on his brother's face.

"Yes," Jake said. "It blew my mind."

"I'm so happy for you." Dan couldn't help but think back over the last year that his brother had, and all he had been through. This happiness couldn't have come at a more important time for Jake.

"You'll be next," Patrick stated. "I bet Kendra will be pregnant by next month."

"Tonight, if I have anything to say about it," Dan laughed. "But we said we should probably give it a little time, let Calle adjust to me being around. I want to start the adoption process with her right after the new year, so that will keep us busy."

"You're not getting any younger," Patrick pointed out.

"Thanks for that, Patty."

"When will that nickname die?" his brother groaned.

"Know what's even worse than the nickname?" Jake asked. "Being the only single one left. Charlie is too young for Stella to worry about, which means her desire to see us all happy and settled is coming your way."

"She won't have a chance," Patrick replied smugly. "I leave in January for filming, and I'll be gone for months. Hopefully I'll be back by the time little Patrick is born."

"You won't be gone that long, will you?" Jake asked.

He shrugged and then sipped his beer. "Who knows, the schedule is six months. Then I'll have to do some voiceover stuff, I'm sure. But I'll come home between filming and whatever I need to do in post, plus they can set me up here to do some of it."

"More and more of a homebody," Dan teased. "But in all seriousness, it will be weird to have you be gone for six months."

"Be a nice break for me," Patrick replied with a laugh. "Maybe I'll miss you guys a bit. It's been a while since we filmed, so I'm missing those guys too. It will be a fun shoot, but I'll be ready for some quiet when it's done."

The family piled into the room with trays of snacks and bottles of wine, with Calle excited to play a present swap game that Charlie had seen on YouTube. Kendra settled in next to him, the room filling with the sounds of laughter and holiday fun, and he realized he had everything he needed right in this room. Staying home to help his brother had ended up fixing all he didn't know was broken in his own life. Winning Kendra back and becoming a dad to Calle filled his future with more happiness and possibilities than he could have ever imagined, and he was excited for what it held for them all.

Acknowledgments

Rachael and Kevin Cronk lost their second child, Calle, to DIPG at just six years old. She was a ray of sunshine, dancing through life with a constant smile on her face. Her older brother Connor adored her and was her hero. When Calle gained her wings, she picked out the perfect addition to their family, sending little sister Maddie down to help heal their hearts. Maddie's infectious laugh and joyful spirit is a gentle reminder of her older sister every day. Calle loved horses, puppies, dancing, princesses, and all things as sparkly as she was. If you loved Calle in this story, you would have loved her even more in real life. Please honor her memory by finding a way to support the battle against DIPG, or by doing something kind for someone today. Thank you, Rachael and Kevin, for allowing me to share Calle with the world.

Kendra's relationship with Brad is fiction, but I know there are people in the world that this might ring true for. Please know you are not alone, and there are people who can help. 800-799-7233 is the National Domestic Violence phone number, in addition to your local police and state resources.

Book Designs by Shae (on IG @bookdesignsbyshae), who created the cover art for me once again with just a few words of input from me, and yet she nailed it. I'm so grateful to have her in my corner. Shae supports St. Jude Research Hospital, so if any readers are looking to make a donation in Calle's name, please consider them as a benefactor.

My friends and family rallied around me when I announced the publication of "Coming Home", and their positive words got me through the writing of this book. I couldn't ask for a better village to be a part of, I am so lucky to have you all in my life.

My parents have always been there to support me in everything I set out to do. They talked me out of my self-doubt on many occasions, and hearing that they brag about my books to anyone who listens keeps me going. I love you both and am so lucky to have you in my life.

Jeff and Danielle, thanks for always being ready with a hug or a laugh. My brother has always been one of my best friends, and when he brought Danielle into our family, I gained another one. You are both amazing people, parents, and friends, and I'm so fortunate to have you in my life.

Brendan, Conor, Timmy, Tessa and Emmy, I love you all! My biggest fans, and the reason I'll keep writing. No one found my first book to be as exciting as Timmy, Tessa and Emmy, who waited anxiously for the package to arrive and had Danielle start reading to them instantly. Keep writing your stories, you'll be right here with me one day!

My husband, Tom, will never read my books, but I'll always find a way to throw in a little piece of who he is in each one. He served our country for so many years, and still finds ways to give back every day. He's always looking for a way to help people and gives back in so many ways to our community. I'm proud of his service, his hard work, and his dedication to his family.

Camden and Calum, my heart beats because of you. You make me proud every single day with who you are. You are as different as night and day, yet share the same kindness and respect for those around you, and I could ask for nothing more as a mom. Keep chasing your dreams and trying new things, I'll always be here to cheer you on.

Stay Tuned

If you have fallen in love with Patrick as much as I have, you'll want to head over to any of the sites below to follow me so you'll know when his story is coming! He has been anxiously standing side-stage while his brothers found their happily-ever-afters, and it's time for him to come center stage so we can all enjoy him! Plus, the Burrows family story will continue with updates from Jake and Shea, Dan and Kendra, Ben and Stella and of course, Charlie and Calle!

Find me on Instagram (@DeniseLathamWrites), Amazon or Goodreads to be alerted when the next book will be released! You can also sign up for my newsletter at www.deniselatham.com to stay up to date on special offers, new releases and giveaways! I love hearing from readers, so please feel free to send me a message as well.

Finally, reviews are what keep new readers discovering Windsor Peak, so please make sure to leave one when you finish reading. I appreciate you all!